ANTHILLS
AND STARS

Kevin Duffy

Bluemoose

Copyright © Kevin Duffy 2006

First published in 2006 by
Bluemoose Books Ltd
25 Sackville Street
Hebden Bridge
West Yorkshire
HX7 7DJ

www.bluemoosebooks.com

British Library Cataloguing-in-Publication data

A catalogue record for this book is available from the British Library

ISBN 0-9553367-0-8

Printed and bound in Europe by The Alden Group

To Margaret Mary Winifred Duffy

Thanks to my family, Hetha, Leo and Cal,
for their patience and understanding.
Also thanks to Al, Chris, Viv, Kev and Lin.

Chapter 1

To a generation who had turned on, tuned in and dropped out, the lure of dark satanic hills, fast flowing streams and cheap property was ideal. And so they came, bearded, beaded, sons and daughters of the Beat generation, eager to live their idyll and commune with Mother Nature. The first rainbow-coloured van arrived at number twenty-three Prospect Street, Broughton at 9.30 one cold wet Thursday morning. Neither Broughton nor its inhabitants were ready for The Permissive Society, especially when it came in the guise of one Solomon Tump. With mills and factories closing every week, the last thing Mrs Hebblethwaite needed was a hippy moving in next door. It may have been heading towards the Summer of Love elsewhere, but the spring of 1968 was proving difficult for this northern town.

Mrs Hebblethwaite was filling the coal scuttle when she saw Solomon Tump arrive. Not trusting her failing eyes, she gave the kitchen window a quick wipe with her pinny. The vision she saw confirmed that hell was only twenty feet away. Mrs Hebblethwaite was from that school of Catholicism which applauded plagues of locusts and encouraged frogs to descend from the heavens. She spat great tracts from the gospels with a forked tongue and the jury was still out as to whether she would kill the first-born of those that didn't believe.

The heathen that got out of the van was well over six feet tall, with a head of hair that was as wild and dissolute as the village drunk. He was wearing a moth-eaten coat and flared jeans that flapped about like a couple of half-dead fish marooned on dry land. Her first instinct was to go out, cut his hair and give him a good scrub with some carbolic but she knew it would take more than soap and water to rid Broughton of its first hippy.

Solomon made several trips into the van and Mrs Hebblethwaite was perturbed to see that books, carpets, pipes, albums, a record player, posters, guitars and even a tin whistle were being carried into the hippies new house. Finally Cass, his girlfriend of ten years, emerged with their eighteen month old son, Leo and they all disappeared into number 23 Prospect Street. Mrs Hebblethwaite seethed like a boiling kettle and after seeing Solomon take the final piece of furniture into the house, she dropped the coal scuttle, took off her pinny, blessed herself and walked as quickly as her ample frame allowed to the presbytery.

Mrs Hebblethwaite had never really taken to Father O'Dowd. He was young, he said Mass too quickly and he dished the communion host out as though he were dealing a hand of poker. However, if Satan and his works were moving in next door then she wanted all the help she could get.

The Church of The Immaculate Conception was situated at the top of Millgate; its grandeur and opulence stood in stark contrast to its barren surroundings. Two massive spires greeted the worshippers, a mini Notre Dame in the wastelands of the North West. The adjoining presbytery was a scaled-down model of the church itself, with a row of statues housed above the doorway imploring the citizens of Broughton to worship.

She knocked on the presbytery door. Miss Mcafferty, the ageing house-keeper, stuck her head round the door like a chastened child. "Mrs Hebblethwaite, you look like you've been chased by the four horsemen of the Apocalypse," she said in a thick Irish brogue that had not been tempered by forty-two years of living in England.

"Is Father in?" Mrs Hebblethwaite said, annoyed that she had to get past this first line of defence. Miss Mcafferty didn't reply. She closed the door, disappeared into the presbytery and returned a couple of minutes later to usher Mrs Hebblethwaite into the house. Miss Mcafferty stopped outside Father O'Dowd's office and said "Father, Mrs Hebblethwaite to see you." She returned to her domestic chores, annoyed that she'd been interrupted.

Father O'Dowd stood up and greeted his parishioner. "Good morning, Mrs Hebblethwaite. What can I do for you?" he said, as he grasped her hand and invited her to sit down.

"Well Father ..." she said, not knowing how to broach the arrival of the permissive society in Broughton. "You'll think me silly, but it's me neigh-bours, they're ..." She struggled to find the right word. " ... they're pagans, Father, devil worshippers, all hair and posters and speakers the size of cupboards and dressed in all manner of things." Mrs Hebblethwaite took out her rosary beads and was rolling them around in her hands. " And pipes, Father! They brought pipes in and you know what they use pipes for *and* they've got a child and I don't think it'll be baptised, do you?" Father O'Dowd wanted to interrupt but knew better. "What are you going to do, Father? Are you going to tell the Bishop, because I think he should know if there's devil worship in Broughton, then he can come down and exorcise them! We don't want our children learning about smoking pipes and listening to who knows what. You've got to do something Father, you've *got* to. Shall we pray now? Yes, that's what we'll do, we'll pray." Mrs Hebblethwaite fell to her knees and prayed very loudly to the Virgin Mary for help. She was about to do a tour of her rosary beads when Father O'Dowd helped her to her feet.

"You don't think you're getting ahead of yourself, do you Mrs Hebblethwaite?" he said. She exhaled with all the contempt of a true zealot and wondered how this supposed priest in front of her had the gall, nay temerity, to profess the word of the Lord. She hadn't spent the best part of her tragic life on bended knee to be told she was ahead of herself. Had she not embraced the Catholic Church happy in the knowledge that it never wavered in its denunciation of sin, that it revelled in making clear distinctions between what is black and what is white? However, she'd always known deep down that come the day sin arrived in Broughton he would be found wanting. And how!

She gave him her Old Testament look and said witheringly "Father Richardson would have done something!" She put her rosary beads into her cavernous handbag. "He was a *proper* priest," she continued, marching towards the door. "He'd 'ave told them what they could do with their bloody drums and pipes!"

Father O'Dowd tried to reclaim the ground he'd lost but found himself talking to her back as she disappeared down the hallway, ranting and cursing and intoning the Holy Scriptures in that punctuated way only elderly women of the church can.

Angry and hurt, Mrs Hebblethwaite bustled down Millgate like an overweight fell runner, barely able to keep her feet on the cobblestones. It was her stout footwear that finally stopped this incensed ball of Catholicism being knocked down by the number twenty-three bus. She was in no mood to brook any nonsense from a vehicle, priest, or long-haired hippy.

Still mouthing tracts from the Scriptures she strode across the market, ignoring pleas from friends who tried to find out what was wrong. She did however smile and wave to Mrs Holroyd, whose husband had recently passed away.

Never in her sixty-eight years as a Catholic had she felt as depressed as she did now. Under her breath she was still chuntering. "Not out of his nappies and he's trying to tell me what's right and wrong," she said. She didn't take too kindly to being upbraided by anyone, especially by a priest young enough to be one of her grandsons. "I bet he doesn't know his chasuble from his cassock!"

A couple of her younger friends noticed her talking to herself, but kept their heads down, in case she unleashed her obvious anger at them. She rounded Der Lane, misty-eyed from her exertions, desperate to get home and find out what was happening. What she found was that the van that had delivered the Permissive Society to Broughton was still there along with its driver, who sat on a wall smoking.

"Typical," she said. "I bet the lazy bugger's never done a day's work in his life." She walked down Prospect Street towards Solomon like Gary Cooper in High Noon.

If Ethel Hebblethwaite hadn't already had enough shocks that day, the next vision nearly killed her. She saw her third-eldest grandson, Gary, who lived across the street with his mum and dad and a sister, talking to the man with the hair and the van. If that deed alone didn't warrant punishment from the Lord himself, what her grandson was actually doing, did: Gary was smoking a strange smelling cigarette.

"Jesus, Mary and Joseph." she said as she blessed herself. She took a deep breath and glared at her grandson. "What the bloody hell are you doing?" she yelled, managing to grab the roll-up from his teenage mouth and toss it over into next door's garden. Gary stood there more frightened than embarrassed. He'd been belted before, but he'd never witnessed his Nan in such a mood. Her eyes bore into him like red-hot coals. "You!" she bellowed, pointing at her grandson, "Get inside and stay there until I say so." She directed Gary to her house and he sheepishly followed her instructions.

Mrs Hebblethwaite put her handbag down and looked at Solomon, placed her hands on her hips and puffed her chest out. She didn't need her

Old Testament stare this time; she just thrust an accusing forefinger at him and shouted "You've only been here a bloody minute and you're up to your tricks, aren't you!" She paused. "I go up to church to have a word, and what happens? I come back and you're passing the bloody peace pipe round with my grandson. First it's drugs and then God only knows – and he's not telling."

Solomon got off the wall and tried to say something. Nobody interrupted Mrs Hebblethwaite, not even Solomon Tump.

"He's sixteen and he should be at work, not bloody day-dreaming with you, smoking you-know-what."

Solomon smiled and put his hand out in a gesture of conciliation. Mrs Hebblethwaite looked at him, then at his hand and said: "I'm not shaking that dirty thing!" As she said it, she looked down and noticed that his nails were beautifully manicured. She looked up.

"Solomon Tump, pleased to meet you." He kept his hand out, but she didn't shake it.

"You may be pleased, but I'm bloody not," she said. Picking up her handbag she walked into the house, ready to give Gary a piece of her very angry mind.

Solomon wasn't annoyed or offended: dismayed perhaps, because he thought Broughton was slightly different from all the other towns and villages they had visited. Solomon, his girlfriend Cass and their son Leo, who was now eighteen months old and had just started to walk, had been travelling around Great Britain for three years. They had chosen Broughton because property was cheap, the countryside was stunning, and there was a burgeoning movement of like-minded people who wanted to get away from city life and live off the land. They'd been on the Hippy Trail in India and were all Ashramed out. George Harrison may have found his Chakras in the foothills of Henley, but those that couldn't afford Nirvana looked to outposts like Broughton to start afresh. One unhappy old lady wouldn't put them off but it wasn't the best of starts. He walked towards their new house, a little concerned that he'd got Gary into trouble with his grandma and reminded himself to apologise to both when the time was right.

Cass came to the door smiling, her long red hair cascading over her shoulders and she flicked the locks away from her face to reveal green eyes which were alluring and beautiful, funny and strong. Although Cass had agreed to put some roots down and stay put for a while, she wasn't that convinced running a shop in Broughton was the best idea. Two years ago they would have laughed at such a turn of events, telling each other that to run a shop and join the rest of the ants, working all hours God sent, would be selling out. How times change when your body clock enters its fourth decade. However, she acquiesced hoping that this move would bring them closer together.

She brought Leo out into the garden.

"Everything OK?" she asked with genuine concern.

"I've upset the neighbours," he replied, his eyes rolling skywards. "Gave a rolly to a lad who turned out to be her grandson." He took Leo from her arms and blew a big wet raspberry on his cheek, which made them both giggle.

"I suppose you're the devil incarnate, and I'm the wicked witch from the west," Cass laughed, reminding Solomon of the onslaught they received from an evangelical minister, who tried to sell them tickets to his tented mission in Salisbury last year. He laughed and threw Leo into the air.

"Come on, let's go for a wander," Solomon said, passing his son to Cass. He locked the door and the three of them left Prospect Street to Mrs Hebblethwaite and her tongue.

Chapter 2

It was twenty years ago to the day that Thomas O'Dowd, a spindly youth of eleven, walked into his secondary school and saw 'The Monk' hovering over him like a beast of prey. Thomas's only thought was that he hoped 'The Monk' wasn't angry, because he had been told at Sunday school that little children were often beaten for thinking naughty thoughts.

"There are anthills in this world, O'Dowd, and there are stars," the Monk said. He'd obviously had a good day because he hadn't laid a hand on him yet. "The anthills are inhabited by creatures of limited intelligence. Their role, to work tirelessly for the good of everyone." The Monk looked heavenward and continued. "The Stars are jewels that light up our firmament with their creativity and boundless energy. They have to be nurtured and treasured." The Monk pointed at him with a long finger and equally long fingernails. Thomas had never seen men with fingernails like that. Everyone he knew had stumpy fat things like sausage rolls.

"You, however, have been allocated to the anthill, so you must work hard O'Dowd. It may not be the best of starts but, with some application and good honest toil, you may get a chance to star! "

Monsignor Dodson took it upon himself personally to welcome the new entrants into the school and it was done with great theatricality. Thomas thanked the priest, who told him he would pray for his soul and with a sweep of his black coat, he was off to care for all the other souls who'd just started their first day.

Father O'Dowd sat in his office, collar off, shoes undone and feet on his desk. He shook his head at the thought of his old headmaster and his fine words of wisdom.

"Thank God for Elvis Presley, the Beatles and Afghan coats," He said to himself. Perhaps if he played 'A Hard Day's Night' to Mrs Hebblethwaite she might undergo some kind of tolerance conversion and embrace her new neighbour. He enjoyed these bouts of fancy and laughed, just in time to see Miss Mcafferty round the corner. He took his feet off the table and rearranged his collar.

She tapped him on the shoulder and said: "Dinner's ready, Father."

"Right," he said, smiling weakly in the knowledge that his housekeeper excelled in many things but cooking wasn't one of them. As she left the room he grimaced at the prospect of yet more tortured cabbage, distressed carrots and minced meat you could play marbles with. When his mother came, and that was often, there was always high tension before his mother realised that Miss Mcafferty lived and worked in the kitchen and it wasn't her place to tell the housekeeper what to cook. He didn't know who the patron saint of lost culinary causes was, but he was desperate to find out.

They sat down at the table which had been waxed and polished for over a hundred and thirty years, giving the table a buffed-up look. However, it did mean that whatever was cooked had an added herb. Beeswax. He addressed the food and said grace.

As soon as his eyes opened Miss Mcafferty looked at him inquisitively. "Well, what are you going to do about yer man Father?" His housekeeper said, biting into her cheese and biscuits. She never had a cooked meal herself, he noticed. Father O'Dowd realised that the man she was referring too wasn't your man in the general sense that she normally meant, but yer man Mrs Hebblethwaite was concerned with.

"Listening at the door, were we?" he asked.

"Well, Mrs Hebblethwaite doesn't hide her voice under a bushel, does she Father?" she said, paraphrasing the scriptures with her usual skill.

"Her new neighbour's done nothing wrong as far as I can see, Miss Mcafferty, apart from wear flared trousers, long hair and smoke roll-ups," he said, viewing the meal in front of him with some trepidation. Every meal was like fire-walking. "And there is nothing in the Bible that says he can't."

Father O'Dowd took the plunge and put the tepid cabbage into his mouth and swallowed, relieved that the pepper he always had at hand managed to give it some taste. The mince created a far more difficult problem because it couldn't be just swallowed, it had to be addressed, drawn and quartered, and then eaten. As he was busy chopping and cutting, his housekeeper asked: "When's your mother coming?"

He had a mouthful of food and gestured to her that he would answer once he'd finished eating. "Two weeks," he replied eventually. She nodded.

Only two more mouthfuls and he could go for his early evening walk. Mouthfuls two and three dutifully followed and the meal was over. He thanked Miss Mcafferty, who seemed annoyed that she hadn't received first-hand knowledge of what Father was going to do. It was one of the perks of the job to know what Father was doing. There were so many ladies in the parish who craved such information, Mrs Hebblethwaite being one of them. He placed his knife and fork on his plate, and said grace.

Father O'Dowd closed the presbytery door behind him and walked leisurely down Millgate, glad to get some fresh air. Ever since he'd arrived in Broughton, he'd taken it upon himself to walk through the town, giving himself a presence, raising the profile a bit and enabling him to try and get to know the town and its people. It also gave him the opportunity to get away from the phone and enjoy the beautiful scenery that hugged the valley to its chest. The hills, which formed a natural amphitheatre, tore through the shroud of greenery like brooding, grumpy teenagers, full of anger and were constantly being punished by the incessant rain. It seemed that in centuries past, some unimaginable slight had been done to the gods and their punishment was to have the heavens open up on Broughton whenever the mood took.

The parish of Broughton was home to several different communities. Father O'Dowd administered to Poles and Ukrainians who both came to the town after the Second World War, and a host of Irish workers who had left the Emerald Isle during the famine. There were a few Italian families that had settled in Broughton, mainly those Italian soldiers that were prisoners of war in a nearby camp and had stayed on after 1945. It was a heady mix, especially when a few pints had been downed.

It was six o'clock and he was the only person about, apart from two young boys who tried to hide when they saw him and his collar approach. They coughed on their cheap cigarettes and giggled as he walked past, fully aware that Mrs Bingley and Mrs Arkwright would not be best pleased their thirteen-year-old sons were already smoking. Most of the working men were in one of the pubs having a pint before returning home for their tea. Those that weren't working would be reading their newspapers, tending their allotments or sleeping.

He crossed over the bridge where the river separated the two Town Halls. He had been told that this had nothing to do with civic munificence, but everything to do with the pride and arrogance of a mill-owner's son.

Father O'Dowd passed the town halls and looked across at the canal, which ran parallel to the river. The canal was a star-gazy pie of a navigation, a watery repository of household waste, a floating tip. The glory days of bringing coal and cotton had long gone; these days it left Broughton rather embarrassed at its own indolence and scuttled off towards Manchester.

Broughton had suffered terribly in the past ten years. Mr Macmillan may have told everyone else that they'd 'never had it so good', but the good folk of this northern town had not. Of the eighteen mills that produced textiles after the war, only three remained. Unemployment was four times the national average and there had been a Diaspora of young men and women in the past five years. The town was battered and bruised, too busy trying to look for gainful employment to notice the Swinging Sixties.

Father O'Dowd had been there only three months and although, as yet, they hadn't accepted him with open prayer books, he was beginning to feel more at home in Broughton. He crossed Water Street and idled by The Flying Swan, one of eight pubs in the town. Mr Hetherington sidled out, a cigarette in his mouth and his cap at an angle that told the priest he'd had a good time. "Good evening for one," he said as he tipped his hat.

"Yes," Father O'Dowd replied without understanding.

The priest looked down the street and saw some colourful clothes approaching, two sets of big hair, and what looked like a small baby. "The Permissive Society no doubt!" he smiled to himself, quite pleased with his detective work. Solomon, Cass and their baby son were also taking in the sights of Broughton.

"Lovely evening," Father O'Dowd said to them. Cass smiled.

"It is, isn't it?" she replied as they passed each other. Solomon didn't speak but nodded in recognition.

"So those are the people who are going to turn Broughton into Sodom and Gomorrah," Father O'Dowd said to a lone pigeon that had joined him for this part of his walk. It was unfortunate for Broughton that where music was concerned the town was at least a decade behind. They had just discarded the big band era and were quiffing up for Elvis when the Beatles arrived. People in Broughton were happily parading around in drainpipe jeans, brothel creepers and beehive hairdos. Afghan coats, patchouli oil and the mystical East were not on the radar, and although Solomon looked like thousands of others in 1968, Father O'Dowd could well understand how Mrs Hebblethwaite felt. He crossed New Road, and down Hill View, before turning into Prospect Street.

"Oh, it's you!" Mrs Hebblethwaite said as she opened the door. She was still angry he thought as he went into her house. He walked through the hall, past the picture of the Pope and also one of President John F. Kennedy, which was quite the norm in Irish Catholic households. Although not a shrine to the Catholic faith, there were four statues of saints: Agnes, who protected virgins; Anthony, who was one for lost causes; Philip, the apostle, and finally Bartholomew, who was flailed to death in Armenia and was chief of the hair shirt brigade. Father O'Dowd guessed these were the Hebblethwaite household's security. They didn't require the services of a dog or an alarm system; these statues were enough to deter the hardest of criminals. Or so they thought. If you drew a line from each of their eyes, in true spot the ball fashion, at the intersection of all four would be the Hebblethwaite fortune. It was common practice, and well known amongst the clergy. It was a good job he wasn't a common-or-garden thief, because he could see straight away where their limited funds were hidden.

Mr Hebblethwaite was at the table, still in his overalls, reading the Daily Herald. He turned, put the paper down, took his reading glasses off and greeted the priest far too warmly for his wife's liking. "Hello Father, good to see you," he said, smiling his toothless smile. "Cup of tea?" He stood up. "Ethel, get Father a cup of tea." His wife grimaced slightly and went into the kitchen.

"So what brings you round here?" he asked.

"Your new neighbours, Sam."

"You mean that thing parked outside?" he said, pointing in the general direction of next door. "Ethel's told me all about them, bloody long-haired louts." Mr Hebblethwaite wasn't the devoutest of souls but he did realise he had sworn in front of a man of the cloth and, although not worried about embarrassing the priest, he was concerned about his wife's response. "He even tried to get our Gary smoking funny baccy, can you believe that Father? Only been here half a day and he's started selling the stuff? Even Vatican Two would have something to say on that, wouldn't they?" Mr Hebblethwaite laughed. He liked laughing at his own jokes, as did the rest of his body, which was quite considerable.

"I've just passed them on the High Street and yes, they may be wearing strange clothes but they seemed decent enough," the parish priest said as he sat down on the sofa that the Hebblethwaite's had received as a wedding present. "I think we should give them a little bit of time to settle in before we start making judgments." The priest looked at Mr Hebblethwaite and smiled.

Mrs Hebblethwaite came in with the tea. "You mean give them enough time to get people like our Gary," she snorted, handing the cup of tea to Father O'Dowd. "Going round getting up to all sorts! By the time you think it's about right to have a say, it'll be too late, won't it Father?" She handed him a biscuit, re-filled her husband's mug and sat down.

"It's like I said to our Jessie about the Pill and the like, putting all these contraceptives into young people's minds, it's not right." Mrs Hebblethwaite was known to pronounce on everything and her opinion was not to be challenged, well not in the Hebblethwaite household ... "Before you know it, there'll be young girls having babies willy-nilly in the High Street and what will you do then, I'd like to know?" She took a biscuit. "No, you have to make a stand somewhere and mine's here." Her dentures demolished the digestive in two angry bites. "They've already had their music on full blast and that was a bloody racket. Sounded like they were killing a cat, which I wouldn't put past them."

Mr Hebblethwaite witnessed what she said and logged it for future reference: his wife swore in front of a priest. She paused, took a mouthful of tea and continued. "And what about the baby, they have a duty to that child ..." Father O'Dowd feared he had walked into a rant, and he was right.

"Mrs Hebblethwaite." He placed his hands together as in prayer, paused and said: "Look, I know you're concerned about the permissive society and –" He didn't have time to finish.

"Concerned? *Concerned?*" She wasn't ranting, she was apoplectic. "I've got seven grandchildren and I don't want them cavorting around with the likes of those with no respect for their own or anyone else's bodies." She didn't pause for breath; she was being fuelled by a divine wind. "They can have their permissive whatever it is in London, but I don't want it next door to me. Bloody music and drugs, chanting like animals and doing heathen things to each other."

Mr Hebblethwaite wanted to know what all these heathen things were and how his wife knew about them. She made a fateful pause and the priest seized his chance.

"Look, I'll go round and have a word –" He didn't get to finish his sentence because she stood up, motioned to her husband, nodded to Father and left the room. If there was one thing Mrs Hebblethwaite detested more than young priests, it was young priests who didn't grab things by the horns and deal with the issue in hand.

"She's not happy, Father, and to tell you the truth neither am I."

Father O'Dowd drank his tea, thanked Sam for his hospitality and went next door.

Chapter 3

S olomon was coming down the stairs, having put Leo to bed, when he saw Father O'Dowd walking down the front path. He called to Cass, who was busy in the kitchen, "Swiss Guard's arrived!" Solomon opened the door before Father O'Dowd had time to knock or announce his arrival. "Come in, Father."

The priest smiled wanly. He went into the front room, which was still full of boxes and books. The only item that had been unpacked and positioned was the record player and it was on, much to their neighbours' annoyance.

"I thought I'd just pop round and welcome you to Broughton," he said and proffered a hand to Solomon. "Thomas O'Dowd." He looked across the room to see Cass enter.

"Hello again," she said.

"I was just saying to ..." He looked at Solomon.

"Solomon. Solomon Tump."

"Yes, I was just saying to Solomon that I thought I'd pop round and welcome you to Broughton."

"That's very kind," Cass said. "Would you like a cup of tea? Coffee? Something stronger?"

He didn't really want anything, having just had a cup of tea at the Hebblethwaite's', but he didn't want to appear rude. "Coffee will be fine, thank you."

Father O'Dowd sat down opposite Solomon. Having just been on the receiving end of one of his parishioners' rants about life, death and ineffectual clergy, he waited for his host to speak. He didn't. Father hated silence and so he always talked, to himself if needs must or to God if everything else failed. Solomon, however, seemed to embrace the quiet and looked up every now and then, smiling. He was preoccupied with rolling a cigarette. Father didn't know whether there was anything strange going into it, as the neighbours would have him believe, but as he couldn't smell any unusual aroma he felt assured that it was only nicotine. Solomon sat cross-legged on the floor, his head bowed slightly, consumed with the activity in hand.

For the first time he could remember, Father O'Dowd didn't want to break the silence, he was content to just to watch and gaze at Solomon. He hadn't really noticed him before when they passed on the street, just that he had big hair which consumed most of his face. Sitting in his front room he saw his face properly, as the curtain of hair was flicked away from each cheek at regular intervals. The priest found himself gazing intently at him and blushed slightly when Solomon raised his head and caught him watching. It was like a child caught stealing some sweets for the first time, but he just kept on looking at Solomon. He had beautifully chiseled features, fine and delicate, and a flared jaw that exuded character. His cheekbones had been stolen from Bridget Bardot and looking down onto them were eyes, incandescent, translucent, emerald green windows that shone with an energy and vigour, as compelling as they were frightening. They seemed to be aware of how he was feeling, how he'd felt and what he may feel in the future.

Solomon was calm, serene, and worldly. Thomas had never felt like this before. The man in front of him, engaged in the erotic act of rolling a cigarette, was doing to Father O'Dowd what nobody had ever done before. He was arousing him, and with such an intensity. He flattened his coat and could feel the erection trying to fight its way out of his soutane, trying to exit any which way it could. He was pleased, offended, angry and annoyed. Solomon placed the lit cigarette between his puckered lips. He drew on it, exhaled and proffered it to the priest. Blushing slightly, Father O'Dowd declined. Cass came into the room with the coffee but he didn't notice: his gaze was still firmly fixed on Solomon. He couldn't think, talk, respond. He just sat there transfixed by the beauty that sat before him smoking a cigarette. He'd never had such an experience before and wanted to get back to church as quickly as possible and ask forgiveness. He'd witnessed the naked gambolling of fellow seminarians in his college, but that had never aroused him. To be aroused so blatantly by a man he had just met, not touched, or had hardly spoken to, was unnerving.

The spell was finally broken by Cass bending down and giving him his coffee.

"Thank you," he said tremulously.

Cass sat next to Solomon and put her arm round him, and kissed him on the cheek. She took the cigarette from his mouth and started to smoke it herself. Nicotine harmony. 'Well, there are some perks of a relationship,' she thought as she blew a perfect smoke ring across the room towards Che Guevara and all his other revolutionary friends.

"Is it about Gary?" Solomon finally asked, combing his hair with his long slender hands.

"Well, I suppose ..." Father O'Dowd checked himself, then continued. " ... in a way. Mrs Hebblethwaite seems concerned that your presence here might lead to him being led astray, so to speak," he mumbled.

"I see. Long hair, flares, roll-ups and music. Is that such a threatening sight?" Solomon said, retrieving his cigarette from Cass.

"No, but you have to realise that some people are not used to –"

"People like us," interjected Cass.

"Yes," Father O'Dowd said, slightly annoyed that his train of thought had been disrupted.

"A little bit of something can add to a community, don't you think, Thomas?"

"Yes," he agreed.

"And we've done nothing wrong, have we?" Solomon said.

"No."

"So what's the problem?"

Father O'Dowd, still erect and confused, was incapable of formulating a Jesuitical response and tried to gain some time by drinking his coffee. "There isn't a problem as such," he prevaricated. "It's just that I'd like you to know that there are some people in Broughton who'll find it difficult to accept you straight away." Father Thomas was not one for debate. "But I'm sure in time they'll get used to you."

"What, like they do cats and dogs?" Solomon asked.

"No. But for the time being, if you could keep a lowish profile ..."

Solomon looked at Cass and laughed. "How can I keep a low profile in clothes like these?" he said, pointing to his orange and maroon flared jeans. "Look Thomas, we just want a quiet life. We're not into anything heavy, we've got a young child and we just want to bring him up as best we can."

"That's fine, but could you just be careful with Gary, he's only sixteen and –"

Again Cass finished the priest's sentence: "Impressionable. Don't worry, Father. We've all been there." She realised what she had said, smiled and continued. "Well, I suppose some of us have been there."

Father O'Dowd laughed politely, thinking what might have happened if he hadn't had the call and gone to the seminary in Rome at the tender age of fifteen.

"We get the message, Thomas, and I promise not to sacrifice any children –" Solomon paused. "Well, not this week anyway." The hippy stood up. "Thanks for popping round, much appreciated."

Father Thomas O'Dowd wanted to stay. He wanted to be in Solomon's company for as long as possible but he wasn't quite sure what would happen if he did. He stood up and he was still erect.

"And if you ever want to come round for a chat again, the door's always open."

Father O'Dowd put his coffee cup down, thanked Cass and Solomon, and took his aroused body out of the house.

He returned swiftly home, making light work of the hill up Millgate. He'd never considered himself gay. As a young man of eighteen he had been propositioned by a much older cleric but had laughed it off, dismissing it as playful exuberance on the older man's part. He entered the presbytery, took his coat off, said 'hello' to Miss Mcafferty, and went into the main body of the church, where he knelt and began to pray.

"Father, forgive me, for I don't know who I am!"

Unnervingly he was still erect, but after a rosary and a full personal confession, he returned to his normal state. He went to bed early, slightly worried what kind of dreams he would have.

Chapter 4

Solomon Tump was thirty-three years old, the same age as the priest. His past was shrouded in secrecy and even Cass knew very little about his family or formative years. He liked it that way. He had spent a great deal of time and energy creating the enigma that was Solomon Tump; he didn't want his past to destroy that image.

"What did you make of that?" he asked her as he sat down.

"Very strange. I couldn't help but notice the way he kept looking at you," she said, sprawling out on the couch. "I think he fancies you!"

"He can't, he's a Catholic priest. Anyway they're celibate," Solomon replied, not wanting to acknowledge the truth.

"Celibate or not, he can still fancy you. I can see the headlines now. Vatican celibacy police to investigate local priest!" Cass laughed out loud.

"Hilarious, but what about all that stuff he was saying, you know, Mrs What's-her-face next door?" He tried to look serious.

"Stop changing the subject. Did you fancy him?"

"No. I don't go for men in skirts." He tried to make light of it.

"I wouldn't mind having sex with a priest, that would be a laugh. What about all three of us? 'The Holy Trinity.' That'd stir things up a bit round here." She giggled and put her arms round Solomon. "I could have sex with the priest, then have confession, and after absolution me and you could get down to some serious business."

She wasn't joking, thought Solomon, as he kissed her.

"I don't think so. We don't want the walls of Jericho falling down round our ears just yet. Anyway, didn't you hear what I said about being here to lead a quiet life?" He began to nibble her earlobe.

"I don't want *too* quiet, Solomon. A little bit of quiet here and there's OK, but too much isn't fun. Is It?" Cass purred.

"No, but we'll do quiet for a little while."

She put her hands down his trousers. "Not too quiet. Well, not just now." Cass forced her mouth onto his and pushed him back onto the couch. "I'll be your priest if you want." She took her top off to reveal her breasts, which Solomon tried to grab.

"Now, now," she admonished. She forced his arms down. "And now, just for tonight the Vatican brings you blood, sweat and orgasms." She climbed on top of him and laughed.

*****

Father O'Dowd turned over in a cold sweat, to hear somebody knocking on his bedroom door. He sat up and heard Miss Mcafferty say "Are you all right, Father?"

"Yes. I was –"

"It's just I heard you call out somebody's name," she said anxiously.

"I'm fine, Miss Mcafferty. I must have been dreaming." He was having the dream he didn't want to have. "You can go back to bed now." He turned over and buried his confused head in the pillow.

Chapter 5

The Bishop was struggling to take the top off his egg when his secretary came into the dining room. The young priest entered without knocking. The Bishop glared at him. "I take it that whatever your message is, it's more important than this egg?"

"It's the phone, Your Grace," the priest said mildly.

The Bishop stood up, threw his napkin onto the table and followed his personal assistant out of the room. The eggy soldiers would just have to wait.

Bishop Bone was tall and angular, with thin greying hair that merely accentuated the fine quality of his skin. He was sixty-seven, but looked fifty. His hands were long and delicate, extremely well manicured and told the onlooker this was a man of letters. He walked with a grace associated with those that had greatness thrust upon them. He glided with an ease given those who held high office. Only occasionally did his gait give the slightest hint that he suffered terribly from bunions.

Malachi Bone had been an exceptional child, a boy so immersed in the teachings of the church that all who knew him at school and seminary were convinced that he was destined for great things. Unfortunately so did he. He had been the youngest priest to rise to the Bishopric. His brilliant mind and knowledge of Canon Law had fast-tracked him to purple before he reached his thirty-fourth birthday. Many in the Catholic Hierarchy had expected him to go all the way to Rome, and if not the pontificate, at least Cardinal. However, his meteoric rise, snarling wit and caustic tongue had created many enemies along the way and so a mere Bishop he had been for the past thirty-three years. He walked towards the telephone muttering under his breath about 'something and nothing'. The Bishop picked up the receiver. "Hello!" he bawled down the phone.

"Is that you, Your Grace?" said Mrs Hebblethwaite, on bended knee next to the Pope in the hallway.

"Yes," said Bishop Bone, annoyed that his egg would now be congealed and cold and not at all receptive to a soldier.

"Oh good, because I wanted to speak to you about Father O'Dowd." Mrs Hebblethwaite was no master of the telephone and she too was shouting.

"Will you give it a rest, woman? It's Saturday bloody morning and I'm trying to get some shut-eye!" roared her husband from the disturbed sanctuary of his bed.

"Sorry about that, Your Grace."

By now the Bishop had all but given up on his egg.

"As I said, it's about young Father O'Dowd, your Grace. You see, I was just filling up the coal scuttle –" His Grace looked towards the nicotine ceiling and asked for divine intervention to help the caller get at least halfway through her tale before the cold linoleum floor started to affect his bunions.

"– when this multi-coloured van arrived and out pops the Permissive Society, Your Grace, a man with hair so long you'd have thought he was Rapunzel's sister and as for clothes, they barely wore any and you know what they say about hippies, Your Grace, and that stuff they smoke, and fornication and pleasures of the flesh, and orgies, they'll be having them won't they, Your Grace and we can't have that in Broughton, so I said to Father O'Dowd was he going to do anything – "

The Bishop looked at his watch. It was eight thirty-five and he was supposed to be chairing a Catholic response to Birth Control later on in the day and he still hadn't finished his opening speech. "Yes, this all sounds very distressing Mrs – ?"

"Hebblethwaite. Mrs Hebblethwaite. Well, that's what I said to Father, Your Grace."

The Bishop's egg was now solid.

"Well, leave it with me Mrs Hebblethwaite and I will have a word with O'Dowd. OK?"

"Thank you, Your Grace."

She bowed, kissed the receiver and replaced it on the phone. She shouted up the stairs. "Don't you 'bloody give it a rest' to me, Sam

Hebblethwaite. If you hadn't been on the beer all night, you wouldn't have to have a lie in, would you?" Sam put the pillow over his head and knew that his day would now be littered with meaningless tasks.

The Bishop knew his egg would be hard, but he still went back to have a look. He tapped it and knew. He hated hard eggs as much as he despised chocolate coffee creams. Putting his mitre underneath his arm as though he were about to score a try, he walked annoyed and hungry to his office.

He was halfway through the introduction to his speech when his personal assistant turned up again unannounced. "It's the phone, Your Grace," he said quietly.

"Don't they teach you to bloody knock at seminaries these days?" barked His Eminence.

"There is no seminary at Knock, Father, just an airport."

Not only was his assistant hard of hearing, he wasn't blessed with the greatest of intellect either. Before he had time to relate the topographical details of the small Irish town, the Bishop was out of the room and marching to the phone.

"Yes?" said the Bishop. When the Bishop was monosyllabic, Father O'Dowd knew it meant trouble.

"Your Grace, it's Father O'Dowd – " He didn't have time to finish off the preliminaries.

"If it's about hippies and orgies and the permissive society, save your breath. Mrs Hebblethwaite has already told me."

This didn't surprise Thomas O'Dowd. "No, Your Grace, it's something a bit more delicate."

"Can't it wait? I've got an important meeting this afternoon and I haven't finished my speech yet," the Bishop said sharply, hopping from one foot to the other trying to alleviate the pressure on his bunions.

"I'm afraid it can't," O'Dowd said rather apologetically.

"Well, spit it out man! It can't be all that bad, can it?" There was a lengthy pause on the end of the line, and the Bishop knew that he would have to write the conclusion to his speech in the back of his chauffeured car.

"Your Grace, I think I might be having unnatural thoughts."

The Bishop looked worried, very worried. Worried enough to forget about the pain from his feet. "You're not thinking about what I think you're thinking about?"

"Yes, Your Grace." Father O'Dowd replied, relieved that he didn't have to spell it out.

The Bishop held the telephone at arms length. "Good God! O'Dowd's thinking of becoming a Protestant."

"What shall I do, Your Grace?" the priest asked, hoping that some words of wisdom from the Bishop would expunge all disturbing thoughts from his mind.

"You must pray, my son. You must pray to the Lord until these thoughts are no more, until they are scattered on ground that is barren and infertile. We are here on a mission to teach and explain the word of the Lord, to shout from the highest mountain the love that God has for us and to welcome those who have not heard that the Catholic Church will always welcome those who have fallen by the wayside. We must be strong in our convictions and we mustn't stray to those perfidious religions that purport to be the truth. They are mere shadows of self-parody. They couldn't walk with our Lord in our garden, our garden of destiny —" Father O'Dowd wondered if the Bishop had been at the bottle this morning. "— Protestantism is in denial, my son."

Father O'Dowd interrupted the Bishop, a brave and sometimes foolish thing to do. "I think we may be talking at cross purposes here, Your Grace."

"I never talk in cross anything O'Dowd, especially when it comes to the word of the Lord," the Bishop said, annoyed that his elegant prose had been halted.

"No, Your Grace, I mean my unnatural thoughts are not about becoming a Protestant."

"Thank God for that!" he sighed. "Well, what can be more unnatural than that?"

"Erections, Your Grace." Father O'Dowd blushed.

"Erections, O'Dowd? What do you mean, erections? Having trouble with your steeple?"

"No, Father."

"Well then, what?" He was getting irritable now and he could feel his ulcer, denied the comfort of the egg, starting to play up.

"Penile erections."

"Sorry?" Intelligent and knowledgeable the Bishop may have been but when it came down to the matter of the human body and its functions he was all at sea.

"Your Grace, I'm getting erections when I see other men. Well, just one man in particular."

Bishop Bone had been in his position for nearly thirty-four years, but to have a priest on the end of the telephone line with an erection was a first. He didn't know what to do. Hippies and pot he could handle, erections he couldn't.

"Thomas, I think we need to talk. I'll call round after my conference and we'll discuss the matter then."

"Thank you, Your Grace." Father O'Dowd put the phone down, pleased to find that he would at last have someone to listen to his troubled thoughts.

The Bishop was concerned, very concerned. He had a vast array of books and literature on Theology and Canon Law, but he wasn't conversant with that aspect of celibacy. He was learned and had read voraciously in order to climb the ecclesiastical ladder. He walked into the library and strolled along the shelves looking for a book he had seen but had not read. "Ha, there it is!" he said to himself, pleased that he had remembered where it was. He picked the book from the shelves and read the title out aloud. *"The Rising Importance of Erections in Secular Society: a Jesuitical Response."* The Bishop smiled. If there were any outstanding issues to be resolved with Father O'Dowd, then he was sure that all the questions would be answered inside this weighty volume. He was in no doubt that when it came to this matter the Jesuits, famed for their intellect, would put the matter straight. Speaking quietly he read out the table of contents, moving his finger slowly down the list. *Chapter one: What is the appeal of Tumescence?*

"Interesting," he said as he moved swiftly through the book before arriving at those chapters which were pertinent to his particular problem. It was chapters nine and ten that caught his eye. *Chapter nine: Homosexuality and its rise in a secular world. Chapter ten: Ecclesiastical erections and how to handle them. (Only to be read by senior members of The Faith)*

He sat down and read and re-read the chapters that would enable him to answer any of Father O'Dowd's queries.

Chapter 6

"Fellow Brothers in Christ," the Bishop said, moving from side to side. From the back of the conference hall he looked like an Irish Dancer caught in glue. "Let us pray." The hall rose to a man. "We beseech you, Holy Father, that with your divine intercession there will be an end to this needless waste of human life." Bishop Bone paused for the full dramatic effect of what he had said to sink in. He carried on. "And we pray that those bra-less woman will realise the error of their ways and refrain from using The Pill."

Although the conference was in full agreement with what the Bishop was saying, they were slightly confused as to the content, as it seemed to stray from the core subject of their meeting. The Bishop was in full flow: " – and heap pox on the man who brought in the Abortion Bill."

A resounding 'Amen' echoed around the hall, followed by a Vatican wave.

"Let us pray that all the wickedness we hear in the music of today may not corrupt the minds and hearts of our children. That they will not go out and buy flares and smoke pot and indulge in the orgy." By this time several of the more elderly clerics were floundering. Some of the younger ones wondered if the rumours about Bishop Bone and the bottle were true. They sat down amidst much rustling of papers and coughing. "Dear Brethren … "

As Bishop Bone launched into his invective, Father O'Dowd paced around the presbytery deep in thought and concern. He hadn't joined the priesthood to worry about his own feelings but to go out and shepherd the flock. After his meeting with Solomon all his thoughts had been about the man, and no matter how many Hail Marys, candles lit and cold baths, the damned thoughts were still there.

"Father, you have a visitor." Before his housekeeper had chance to tell him who it was, the bustling form of Mrs Hebblethwaite burst into the room. She positively glowed below her own personalised halo. She was about to speak but was stopped by the hand of O'Dowd. "I know you've spoken to the Bishop: he's coming round later."

Mrs Hebblethwaite was momentarily deflated but she drew up a chair and sat down.

"Hippies, Father. I've been doing a bit of research down the library; got a few queer looks from Miss Temple mind, but when I put her in the picture she was very helpful." She pulled a piece of paper from her pocket and read: "Hippies: people of unconventional appearance, typically having long hair – that's him then, isn't it? – and wearing beards. Associated with a subculture involving the rejection of conventional values and the taking of hall-u-c-i-n-o-g-e-n-i-c drugs. Beatniks. Dropouts. Flower Children." She put the piece of paper away, looked at Father O'Dowd and continued: "Druggies, Father, unconventional. Shall we cut his hair off, Father, would that help? I mean if he hasn't got the hair, you know like Samson, then perhaps he'll go back to normal and stop taking drugs and go to church and the child won't go to hell."

A little bit of knowledge was dangerous in the hands of a fanatic. He put his hands together. "Tolerance, Mrs Hebblethwaite. Tolerance." She didn't hear a word zealots have a problem with listening.

"I've called a meeting of the Catholic Mothers' Group and also The Prospect Street Committee, to look at what we can do to nip this hippy thing in the bud."

"Good God!" thought Father O'Dowd. He'd been told the last time the Prospect Committee met was to organize V. E. Day, and that turned into a drunken brawl on such a monumental scale that ambulances from three districts had to be called in. As for the Catholic Mothers, they were Vatican Gauleiters who were not to be challenged on theological matters. Mrs Hebblethwaite was chairman of both and as Parish Priest he would have to attend the meetings.

"I've already spoken to Miss Mahoney. She wanted to tar and feather that heathen Tump, but I managed to persuade her that it wasn't a good idea."

Father O'Dowd raised his eyes heavenwards.

"Yet!" she added.

Miss Mahoney had set up a factional movement of the Catholic

Women's Group after the introduction of the Abortion Bill. She was a dangerous zealot who made Mrs Hebblethwaite look like Gandhi. The priest had heard on the ecumenical grapevine that she'd been over to the United States of America and had been engaged in some underground guerrilla activities. He put this down to mere gossip. Mrs Hebblethwaite knew different.

"I'm sure the Bishop wouldn't approve of any violence," he said, knowing that she already deemed him spineless when it came to standing up for the church.

"Father, what will it take for you to get off the theological fence and defend your parishioners from the evil that is here in Broughton? It is living next door to me and giving your man Mr Hebblethwaite a terrible time with his sleeping habits. If its not all that damned music, it's the moaning and goings on that gives a healthy man like Mr Hebblethwaite ideas that shouldn't be encouraged, he being seventy three. Does the Devil himself have to come riding up the street naked on a motorbike for you to do anything?" Father O'Dowd quite liked her analogy.

Fundamentalist, zealot, bigot. These were all tags you could pin on Mrs Hebblethwaite, but she was above all a mother, wife and grandmother. She was a woman and was as perceptive as Cassandra.

"Are you concerned about anything else father?" she asked, dipping her rod into the dark pool that was Father O'Dowd's conscience.

"Concerned! Me?" He laughed at the very idea, but his conviction was as hollow as a politician's at election time.

Mrs Hebblethwaite knew the wiles of man and she also knew that Thomas O'Dowd was what was known as a Mother's Vocation. How did she know? She just did. The church was full of them, boys in men's clothing trying desperately to make their mothers happy by joining the priesthood. Father O'Dowd may know how to give the sacraments but his heart wasn't in it. He was easily distracted and she knew. Hadn't she been married nearly fifty-five years and studied the wiles of man? There was nothing she didn't know about lying, and the Parish Priest was doing just that. Lying.

"Father, can I ask you straight?" Mrs Hebblethwaite said.

"Is there any other way?" he grimaced.

The bosomed one squinted at him. She had her prey in sight and she wasn't going to be deflected by ecclesiastical humour. "Is it the drink?"

"No!" he said with feeling.

"Because you know, Father, you wouldn't be the first priest we've had here who liked more than the occasional glass of whisky." She tried to give him an escape route, but he was adamant.

"I don't have a drink problem," he reiterated firmly.

"Well, it must be the women. Have you found yourself a bit troubled with some of the younger woman, Father? I mean I know you're a priest an' all but it must be difficult, you only in your thirties and still with, you know, feelings in that department."

This was getting out of hand. Father O'Dowd felt like it was he who was in the wrong, he who should have been in the confessional. He was also annoyed that he'd let a parishioner try to get him to divulge what really was the problem.

"Thank you Mrs Hebblethwaite, but I'm all right." He looked at her and could see her furrowed brow thought otherwise. "Honestly, I'm OK."

"I'm not convinced, Father. I think you should go on a retreat, you know, down to some Abbey in Devon and talk to the trees and stuff. Relax, take the weight off your crucifix. You're young, you'll bounce back."

Mrs Hebblethwaite was good, thought Thomas; she was very good. She'd nearly convinced him that, yes, he should have a break, but then he knew that she just wanted him out of the way so she could drive the Tumps out of town. She wanted to cleanse Broughton of the permissive society.

"It'll take more than one suspicious cigarette to bring Armageddon to this town!" he said. Mrs Hebblethwaite quickly changed tack and started to talk about direct action. Father O'Dowd tried to deflect her. He failed.

"Father, we have to defend ourselves from their polluted thoughts and actions, and if that means we have to resort to some strong-arm tactics then so be it." She was already talking of taking it to the highest ecclesiastical authorities.

Father O'Dowd had enough on his plate already, what with Solomon, impure thoughts and the impending arrival of the Bishop; the last thing he wanted was all-out warfare on Prospect Street. He wanted to warn Solomon and Cass that danger was afoot, but he didn't want to visit their house lest his impure thoughts get the better of him. And he knew they would.

"Could I ask you, Mrs Hebblethwaite, if not for my sake then the Church's, not to arrange any meetings until after the Bishop has been and I have had chance to speak to you and to Solomon and Cass?" There was desperation in his voice, and he knew it.

So did Mrs Hebblethwaite. She thought for a few seconds, looked at Father O'Dowd and said: "OK Father, but that doesn't mean we're not going to. It just means we'll be putting it on the back burner for a while."

She said good-bye and left his office, walking calmly down the hallway in the way only those that think victory has nearly been achieved can.

Father O'Dowd returned to his chair and thought for a while. He didn't want some kind of sectarian divide in his parish, he wanted it to be inclusive, those with flared jeans praying with those with drainpipe jeans, but he could see that soon, oh very soon, the jean war could be on the front page of every newspaper in the country. The last thing he wanted was journalists snooping around the town looking to sensationalise the situation.

Chapter 7

There was nothing extraordinary about a nineteen-year-old girl having an all-consuming crush on somebody. It was only to be expected and Margaret was a very attractive girl indeed. In fact, her mother had been a little worried that her interest in the opposite sex had taken this long. Broughton female lore stated that every girl should be married and have a family before her twenty-fifth birthday. To be a spinster in Broughton was virtually a crime and the culprit was looked upon with suspicion and pity. Lesbianism was an urban trait and Broughton women were not afflicted, or so they thought. So, when Margaret displayed all the signs of infatuation, her mother for one was delighted. The house was full to bursting anyway, so losing a child would free up a bit more space and the food bill wouldn't be so big. Her grandmother was also pleased. She too remembered those first heady days of love. Of course being married for over fifty years had dulled the memory, but she was delighted for Margaret. Briefly delighted, that is.

It was only when she realised who her granddaughter's favours were being bestowed upon did she start to worry. Margaret's infatuation was with the flared one. He with long hair and worrying rolled-up cigarettes. Yes. Solomon bloody Tump. Mrs Hebblethwaite wasn't one for paranoia, she being a devout Catholic who didn't have to worry about such things, because Prayer was solid and certain. She knew what was right and what was wrong. However, she was distressed that her new neighbour, who had already introduced her grandson Gary to the wicked weed, seemed hell-bent on ruining the lives of all those closest to her.

She first saw them the night after she'd phoned the Bishop. Solomon was walking down the street, all hair, eyes, flares, and colours. She snarled at him through the net curtains and wrote down in her pagan-busting diary the time, date and where he was heading. She was determined that the

Bishop would have at his fingertips as detailed a list of events as possible. "When you're dealing with evil, you have to be precise," Mrs Hebblethwaite said to the Archangel Gabriel. She was about to let the net curtain go when she saw her granddaughter Margaret skip down the road after HIM, stop, and then *engage him in conversation.*

"Jesus, Mary and Joseph!" she said, blessing herself before the picture of the Pope. Before you could rattle off the names of the twelve apostles she was in her shoes and coat, and out the door. Broughton's only Catholic sleuth.

"Hiya!" Margaret said, pulse racing, breasts heaving, and stomach rippling with anticipation.

"Hello," replied Solomon, flicking his hair from his face so he could get a look at who was speaking. There was a pause that seemed to last an eternity to Margaret. She tried desperately to subdue the giggles that seemed imminent. They carried on walking in silence until she said: "I saw you move in yesterday." She tried to think of something else to say. "I like the van. Do all your lot drive things like that?" She didn't know where her new-found confidence had come from, but glad nonetheless that she'd said something.

"Yeah, suppose so."

"Who did all the painting?" Margaret didn't want to stop talking.

"I think we all had a go. We all mucked in."

"All? I thought there was just you and your lady friend." Margaret wanted to know more about Solomon's lady friend.

"Well, everyone kind of helps out, you know. If the van needs fixing someone will give you a hand. It's what communal living's all about. Have you read any Marx?"

Margaret was confused. "No." She plumped for honesty.

"Well, when you've got time we'll go through what he has to say." Solomon said, happy that he had an eager student. Eager she was, but not for dialectical discourse.

"That'd be great," Margaret said. She'd go to the library tomorrow and find out who this Marx chap was. She didn't want to look foolish in front of Solomon.

Chapter 8

M rs Hebblethwaite's apprenticeship in the dark arts of surveillance had come from the television and in particular, Z-Cars. She was staying as close as possible to the suspects as she could without being spotted. To the casual observer, which meant every house in the street, she was anything but inconspicuous. Trying to hide a 60–60–60 figure in a green anorak at seven-thirty in the evening was never going to be easy. Although she was an avid viewer of detective programmes, her surveillance skills were abysmal. Crouching as best she could, she followed them down the street using the privets as camouflage. If it were hard enough for Mrs Hebblethwaite to follow them, it was doubly difficult as she was trying to write down what she heard at the same time. She wanted the notes to be contemporaneous, whatever that meant, but it seemed important, because that's what the courts wanted, so she expected the Bishop would want similar too.

Solomon being Solomon, granite chin, eyes to die for, and West Coast Surfing looks, was used to admirers, sometimes even Catholic Priests. Usually it was young women; being a healthy male he always took advantage of situations that presented themselves. He and Cass had an open relationship and always told each other who they had slept with. They were totally honest. This was normal practice amongst their friends. He never forced anyone into sleeping with him, but the sheer force of his personality meant that he was rarely without a different partner two or three times a month. Obviously, when they were on the road it was different, but they had settled in Broughton and, although he didn't expect as a right to lay half the female population, he knew that the opportunities would arise at some time or other.

"I'm just off to get some tobacco: do you want to come with me?" Solomon asked.

It wasn't the greatest line that Margaret had heard. Having been brought up on the classic films of the forties and fifties, she was expecting something a little bit more romantic.

"Yes please!" They carried on walking, not saying too much, with Margaret ready to hang on to every word Solomon might say. She wanted to try and remain cool and so said nothing. Margaret liked being with him because he was different from all the boys in Broughton. They constantly flexed their muscles and talked of doing of great things that everyone knew they wouldn't do. And then she did something quite out of character: she held his hand. Turning, Solomon smiled at her. Margaret's knees nearly buckled and something happened that felt, well, good.

They both heard a rustle and turned round just in time to see a green ball of plastic disappear into Number Thirteen's hedge. They both rushed back and tried to retrieve the lost soul.

"Probably Mr Hampson," Margaret said. "He's always having one too many." Solomon smiled, and reached down to try and grab an arm or a leg and pull Mr Hampson from his leafy confines.

"Get your bloody hands off me," said the hedge; it wasn't Mr Hampson, unless he'd started impersonating women in his spare time, which according to Margaret's mother was possible, as anything was possible in the Hampson household.

"You're not going to have your wicked way with me, you long haired, drug-crazed disciple of Lucifer," said Mrs Hebblethwaite as she emerged from the hedge like Raggedy Ann.

"Nan!" exclaimed Margaret. "What are you doing in that hedge?"

Mrs Hebblethwaite had always known that her granddaughter had not been blessed with the sharpest of intellects, but to think she would want to hide in a hedge as a matter of course took the biscuit. In fact it took the whole barrel.

"Well, I'm not in there for the good of my health now am I?" Mrs Hebblethwaite said removing bits of twig from her hair. She spat out a leaf and pointed to Solomon.

"What the bloody hell are you doing with this . . ." She looked Solomon up and down as though he were from outer space. " . . . *specimen*? He's only after one thing, Margaret!"

"And what would that be, Nan?" asked her granddaughter, fully aware of what her Nan was thinking but wanting her to spell it out.

"You know perfectly well what I mean, so don't come the innocent with me, young lady." Mrs Hebblethwaite waved her famous finger at Margaret. To any other citizen of Broughton this would have been warning enough but to her grandchildren and especially Margaret, who'd been accustomed to the wagging of the finger on many occasions, it had little authority.

"Nan, I was just walking to the shops with a neighbour. Doesn't it say in the Bible we must love our neighbour?" Margaret said, throwing a bit of scripture back at her Nan.

"Don't blaspheme, girl, don't you blaspheme with me, Margaret. You know very well that love in the Bible doesn't mean S-E-X," shouted her grandmother, who was so annoyed she dropped her Pagan Diary onto the floor. This was the first time Margaret had heard her Nan use the term sex and she was pleasantly shocked.

Margaret picked the diary off the floor. "What's this?" she asked, leafing through the first few pages.

"It's got nothing to do with you Margaret, now give it here." Mrs Hebblethwaite was getting slightly worried, a state Solomon hadn't seen before. He'd seen her angry, irate, annoyed, but never embarrassed.

"It's just a shopping list," she lied. That would be four Hail Mary's.

Margaret flicked through a few more pages, then turned to the front cover and read out loud. "THE PAGAN-BUSTING DIARY. HOW TO ERADICATE SIN AND SOLOMON TUMP FROM BROUGHTON." She handed the diary to Solomon.

"Nan, what's all this about?"

Solomon looked at a few pages and gave it back to Mrs Hebblethwaite. She grabbed it eagerly.

"I'm working for the Bishop. He said I have to monitor the goings on at Number twenty-three." Mrs Hebblethwaite said. It was a lie but only a wee one, which would probably mean only a few extra days in Purgatory.

"But we're not doing anything!" pleaded Margaret as she looked at Solomon longingly.

"Margaret, the Permissive Society is just a rolled-up cigarette away, and I'll be damned if I'll let my granddaughter be deflowered by this good-for-nothing layabout," Mrs Hebblethwaite said with all the conviction one would expect from the Chair of The Catholic Women's Guild.

"Nan, I was just talking to him! And I wasn't smoking," she said, outraged.

"Well, it starts off that way, and before you know it your face'll be all painted up like some bloody tart, and then he'll have you running naked through corn fields, banging a drum and chanting the Devil's music!"

"We don't have corn fields in Broughton."

"Look. I don't want you cavorting with him," said Mrs Hebblethwaite, pointing at Solomon."He's trouble, Margaret. You mark my words." She took a deep breath. "And besides, what will the neighbours think, you walking down the road at all hours with a hippy?"

"Nan, I don't care what the neighbours think. I'm not doing anything wrong," implored Margaret.

"Look, it's OK Margaret. If it's getting you into trouble –" Solomon was about to agree to compromise but Margaret was having none of it.

"No, Solomon. I'm nineteen and I can walk to the shops with whoever I want to." Margaret grabbed hold of his hand and they went on their way.

Mrs Hebblethwaite stood there stunned that she had been defied by her own granddaughter. Waving the Pagan Busting Diary at them both she shouted for all the street to hear: "I'll phone Father O'Dowd and tell him to come and speak to your mother. Hopefully she can talk some sense into that teenage head of yours."

She turned and walked back to her house, noting in her diary that her granddaughter had carried on regardless with one Solomon Tump, hippy of the Parish of Broughton.

They finished what little shopping Solomon had to do and left the newsagents. Margaret still had hold of his hand and they just carried on walking away from Prospect Street. Very little was said, but Margaret was experiencing a female version of what her parish priest felt. "Why did you come to Broughton?" she asked.

"Well, we just got kinda sick of moving around. It wasn't that bad when it was just the two of us, but when Leo came along, it made things more difficult," Solomon replied.

"How old is he?" Margaret wanted to find out as much as she could about Solomon and his family.

"Eighteen months."

"Lovely looking boy."

"Thanks."

"How long have you and your ...?"

"Girlfriend," supplied Solomon, smiling.

"Yes," Margaret said, blushing.

"Must be over ten years now."

"Aren't you married?"

"No," Solomon said in utter horror at the prospect.

"You couldn't live in Broughton for that long together and not get married," Margaret replied with a pained expression.

"Why not?"

"Because you couldn't, there'd be all hell to pay. For one, your mum and dad wouldn't speak to you if you didn't get married, and if that didn't work the priest'd be round telling you all about Sodom and Gomorra, gnashing of teeth, plagues of this and that, and if that didn't work, he'd play the master card."

"What card's that then?"

"The Eternal Damnation card, of course."

"Heavy!" laughed Solomon.

"It's no laughing matter," Margaret said seriously

"No, I suppose it isn't." There was a couple of minutes' silence.

"Is that why your Nan's giving me such a hard time?"

"Probably, but then she gives everyone a hard time who doesn't do as much for the church as she does. The Virgin Mary would have a struggle keeping up with her."

Solomon started to laugh.

"What you laughing at?" she asked, thinking he was laughing at her.

"Just what you said, it made me laugh." Solomon kissed her on the cheek. "It was just funny." Margaret squeezed his hand and said nothing. The two meandered through the town and walked up one of the pack-horse trails that led up to the tops.

"Have you always travelled?" asked Margaret.

"I suppose I have really. Even when I wasn't travelling I always wanted to be somewhere else."

"Daydreaming, you mean."

"Yes," Solomon said, looking around the hills that had been trussed up together like a side of beef. Outcrops of rocks were desperately trying to flee from their underground prisons, only their escape route was blocked by the elements, forced back to stay in their inhospitable surroundings. "The day you stop dreaming is the day you stop living," said Solomon the Sage.

"Know what you mean. My old man used to take his belt off to stop us daydreaming. He said it helped to concentrate our minds." Margaret had never told anybody this before. "It didn't work; it just made us dream even more of getting away."

Solomon stopped walking and, facing Margaret, put his large soft hands to the sides of her face and asked " Why haven't you?"

"Why haven't I what?" Margaret looked puzzled.

"Left home!"

"Girls don't leave their parents' home unless they're in a box or they're getting married."

"Really?" Solomon was genuinely shocked.

"For somebody who's travelled the world, you're pretty naive aren't you?" It was Margaret's turn to laugh and she was laughing at him, not with him.

Solomon just pursed his lips and they carried on walking.

"If I left the house, me dad would beat the living daylights out of me."

"Why?"

"Because I'd be bringing shame onto the family. Everybody would know that I was pregnant and had to leave." It was Margaret's turn to be the wise one.

Solomon chose ground he was more sure of and said: "Violence doesn't work. Look at Vietnam!" Margaret didn't know what he was talking about, so she just looked at the sky. "Where's Vietnam"

Solomon smiled. "It's in the far East. The Americans are using it for target practice."

"Oh," replied Margaret. "Have you been there, then?"

"No. We wanted to, but then the war broke out." Solomon said matter-of-factly.

"Wouldn't be much fun travelling when there's a war on." Margaret laughed.

Solomon looked at Margaret, gently stroked the hair away from her cheeks, and placed the softest of kisses on her mouth. She would later describe that kiss as a snowflake gently falling on her lips, because Solomon had told her that snowflakes always find the right place to land. Her mother would nearly vomit when she was told the tale.

They had walked over a mile and a half before they stopped and leaned on a large boulder "Are you a virgin?" Solomon asked. He sat down and started to roll a cigarette. He looked up at Margaret who was visibly shocked by the question.

"What kind of question's that?"

"Perfectly normal question." Solomon lit his cigarette. "You don't have to answer if you don't want to." He was all gentleman.

Margaret didn't want to answer because he would be shocked that she still was. She bet he didn't know any nineteen year old virgins. She bet all his girlfriends were dead experienced at sex and the like. She would give her right arm to be as confident as all his female friends were. Liberated, on the Pill, having orgasms on the hour every hour whether they wanted them or not. She wished he'd never asked, because it kind of ruined what they had. She knew she wanted to sleep with him, and she knew she would, but not like this. Not being quizzed, not being sneered at for not losing something she didn't want to lose. When she lost her virginity it would have to be at the right time, and this time, it wasn't.

"I think I better get back now, it's getting late." Margaret was crying, so she tried to turn her face away from Solomon. "So I'll see –"

Solomon stood up and grabbed her arm. "I didn't mean to offend you." He tried to give her hug but she pulled away.

"Well you did," she managed to say through the salty tears that just wouldn't stay where they were supposed to stay.

"I'm sorry." And he was. Solomon was genuinely sorry.

"So you should be. I was having such a nice time and then you go and say that, and laugh and sneer because I don't immediately stick my legs in the air."

Margaret walked off and managed to wipe her eyes before he caught up with her. She marched off again keeping some distance between them. They arrived in the town centre and Solomon ran in front of her.

"I'm sorry Margaret. Truly I am." Solomon sighed. "Can I see you again?"

Margaret did want to see him again. "I'll see." She'd managed to dry her face, and so turned round. "But if you ever say anything like that again you won't."

"OK" Solomon felt well and truly admonished. Margaret smiled and walked back home.

Chapter 9

S olomon, Cass and Leo headed for the town centre. The reason for coming to Broughton was to put down some roots, for themselves, but mainly for their son, Leo. They'd done the Magic Bus thing, and were Chakra'd to the eyeballs. They'd eaten cheese and drunk red wine on the left bank in Paris and listened to Jean Paul Sartre talk about whatever he was talking about, which didn't seem much. They'd danced and debated and had passionate sex in apartments off Montmartre. Squats in London had been drug-fuelled heaven, but when the drugs ran out and the squalor kicked in, reality was only a sober morning away. No, they'd convinced each other to set up a workers cooperative somewhere in England and sell organic foods and oils and nuts and books. Healthy stuff that gave everyone an opportunity to earn a reasonable wage. Theirs was to be the first beardless co-operative enterprise.

That's what Solomon thought they both wanted. When he went on one of his 'we'll change the world' talks about cooperatives and workers of the world united against the suits, Cass used to smile in all the right places and laugh at the same old jokes. She wanted to believe what he said, as she had in the past, but now that she'd lived with him for so long she knew what he was really like. Solomon was like those plants that can live in a bottle without roots or soil. He was frightened to put any roots down in case he couldn't dig them up and leave. She was amazed they'd got this far, and to give Solomon his due he was certainly trying to play the part. And then there would be the women. They'd both played the field and had told each other whom they'd slept with but Cass was in her mid thirties and getting bored. Not with sex, but the competitive nature of it, trying to keep up with Solomon's conquests, keeping the flame of feminism burning bright. What she wanted really was some loyalty, but once you've burnt your bra the sisters expected you to compete with the men. The game was beginning to become tiresome.

On their way to the estate agents they called into the only café in Broughton. It was called *'Everything But the Squeak'* in a rakish attempt at humour. They fried, toasted, and boiled all that came from the pig, even the residual pig-swill from their stomachs was used, but no one was brave enough to ask the proprietor what its use was. The decor was nicotine brown, the tables were laid with yellow and green checked cloths, and the ceiling was Artexed in grease. As soon as the newcomers walked through the door, five faces from separate tables slowly turned round. It could have been a scene from one of Hitchcock's more ghoulish films. The diners were an assortment of Broughton's less well-adjusted citizens.

Ken, the bag man, who spent his life looking through bins for tin cans because he was building a boat, was the first to speak. "Is it Pantomime season already?" laughed the landlocked sailor. He was referring to their dress, which seemed quite strange to Solomon as he thought they'd dressed down for the occasion. The four other café-dwellers joined in laughing and pointing.

"Come on Sol, let's go," Cass said, tugging at his arm. She was ready to leave.

"No." He half turned and smiled at her, took Leo in his arms and walked to the only vacant table.

Mrs Butterworth, the owner, looked concerned because she knew that incomers were not well liked, especially when they wore pyjamas twenty-four hours a day. She was large, knew her trotter from her snout and was holding a large and very greasy ladle. "Now I don't want any trouble. D' you hear me?" She pointed the ladle first at Ken and then at Sol, before moving it around the room in some kind of Shamanic ritual, making sure that everybody knew what she meant. They did.

"Could I get everybody a cup of tea, please?" Solomon said, smiling. "While we decide what we'd like to eat." This act of generosity stumped the locals, especially Ken who was known to throw his money around like a man with no arms.

"That's five teas then." Mrs Butterworth moved her bulk towards the tea urn that rose above everything else like a giant cooling tower.

"Ah'm not having any tea from some ponced-up, long haired how's-your-father, thank you very much. No, I've bought me own for over fifty year and Ah'm not changing now," said Ken who had suddenly decided to be neither a lender nor borrower.

Mrs Butterworth turned round. In thirty-five years as proprietor of 'Everything but the Squeak' she had never known Ken to turn down anything. After the initial shock she looked at the other four, pointing her spoon at them one by one, clarifying whether they too were going to take the high moral ground and affect her cash flow.

"Tea," she said in turn, and all accepted. Ken was appalled and walked out of the café in disgust, which was a novel twist. It was usually fellow diners who walked out at the sight of Ken and his eating habits. His morning ritual started with him taking out his false teeth, rinsing them in his cup of tea and then attacking his Full English Breakfast.

"OK. Four teas it is then. Thank you, young man," said Mrs Butterworth, who wasn't fazed by long hair or loud clothes, having been a hairdresser's apprentice some forty years ago.

Solomon sat Leo next to him on the bench. Cass leaned over to see what was on the handwritten menu. Sausage. Sausage and Egg. Sausage, egg and chips. Sausage, egg and chips, beans and three rounds of fried bread. Sausage sandwich. Bacon, egg, mushrooms, beans, chips, tomatoes and three rounds of fried bread. Black pudding. White Pudding. Trotters deep fried and chips. Belly pork and mushy peas. Belly pork and any combination of the above, with chips.

Solomon stood up and walked to the counter. "Do you do a Veggie breakfast?" he asked naively.

"What?" said the chef.

"Veggie. Vegetarian. We're Vegetarian."

"Never heard of it!"

"No, it's not a place, it means without meat. Meatless," Solomon explained.

"Without meat! Why would you want a cooked breakfast without meat?" she said, trying to get her head around a concept that would mean her business would go under within a fortnight. Her fellow meat-eaters to a man agreed in a state of puzzlement. It was difficult enough to accept this man with long hair and strange clothes, but to hear him say that he wanted a cooked breakfast without meat, well ... 'Everything But the Squeak' had never seen the like. A gasp went round the café.

"It's just that we don't eat meat," Solomon said.

That would explain a lot, thought Ronald White who sat four benches away from them. He whispered to Arthur Nolan, one bench behind, that it was a well-known fact that if you went without, your brain became addled. Arthur Nolan wanted to know what you went without to make your brain addled, because whatever it was, he wanted some quick. He'd heard about Ronald's whispering and where it led. He slid up the bench lest somebody saw Arthur's mouth very close to his ear. Things like that could lead to a lifetime of abuse in Broughton. Fortunately nobody saw.

"If you don't eat meat why have you come into a café that serves only meat?" Confused, Mrs Butterworth took the four teas to her customers. Cass smiled at her when she went past.

"Two lots of beans and toast then, please," the vegetarian said, looking at Cass to see whether he had made the right decision. She nodded. Leo managed to grab the salt-cellar and empty its contents onto the table. Cass tut-tutted, smiled at her son, and asked Solomon if he could get a cloth.

*****

Mrs Hebblethwaite strolled imperiously through the town centre, satisfied that her morning's work had come to fruition. Several people noticed the difference from two days ago, when word went out that she was possessed by something and if it wasn't the Devil it was somebody very similar. She nodded and waved and passed the time of day with all and sundry. She even acknowledged Mrs Harding, who she'd not spoken to for three years since the brazen hussy had run off with the Pools collector.

She happened to glance through the window of 'Everything But The Squeak,' and her momentary delight in all things crashed to the floor. She couldn't believe her eyes; it was like seeing her husband sober on a Friday night. These things didn't happen, hippy, wife and child in her café eating, drinking and being merry.

"What the –?" She did a double take. "Right!" She fired herself through the door of the café as best somebody could whose measurements were sixty, sixty and sixty. She went straight up to the counter to confront the proprietor. Mrs Butterworth turned round. "Hello Ethel, how are you?"

Before her potted medical history could be revealed to the eager ears of the café, Mrs Hebblethwaite took the café owner to one side. A scrum developed. "Lizzy, what the hell are you doing serving them people in your café?" she exclaimed, feeling the effects of the whalebone corset her Ada gave her for Christmas. "He's a known druggy," said Mrs Hebblethwaite, now conversant with Hippy Lore and Language. "He tried to sell our Gary some stuff the day before yesterday."

"No!" exclaimed the tea maker.

"And they play the Devil's music all night and cavort." The trowel was being used and thickly.

"You don't mean?" She couldn't bear to use the S word and mouthed the words P-E-R-C-Y F-I-L-T-H.

"Not only that, but there are lots of them writhing around at the same time. Men with men and women with women!"

Mrs Butterworth went as red as her three-tier grill. She put her hand to her face and said, "No! In Broughton! There's a law against that, isn't there? And if there isn't, there should be."

"Apparently they used to live in India but got thrown out for you-know-what."

In the context of the conversation, 'you know what,' could mean any of a thousand things and, with Mrs Hebblethwaite already having mentioned THAT and drug taking, Mrs Butterworth was at a loss to come up with anything else that could be as bad. "No I don't, Ethel. You'll have to say."

"Well, I saw with my own eyes books about –" She huddled even closer to the chef, if that were physically possible between two women whose combined chest measurements came to 115. "– Devil Worship"

Well, that was it. Mrs Butterworth was a fair woman and she'd let them buy everyone a cup of tea. Long hair she could cope with, clothes not too much of a problem, but kneeling at the altar of the cloven-hoofed one, well enough is enough.

"Out! Come on, I don't want your sort peddling that kind of malarkey round here. You can do that sort of thing in London, but not round here. So come on, shift."

Solomon stood up and tried to plead with the proprietor, but she was having none of it. "Out! Come on, I've told you once, now shift."

Solomon took hold of Leo, who by now was crying at all the shouting. They left the café.

"That was a near thing, Ethel. Why didn't you tell me before, I would have put a sign up: NO FLARED JEANS.

"Well, I've been busy up at the presbytery trying to get that priest of ours to do something. And can I? Can I bloody hell. He's about as much use as a chocolate fire-guard. Anyway, I had a word with the Bishop this morning and he's coming over to sort it out this afternoon."

"How's your Gary?"

"I gave him what for, but you know what these teenagers are like ..."

Mrs Butterworth nodded in agreement. She had three boys who had all left Broughton trying to find work.

Solomon and Cass stood on the pavement outside the café and glared at each other. Then they looked into the café, saw the four people drinking cups of tea bought by them and began to laugh. None of your polite, back of the throat kind of middle class laugh. No, they roared with joy. Solomon and Cass had been on umpteen political marches and campaigns, arrested on numerous occasions for trespass and the like, but this was a first, being thrown out and banned from a café. The students in Paris were about to take the Sorbonne and start a movement that would have massive ramifications world-wide, and here in this northern enclave they had been banned from the café. Good name for a band, thought Solomon as he put Leo onto his shoulders.

Mrs Hebblethwaite and Mrs Butterworth were discussing at length what their next move should be to rid Broughton of this family when they saw that, despite being ejected from Broughton's only café, the hippies were laughing at their plight. Most people would have been positively shame-faced. Most normal citizens would have had the decency to move away as quickly as possible. Not the hippies.

"It'll be the drugs Ethel. I was reading that they can make you hyster-ical."

Mrs Hebblethwaite nodded in agreement. Her interest in all things hippified had led her to read all manner of worrying texts, although she hadn't, as yet, opened up the book on the Kama Sutra. Mr Hebblethwaite had.

"They say drugs can make you laugh that much you go delirious and fall off buildings and wander into oncoming traffic and hit policemen." Mrs Butterworth knew how to over-egg the pudding. "And in America one man laughed that much his wife took a gun and shot his head off."

Mrs Hebblethwaite wasn't too convinced of the latter tale, but she still nodded in agreement. "There's nothing worse when you've told somebody off and then they start laughing. In fact, it's bloody infuriating." Mrs Hebblethwaite's dander was up and she was all for going outside and wiping the smiles off their faces. She was about to launch herself through the door when a gnarled and leathery hand took a grip of her shoulder.

"Nay! Don't give them the pleasure, Ethel." The chef was known for her strong opinions and Mrs Hebblethwaite stayed put.

"Come on, sit down and we'll have a strong cup of tea." She manoeuvred her friend to a bench and went to make the tea.

Solomon stuck his head round the door. "I didn't pay you for the tea."

A large wet Co-op flannel that had done over six months service at the café flew through the air and hit the wall just to the side of Solomon's head. Solomon decided that payment wasn't required.

"Cheeky bugger! The Bishop can't come soon enough if you ask me." Mrs Butterworth continued to pour the tea out. It was that strong you could stand a dead mouse in it.

The four other tea drinkers kept their heads down. It was an unwritten law in Broughton that when two elderly women were 'in conference' they were best left alone. To interrupt was to put your life in danger. None of the four men present raised their heads until they'd finished their drinks. Then they left. Quietly.

Chapter 10

Solomon and Cass had seen a property that was to be part of their 'grand plan.' It was the old Co-operative building in the centre of Broughton. It still had the original stained glass frontage and big oak doors. He'd arranged to meet the estate agent that morning to discuss terms. The café incident hadn't been a great start to the day but he wasn't bothered. "I shouldn't be long," he said, picking Leo up and throwing him in the air. "So I'll meet you in . . ." He looked at his watch. "At elevenish." He put Leo down, gave Cass a kiss on the cheek and walked down the High Street to Griggs Estate Agency.

In some respects Cass hoped that they didn't get the property and would have to move on, but that would only be delaying the inevitable. She knew that if they did get the shop, Solomon would be enthused for a while but would soon lose interest and she'd have to pick up the reins. He'd end up spending most of his time smoking, putting the world to rights and trying to get as many of the local women into bed as possible. She was sure that he'd already found somebody. She knew him only too well.

Whilst Solomon was sorting out the legalities of the shop, Cass and Leo strolled slowly into the park. All parents are terribly proud when their offspring start to walk and Cass was no exception, though Leo wasn't walking as such: it was more of a controlled stumble. Gradually they meandered towards the swings and past the statue of one of Broughton's local boys made good. Leo wasn't interested in the statue, he was trying to catch a pigeon that was using the statue as target practice.

The park was a huge natural amphitheatre of trees and fields, with a bandstand in the middle and swings and roundabouts next to the bowling greens. Cass carried Leo over to the swings where two other mothers were playing with their children.

"Who does she think she is?" asked the larger of the two.

"Looks like the fairy from the bottom of the garden, if you ask me," her friend giggled. They took their children off the swings and moved over to the slides. They'd heard of hippies and didn't want to get too close. A Hippy Health Warning was being observed.

Cass didn't say anything; she just placed Leo on the swing and pushed him.

"Michael, get over here!" his mother said, but it was too late. Cass's strange clothes had intrigued the youngster and before his mum could stop him he was tugging at Cass's dress.

"Why are you wearing curtains?" the little boy asked.

"Well they're not exactly curtains, but –"

"Come here you little bugger." His mother picked him up with one arm. "What've Ah told you about speaking to strangers?"

"It's OK," Cass said.

"Is it, and how would you know?"

"He was just asking –"

"Ah know, and asking gets you into trouble, doesn't it Michael? Come on, let's –"

"Hiya, my name's Cass." Cass put her hand out but it remained a solitary hand hanging in the air. "And this is my son Leo, he's just eighteen months and I was wondering –"

"You can wonder all you like, love." She was making her way over to her friend who was beckoning her to get away from the Mad Dangerous Hippy. Sanctuary was a wooden bench.

Cass was not happy. "Oh, piss off then, you miserable tart." She'd had enough with Mrs Hebblethwaite, so she certainly wasn't going to take any nonsense from these teen mums.

"What did you say?"

"You heard." Cass replied.

"You cheeky bastard, you come here with your –"

"Change the record, love. I thought at least with you being younger you'd give us a fair crack before making your mind up. Look," Cass said, taking the wind out of the peroxide blonde's sails, "I'm here in a new town with my son and I hoped I could meet a few friends with kids. You know, so they could play together. Is that so bad?"

Peroxide halted. Thought for a moment and walked over.

"No, but you're different."

"Am I? So did I give birth and have the same shitty time like you?" The blonde started to smile. "And do you get woken up in the middle of the night because your husband's sobered up and wants mad, passionate, beery, five-inch, two-minute sex?"

Teen blonde laughed. "Yes!"

"And do you have enough money to put decent clothes on your children's backs?" Cass asked.

"No."

"Well, I'm not that different then, am I?"

"Suppose not." The two women sat down.

"My name's Cass." She held her hand out again and this time the gesture was acknowledged.

"Martha."

"Pleased to meet you, Martha."

"So, you've just moved here?" The questions started to flow. Broughton woman was nothing if not inquisitive.

"Yes, couple of days back, moved into Prospect Street, number 23."

"Not next to the Vatican?" Martha said.

"Mrs Hebblethwaite, you mean?"

"Yes. She's a nutter."

"You're telling me. She's already had the priest round to check us out."

"No!"

"Yes, but he couldn't take his eyes off Solomon."

"You're not saying he's a bit ..." Martha moved a limp wrist around. "Poofy, like?"

"I don't know, but he didn't take his eyes off him the whole time he was there. "

There's nothing like gossip to break the ice.

"Sheila, come here and listen to this," Martha shouted to her friend. "You'll never believe what Cass has just told me."

Cass smiled. She probably wouldn't become soul mates with Martha and Sheila, but it was good to strike up some sort of friendship with two women from the town.

Chapter 11

"**M**orning," said the receptionist when she heard the door open. She didn't look up immediately, engrossed as she was in a book. Turning it over, she raised her head and saw Solomon standing in front of the desk, smiling. Only sixteen, Doreen Ellis had led a sheltered life; her experiences came from the pages of the many books she had read. She had never seen the like before. She was used to businessmen in suits or supervisors from factories in their overalls and ties, but not this. Not long hair and yellow flares. Not in Broughton. She put her hand over her mouth and with all the professionalism she could muster she addressed the long-haired one. "How can I help you?" she squeaked as she feigned a smile.

"I have a ten o'clock appointment with Mr Griggs" Solomon said politely, sweeping his hair back from his forehead. Doreen looked at him again and realised she'd met him before, three books ago in an Arthurian legend where he stole the heart of Lady Blethwyn. He was doing the same to a dreamy receptionist.

"I'll just get him," she cooed, pursing her lips. She strode Mae West-style to Mr Griggs' office. She hadn't mastered the walk and nearly demolished the office Yucca in the process. "Mr Griggs will see you now," she said on her way back.

The business community had already been alerted to the hippy in the town, and Gordon Griggs, a small, pale figure, all nose, cheekbones and elbows, smiled behind his thick black-rimmed National Health glasses and greeted Solomon as he came into his office. "Please sit down," he said. Griggs was an accountant, where appearances were of no consequence if the client had enough money. His task, at which he was adept, was to find out how much Solomon had and how much he could extract for the property he was looking at. "So, you've been looking at the old

Co-op I believe?" the accountant said, leaning forward across his very large desk.

"Yes," Solomon replied, not wanting to appear too enthusiastic. Enthusiasm always meant a higher price when dealing with professionals.

"What would you be doing with it?"

"Health food shop, oils, books, etcetera" Solomon replied vaguely, not wanting to give too much away.

"Not much call for healthy food round here, Mr Tump. You may have gathered that Broughtonians are simple folk with simple tastes. If it has a heart, then they'll eat it."

"Should do well with lettuce then!" Solomon replied. His attempt at humour fell on stony ground. The accountant looked puzzled.

"Lettuce?" It took a while for the joke to work its way through his abacus-like mind. "I hope your business acumen is better than your humour," he replied.

Better stick to business, thought Solomon.

Mr Griggs pulled opened a file that lay on his desk. "Right. The old Co-Op buildings ..." He leafed through the sheets of paper. He took his glasses off, looked up at Solomon.

"Eighteen pounds a month rent, with rates at twelve," he said.

"Right." Solomon made a quick mental calculation. "Can we make an appointment to see inside the building?"

"Certainly." He buzzed through to his receptionist who came into his office hips a-swinging. 'Too much Hollywood' thought Solomon as she handed the diary to her boss.

"Monday morning, say ten-thirty?" he said, looking up at Solomon.

"Great," Solomon said as he got up. He was about to shake Mr Griggs' hand but the accountant had already negotiated the desk and was opening the door, ushering him out.

"Right, see you on Monday morning." Solomon nodded. That was the quickest transaction that he'd ever done. In fact it was the only transaction he'd ever done. Solomon said goodbye to Doreen and smiled coyly.

He walked to the park and received several wolf whistles from some myopic demolition workers. As he drew nearer to the site, they realised their error and the whistles turned into wholesale derision and abuse. Whistling at men was a hanging offence in these parts. Cass was still there, firing Leo down the slide, but her new friends Martha and Sheila had gone. Cass saw Solomon and waved. Solomon waved back, wondering whether their new project was really such a good idea.

Chapter 12

The Bishop had chaired a successful conference and was basking in the many plaudits he'd received when he remembered that he had to go to Broughton and sort out their troubles. A hippy and a homosexual priest. 'A Bishop's worries are many,' he whispered to himself as he got into his car. "Broughton Parish Church," he told his driver.

The Bishop had not been to Broughton for over five years and was shocked to find how little of it still stood. The massive factories that used to dominate the town had all but gone. Mounds of brick lay where once hundreds tended the looms. The church was still there amidst all the rubble, but he was still taken aback as they approached the presbytery. Behind the net curtain Miss Mcafferty spied the Bishop's car. Flustered, she let the curtain drop and gave the desk another quick polish. "Cleanliness is next to godliness," she said as she circled the desk with her duster. Dust was the devil's work, according to Miss Mcafferty. Dusting was endless and never done. Her own personal hell would be constant dusting.

"Dust is ninety per cent dead skin," Father O'Dowd had told her once and she didn't like to think of moving the priest around the presbytery, even if it was only his dead skin.

"Would that be dead skin from all over your body, Father?" she had inquired tentatively.

"Yes."

"Good God!" She was horrified to think that she'd been moving the priests' private parts around all areas of the presbytery. Including his bedroom. The thought had nearly killed her and she had to embark on a marathon confession to cleanse her soul. From that day on she always wore two pairs of rubber gloves when dusting.

"He's here!" she shouted.

Father O'Dowd was upstairs, working out what he would say. He wished he'd never said anything now, but in the heat of impromptu sexual encumbrances his mind was a chaos of irrational thoughts.

"Right. I'll be down in a minute," he replied.

To the Catholic Church, assignations with housekeepers were not unknown. Affairs with parishioners were becoming a worrisome problem, but homosexual activity with known hippies was a first. The Bishop had contacted the Vatican Sex Unit, which specialised in the Catholic Church's response to the sexual conduct of its priests. They had found several references to Homosexuality but they drew a blank when it came to Hippies. The Cardinal in charge of the department was so worried about this that he'd contacted the Bishop of San Francisco and was awaiting a report on how they deal with such problems. The Bishop got out of his car and walked towards the presbytery. Miss Mcafferty had taken off her rubber gloves and opened the front door. She curtsied, bowed and kissed his ring all in one go.

"Good afternoon, Your Grace." She moved backwards down the hall, still in a crunched-over position. She finally disappeared into the kitchen, to right herself and continue the day's chores.

Father O'Dowd walked into the hallway.

"Hello, Your Grace." He too, kissed the Bishop's ring. "May I take your coat?" The Bishop disrobed. "How was the conference?" Thomas O'Dowd was all nervous energy, firing questions off left right and centre.

"O'Dowd, enough of the questions, there's time enough for those and it will be me who'll be asking them. Meanwhile I would like a cup of tea. One sugar, please."

"Sorry." He turned and pointed to the kitchen.

"I'll just go and ask Miss Mcafferty to make us a pot. Biscuits?" he asked lamely.

"No, thank you. I have an hour, O'Dowd. That'll be a half hour for you and a half hour for the lady with the hippy problem. What's her name?"

"Mrs Hebblethwaite. "

Father O'Dowd walked briskly to the kitchen. "A pot of tea for two, Miss Mcafferty. No biscuits."

"Yes, Father." She was already boiling water in anticipation.

Father O'Dowd followed the Bishop into the office. He closed the door behind him. The Bishop had already sat down.

"Erections, O'Dowd. Homosexual erections. You know the church doesn't believe in erections per se unless they arise in the confines of a marriage, and then only if they are for the procreative act. Erections that lead to the creation of life are embraced by the church. In fact the Holy Father encourages erections in those cases. However, erections outside of marriage are frowned upon, and must be discouraged, either through prayer or showers. Cold showers. Homosexual erections however, do not have a place in the Catholic Church. Never have and never will. The Homosexual erection doesn't bear fruit. It is seedless and leads to sin, and we know that sin is wrong."

This wasn't a discussion, thought Thomas, he was being lectured.

Miss Mcafferty brought the tea into the office, slightly concerned at what she had heard. She thought she heard the Bishop talking about homosexual erections and it took all her fortitude to keep the tray from falling onto the floor. She made a point of coughing and shouting that tea was now ready. She didn't want to walk in on any erection talk or the like.

Father O'Dowd took the tray from her. "Thank you."

The housekeeper left, wondering just what went on underneath the Catholic Cassock. Father poured the tea and gave a cup to the Bishop. He took the cup and continued his speech.

"The Holy Father has ordained you in the name of God to serve him. We don't need erections O'Dowd. Erections are distractions, and we don't need distractions in the delivery of our ministry, do we?"

"No, Your Grace. But –"

"There are no buts where erections are concerned, Thomas. Too many buts and before you know it you've committed a grave sin, and grave sins lead to eternal damnation. You don't want to be led by your weakness into hell fire, now do you?"

Father O'Dowd immediately visualised the scene and he wanted to laugh, but laughter at such a juncture would have been disrespectful to his boss, who although erudite on this subject was nonetheless in some discomfort talking about it.

"So we'll have no more talk of arousals. Will we, O'Dowd?" He leaned forward and looked the priest forcefully in the eye. Father O'Dowd didn't respond straight away, which was tantamount to disagreement in the Bishop's eyes.

"Will we?"

"I can't honestly say," came the reply.

The Bishop hadn't bargained for this response. His directions were usually accepted and acted on without comment. "What do you mean, you can't honestly say?"

"I've never questioned being celibate and up until now it's never been a problem, but if I have these feelings that I can't control, what can I do?"

"We all have feelings, O'Dowd."

Father O'Dowd silently disputed this but let the Bishop carry on uninterrupted.

"But it is how we deal with these feelings that marks us out as different. It behoves you to disregard what you personally feel and continue to deliver the gospel to your parishioners."

He didn't want to tell the Bishop that while he read the Gospel last week he was in an aroused state and spent the whole of the Sunday afternoon on his knees asking for forgiveness.

"Now that's an end to it, O'Dowd. We'll have no more talk about such things, and I don't want to be contacted on such a topic again. Do I make myself clear?"

"Yes Your Grace. But –"

"And there certainly won't be any buts on the topic."

Father O'Dowd acquiesced, annoyed that he didn't have the resolve or moral courage to stand his ground. Solomon wouldn't have had such problems, he would have listened and then questioned. He just sat there and drank his tea. The Bishop sat back content that he'd resolved another problem. He might just reward himself with a biscuit after all.

Mrs Hebblethwaite was on time. She was always on time, and proud of it. Miss Mcafferty let her into the presbytery. The two ladies nodded and smiled to each other, the way two tennis players would before a match, each respectful of the other's attributes but not wishing to give too much away. The fight to be the number one female in the parish was a long and arduous struggle, and it wasn't over yet. Father O'Dowd showed her into the office where she saw His Grace finishing off his cup of tea. She bowed.

"Good afternoon, Your Grace," she said meekly, aware that she was in the presence of holiness. Father O'Dowd had never seen her do meekly before and was taken aback. He wondered if he wore more purple it would have the same effect.

The Bishop held out his hand and she kissed his ring.

'All that saliva,' thought Miss Mcafferty as she returned to the kitchen.

"Please sit down," the Bishop said, making himself comfortable in the large red armchair. "And tell me about these hippies."

"Well, Your Grace," Mrs Hebblethwaite held onto her handbag tightly; moral and spiritual fortitude was required. "Two days ago I was busy in the house when this van turned up, I say a van, it was more like a multi-coloured wreck, Your Grace, what with all the colours of the rainbow over it, I'm surprised the police let it on the road. However, this thing pulls up, and a man with hair you've not seen the like of before, down to his back-side Your Grace, can you believe it, must be festering with lice. He gets out and he's wearing, well, he's wearing clothes that would knock you over, I mean colours I didn't know existed. He then starts carrying books out of the van, books on magic, and Devil worship, Your Grace." She paused to bless herself. "Can you believe it, Devil worship in Broughton? And then the pipes come, Your Grace, pipes of all shapes and sizes and you know what they're used for?" He didn't, but let her carry on regardless. "And records that have strange chanting sounds and noises of people having –" She took a deep breath, shifted uncomfortably in her chair and said "Sounds of people fornicating, Your Grace." The Bishop didn't move an ecumenical muscle. He'd never heard anybody having sex and so wouldn't know what it sounded like anyway. For all he knew he could have such a record in his collection and be playing it every day.

"Then there was all the posters, Your Grace, of people with beards and Russians, and Che whoever. It's all posters and magic and the poor baby will be going to Hell, and they're up till all hours with their naked behaviour, Your Grace, and we can hear them and it's giving Mr Hebblethwaite below-the-belt ideas and at his age it's not natural. The other day I caught this Solomon Tump fellow smoking rolled-up cigarettes stuffed with drugs and giving my grandson some! Well, before we know it they'll all be addicts running around Broughton having you-know-what in broad daylight and all the young girls will be having babies in the bus stops and the Church needs to do something, Your Grace, and quickly!" Now that she had finished she placed her handbag on the floor.

The Bishop coughed slightly. It wasn't that he was ailing; it was to give him more time to take in what he had just heard. For a man who prided himself on having the answer for most things, this afternoon's trip to Broughton had posed him problems he'd never encountered before. Although he wasn't floundering for a response, it was taxing his intellect.

"This all sounds very dramatic, Mrs Hebblethwaite, but I'm not sure we can act on religious grounds just because somebody has long hair and wears coloured clothes. However, if we were sure that any kind of ritualistic Devil worship was afoot, then I certainly would get involved."

Mrs Hebblethwaite looked pleased. She looked across at her parish priest and smiled as if to say 'I told you so.'

"Listening to chanting music of whatever hue, whether it be copulating couples," Mrs Hebblethwaite blanched at his terminology and wanted to rinse her mouth out with a weak glass of bleach. "– in the confines of their own homes is a private matter about which we can do nothing. Now," he pointed a manicured digit in her direction, convinced that what he was about to say was correct, having delivered a speech to the Catholic Bishops on Drugs and Drug Abuse last year. "The drugs issue is a different matter. It is illegal in Common Law and as such is a matter for the police and the courts. If you have any information as to the smoking or supply of narcotic substances you must inform the authorities and they will take the appropriate action." The Bishop sat back in his chair, and folded his arms, contented that he'd made another follower of Christ happy with his moral and spiritual certainty.

"Thank you, Your Grace. So let me get this straight. I can't do anything about the hair and clothes –" The Bishop nodded. "– but with the Devil worship and drugs we can do something." The Bishop said yes and looked across at Father O'Dowd for affirmation that he was on sound spiritual ground.

"That's wonderful, Your Grace, but I'm not too happy about The Other." The Bishop didn't know what other problems she meant and asked accordingly.

"I mean, Your Grace, and I don't wish to appear impertinent, but all the ..." She couldn't bring herself to say the actual words out loud so she mouthed them to the Bishop very slowly. "S-E-X-U-A-L I-N-T-E-R-C-O-U-R-S-E" The Bishop leaned forward but was still unable to understand what she was saying.

"You'll have to speak louder, Mrs Hebblethwaite, I can't hear you."

Mrs Hebblethwaite never blushed but she too shifted rather uncomfortably in her chair. She picked up her handbag for support. "SHAGGING, YOUR GRACE," she shouted.

All this Hippy and Orgy nonsense had softened Mrs Hebblethwaite's attitude towards using expletives. Father O'Dowd thought it most unlike her, and before Solomon arrived on the scene, it was.

A crash could be heard from the kitchen, where Miss Mcafferty was trying to dry the dishes. She was merrily singing an old Irish ditty when she heard Mrs Hebblethwaite mention three words that left her speechless. Had it not been half an hour since, that the Bishop had been talking about homosexual erections, and now she was hearing that Mrs Hebblethwaite wished to engage in full frontal active nakedness with His Grace? She came over all funny, went to sit down and, for the first time in her life, went for the sherry. A tumbler full. In one. She passed out.

She wasn't the only one in the presbytery to suffer a reaction from hearing these words. The Bishop didn't react because he had never heard the word before and was still sitting there nonplussed. Father O'Dowd's heart skipped several beats.

"Shagging, Mrs Hebblethwaite? I'm afraid I've never come across shagging before. What is it?" asked the Bishop, unaware of what he had let himself in for. Father O'Dowd wanted to intervene to save His Grace's blushes, but he knew how his boss hated being interrupted, especially by the lower ranks. Mrs Hebblethwaite, too, baulked at answering immediately because she didn't mean to use that word, it shot out of her mouth and she was slightly distressed that it did. It wasn't a word she'd ever used, it was a term that Mr Hebblethwaite used when he'd been on the pop and wanted Percy Filth. He never got it but he always tried, and he always used that word.

"Sorry, Your Grace, I didn't mean to use that word. What I was trying to say was, what can we do about all the ..." She paused, searching for the correct word. " ... sexual intercourse."

"Ah, I see. I'm afraid, Mrs Hebblethwaite, that the State allows such activity in the confines of ones own home. The Church may take a different view if those engaged in copulation are not married. However, we are toothless in the face of this permissiveness, bar praying for them and lighting the odd candle for their souls." The Bishop put his hands together and in act of modern contrition said: "Let us pray for those unmarried shaggers in Broughton, that they may see the error of their ways, and follow in the true light of God."

There was a minute's silence before he added: "Is there anything else you wish to ask, Mrs Hebblethwaite?"

"Yes, Your Grace. Is it OK if I keep you informed of all the Pagan goings-on and Devil worship?"

The Bishop was tiring and for an easier life merely acquiesced. "That would be most welcome, Mrs Hebblethwaite. If you could pass it on to Father O'Dowd, I would be most grateful," he said.

"And if I see them having drugs, or selling them, I'm to contact the police?" she asked.

"Yes, that's right. Well," the Bishop stood up, "If there's nothing else, O'Dowd, I'll be on my way. It's been a long day."

The Bishop left the office and Father O'Dowd followed him to his car. The driver was asleep in the back, but quickly regained consciousness when prodded in the stomach by His Grace. The withering look the Bishop gave the driver told Father O'Dowd this wasn't the first time he had been caught sleeping on the job.

The car drove off and Father O'Dowd returned to the presbytery feeling a tad uncomfortable. It wasn't merely that his problem hadn't been sorted out, or discussed for that matter, it was the idea that he was told to just stop thinking about it and forget it ever happened. Of course this was impossible to do, as he was bound to bump into Solomon on his many walks through the town. Secondly he would have to confront Mrs Hebblethwaite; she'd be all smugness and light, convinced that right had always been on her side. She would make his life hell, now that her convictions had been ratified by a higher spiritual authority. She stood at the front door, radiant, glowing like a celestial moonbeam.

"That's just what I need!" he muttered under his breath as he walked towards the front door.

"Well, it seems me and the Bishop are on the same wavelength, doesn't it Father?" She paused. "It's a pity that the younger generation of clergy doesn't listen and learn from those more experienced in following the Gospel." She smiled the sanctimonious smile of those who know their path to salvation has already been mapped out. "Good day Father, I'll see you at six-thirty Mass." She walked slowly down Millgate.

Chapter 13

Father O'Dowd was in need of a drink. A large drink. He walked disconsolately back into the presbytery, aware that none of the issues raised had been dealt with. He walked into the kitchen to find Miss Mcafferty lying on the floor next to an empty bottle of sherry. "Oh my God!" he shrieked and ran over to where she lay. He rolled her into the recovery position and started to slap her face gently.

"Miss Mcafferty, are you all right?" This was an inadequate response in the circumstances, as it was plainly obvious that she was not, but it gave some sort of solace to Father O'Dowd. He kept slapping her face, hoping she would come round before he had to do any mouth-to-mouth resuscitation. At last her eyes began to roll around and finally she regained some semblance of control as she sat up and started to mutter incoherently. Father O'Dowd was convinced she was in some kind of delirium because she kept talking about erections and Mrs Hebblethwaite shagging the Bishop. He propped her up against one of the cupboard doors and went to make a cup of very strong coffee for both of them. She was still talking about erections when he brought the coffee over.

"Now drink this Miss Mcafferty, you'll feel much better with a hot drink inside you." He handed her the coffee. "And then we'll get you to bed."

The mention of Father O'Dowd putting her to bed, on top of everything else she'd heard mentioned between the Bishop and Mrs Hebblethwaite, sent Miss Mcafferty into a relapse. She attempted a raid on the drinks cabinet. She was all arms, legs, and mystical mutterings. She tried to stand up, but the events and the occasion were just too much and she fell over. Father O'Dowd managed to catch her before she hit the floor. Being caught in the arms of her employer was too much and Miss Mcafferty fainted.

The priest managed to get her upstairs and into bed, although her dead weight played havoc with his back. He propped her head to one side in case she was sick in the night and telephoned the doctor. The locum on duty told him not to worry, but to keep an eye on her.

"Thanks, doctor." Father O'Dowd put the phone down and went to get a drink of whisky. He took the whole bottle, had one large one and then got ready to say the six-thirty Mass. Mrs Hebblethwaite was in victorious attendance. He whizzed through the service, as Mrs Hebblethwaite knew he would, and was in his kitchen by five past seven enjoying an omelette and another large glass of whisky.

The telephone rang.

"Thomas, it's mum, just phoned up to see how you are?" his mother said cheerfully. A less cheerful moment in his priesthood he couldn't imagine, but he couldn't let his mother know how he felt. She thought all he had to do to be in temporal bliss was don the cassock and assume the role.

"OK Mum. And you?" he inquired.

"You don't sound OK, Thomas. Are you sure everything's OK?"

He hated his mother's intuition. "I'm fine," he replied rather too force-fully.

"You're not, you know, I can tell," she insisted. "Now come on and tell me or I'll be down there first thing tomorrow."

Intuition he could just about stand, but not combined with threats. He would just have to tell her. Well, tell her half of what was going on.

"It's just a problem with a new family who've moved in next door to one of our biggest Catholics, and the family are, how shall I put it, different to most," he said.

"What do you mean, different?" she asked, sitting down on the chair next to the phone. She was in for the duration.

"Just a family of hippies, mum, you know. It's just that they wear different clothes and don't look like your average Broughton citizen."

"Why's that a problem then?"

"Mrs Hebblethwaite thinks they're devil-worshippers and drug addicts to boot. Now mum, I've had a really hard day, Miss Mcafferty's not too well and –"

Before he had time to finish the sentence she said: "Right, I'm coming down tomorrow to look after you both. We can't have you living off sandwiches and the like if Miss Mcafferty isn't too well. I'll see you tomorrow, Thomas." She was off the phone before you could say 'come into my parlour'.

This was just compounding the problem. What with Mrs Hebblethwaite, Solomon, the Bishop and now Miss Mcafferty not feeling too good, the last person he wanted to see was his mother. Three women, a kitchen, a man who gave him erections plus a Bishop who was on his case ... Things couldn't get any worse! He poured himself another large whisky.

Some would say that Thomas O'Dowd's call to the church was a mother's vocation. That his was no Damascene conversion but one to please his mum. Thomas knew she'd had a pretty awful time of it, even after they'd left his dad. He'd never really known him and knew his mum had struggled to bring him up single-handedly. Of course he was grateful, but that didn't seem to be enough. The emotional string just got longer and longer. As a youngster he was constantly trying to please his mum with all the things he did. He just wanted to see her smile. Thomas felt terrible when he failed his Eleven Plus because she didn't smile. She tried to but you can always tell a false smile, it comes with cracks round the edges and lasts half the time of a proper smile. He caught her crying upstairs and he cried, too. That was when he decided he'd make her happy forever. He'd become a priest.

At eight-thirty he went upstairs to look in on Miss Mcafferty. He gently opened her door and peeked in to find she was fast asleep. He slowly walked towards the bed to see if she'd been sick, but found that she seemed OK, was still alive, and breathing normally. He stood over her and said a little prayer. He walked slowly out of the room and closed the door.

Miss Mcafferty could smell malt whisky and carefully opened one eye to see the figure of Father O'Dowd slowly closing the door to her bedroom. She sat bolt upright and looked around, worried to find herself in bed but with no recollection of getting into it. *Whisky, priest, bedroom, woman.* She quickly went through the permutations and started to panic. Had they all not been talking of things that go on in the other world, the world of debauchery and sin and *lipstick*? Had she been drugged so they could all have their wicked way with her, a virgin from Kanturk? A tear formed in her left eye as she lifted up the counterpane to check whether she was still clothed. She was. Relief. She checked her corset was still in place. It was still intact. She always fastened it with the skill and precision of an engineer. The final check was the industrial underwear she always bought from the chastity section in Marks and Spencer's. They too were in position. She sighed and gave a prayer up to Saint Bernadette and went to sleep, with a golf club next to her just in case.

Father O'Dowd finished off the whisky, said a few prayers and retired to his bedroom to read the morning paper. He read the first two pages and fell asleep still clothed.

*****

Mrs O'Dowd arrived in That Hat. She had two hats, one for everyday use and the other for special occasions. Today was a special occasion. Her son hated it for obvious reasons: it was large, pretentious and vulgar. Its only redeeming feature was that you saw it several minutes before the occupant arrived. It gave you time to finish off the dusting or whatever it was you were doing. It was a black affair, sculpted into a bowl that sat awkwardly atop her hairdo, with an enormous black ostrich feather sticking up from the side like a TV aerial. She was also laden with food, intent on taking over the culinary chores now that the housekeeper was laid up.

Thomas opened the door and smiled. "Hello mum," he said with little conviction.

"Hello – quick, get these bags before they tear my arms out of their sockets." Her plump face was reddened from the exertion of carrying the food up Millgate. Thomas grabbed both bags.

"What the –!" His knuckles nearly hit the floor with the weight. "Mum, what have you brought? I've got a fridge full of –"

"Well, it's obviously time you had some proper cooking, what with the cook laid up and –" She tweaked his cheek like flatulent elderly aunts do. "– you're not looking too good yourself, Tom. Looks like you've lost a few pounds. Well," she said as she went into the presbytery, "We'll soon have you right as rain. I'm doing Lancashire hot-pot with red cabbage. Your favourite."

She wasn't wrong, he thought as he lumbered down the hallway with her Red Cross parcels and followed her into the kitchen. As soon as he'd put the bags down, she'd taken off her coat and the pinny was on. She grabbed one of the bags. "I'll put these away while you make me a cup of tea."

What she really meant was that whilst he was making the tea she would be doing a recce, ready to move everything around to how she liked her kitchen. Hell hath no fury like a mother who doesn't run her son's kitchen.

Chapter 14

Solomon and Cass were to have a house-warming party. It wasn't so much as a house-warming as an open town musical extravaganza that would start in the hills above the town and cascade down into the streets and alleyways, music permeating into every pore and every brick, apart from Mrs Hebblethwaite's. She plugged her pores up with religion and tea. If the party were to happen, then that would be the day long hair and Bob Dylan would win; Mrs Hebblethwaite would do everything in her temporal and spiritual power to stop it.

The second van arrived on Wednesday the sixth of May.

Wednesday was baking day for Mrs Hebblethwaite and she was slicing the potatoes for her Lancashire hot-pot and listening to the radio. Engelbert Humperdinck was wooing the housewife when she saw it arrive. "Oh no!" she said, looking out of the window. She put the potato peeler down, wiped her hands on her pinny and went outside. "Two of the buggers!" She had never indulged in swearing before the arrival of the Permissive Society but it was now creeping into her vocabulary. She went back into her house.

"Hello," she shouted down the phone to the Bishop's secretary. "I want to speak to His Grace." She had decided to speak straight to the Bishop because Father O'Dowd wouldn't have done anything.

"I'm afraid he's busy," came the curt reply.

"Not too busy to stop evil and fornication from stealing the souls of our youth, I hope?"

The secretary had to handle many of these calls and was used to it. "As I said, he's busy at the moment dealing with evil in another part of the diocese, so if you want to leave a message, I'm – " He was cut off mid sentence.

"Leave a message? I can't leave a message. When the Devil's work is afoot, you can't leave a message. Leaving messages won't stop the cloven-footed one from doing his work. Our Lord didn't wait for messages, he acted straight away lest the beast of Beelzebub took root. You'll look a bloody fool if the end of the world's nigh and you haven't informed His Grace, won't you, hey? God wouldn't thank you for that would he? We have to be vigilant! Now go and get the Bishop before the Devil does!"

The secretary duly obliged.

The Bishop was indeed busy: he was having his monthly pedicure. His bunions were undergoing their monthly MOT. He found preventative medicine, like religion, the best way to stay healthy. With medicine it was monthly health checks; with religion it was keeping that cupboard full of prayers.

"Yes, Mrs Hebblethwaite," the Bishop replied, barefoot with little bits of cotton wool stuck between his toes.

"There's another one, Your Grace. They're multiplying! If it carries on like this, the town will be overrun with them copulating to Bob Dylan and the like." The Bishop didn't know who this Bob Dylan fellow was, but he was sure that the Catholic Church disapproved of people watching the procreative act.

"Another one?" he said.

"Another van. There's two vans now. What are we going to do?"

The Bishop didn't want to do anything at this precise moment other than get his feet done. "Have you told Father O'Dowd yet?" He was stalling for time.

Mrs Hebblethwaite didn't want to hear this. "No, but I thought . . ."

"I'll tell you what to do Mrs Hebblethwaite. Ring Father, explain that you've talked to me and that I want you to write down everything that you see, report back to him your findings and then he can call me, and we'll go from there. Of course, I'll say a full Novena for your plight."

It wasn't what she wanted but a full Novena from a Bishop was not bad.

"Thank you, Your Grace." She put the phone down and rushed to the window to see if any more of the vans had arrived. They hadn't. She returned to the hall.

"Hello, is Father in?" she asked, not recognising the voice on the other end of the phone.

"Who shall I say is calling?" said the voice in a non-Irish accent. This wasn't Miss Mcafferty, thought Mrs Hebblethwaite.

"Mrs Hebblethwaite."

"I'll just get him for you," said his mother, leaving the caller in some confusion.

Mrs O'Dowd went into the kitchen where her son was eating his breakfast.

"That hippy woman is on the phone. Shall I tell her you're busy?" his mother said wishing to screen her son from any unnecessary inconvenience.

"No, it's OK. I'll speak to her," he muttered through a mouthful of toast.

"Mrs Hebblethwaite, how can I help?" He sounded like an Insurance salesman trying to get her to buy a policy.

"I've just spoken to His Grace, and he says I've got to write everything down, hand it to you and you're to report it to him." Clear as mud the priest thought, trying desperately to work out what the hell his parishioner was going on about.

"Report on what exactly?"

"Have you forgotten already? Sex, Drugs and Rock and Roll, next door to me." She would have made a good newspaper editor.

"Well, if the Bishop wants you to do that, then I suppose you must," Father O'Dowd replied, realising what the Bishop's intentions were. He said goodbye to Mrs Hebblethwaite and went back to finish his breakfast. His mother would want to know every detail of his conversation, so she could dissect it, mull it over and then tell him that his response was wrong. She did just that.

Chapter 15

Cass delighted in annoying those who went out of their way to provoke those she loved, knew or befriended. She didn't like Mrs Hebblethwaite and, although a DIY Buddhist of the Californian variety, she wanted to teach her neighbour a lesson. A bit of bad karma didn't do anybody any harm.

"Good morning Mrs Hebblethwaite. Lovely weather we're having," Cass said warmly. Mrs Hebblethwaite didn't respond. She didn't want to encourage any conversation until she'd converted all of them to her way of life. She held up her crucifix.

"Get behind me Satan!" the religious one pronounced with a sense of gravitas afforded to those who spend their entire life on bended knee.

"I thought Satan was a man?" Cass replied.

Mrs Hebblethwaite was puce with indignation. How dare somebody with long hair and breasts that waved to all and sundry tell her about scripture! Wasn't this the woman who indulged in Percy Filth, and was loose enough to let every man in the street know about it, what with her cries and grunts and screams? The whole street knew what she did and Mrs Hebblethwaite was not best pleased.

"Don't you come telling me about the Good Book, my lady. You wouldn't know the first thing about God, and prayer and devotion. All you're interested in is drugs and fornication and screaming all sorts in the middle of the night." She held the cross up at this latter-day Mary Magdalene. "Mr Hebblethwaite doesn't know where to put himself."

"Well, if he wants a few lessons on how to enjoy himself, he can always come round and watch." Cass smiled wryly. "Might come home with a few tips. You never know, it could be you a-screaming an' a-hollering next Friday." Cass half expected Mrs Hebblethwaite to explode.

She very nearly did. Her corset straps were under undue pressure from her bosom, which was rising with anger at Cass's remarks, and she could feel a sharp pain. She was about to lash out at her insolent new neighbour but managed to rein in her anger, merely falling to her knees to pray, which shocked Cass. She was expecting at least a slanging match and possibly the odd fist, but not prayers for her soul. It took the wind out of her. She went over to where Mrs H was praying and handed her a piece of paper. The neighbour took it, but didn't look at it straight away lest it distract her from her soul-saving rosary.

Cass went inside somewhat deflated. Mrs Hebblethwaite finally sat down on the deck chair, unfolded the piece of paper she'd been given and read in horror that they'd been invited to a party. With music, long hair and well, goings on.

You could have knocked her down with the Bishop's after-shave.

"That's it!" she said, standing up. "Enough's enough." Which is true because they're spelt the same. "This calls for police intervention. I can leave the spiritual matters to him upstairs but when it comes to Percy Filth and five-a-side wife-swapping next door, then it's up to Sergeant Baldwin to act." She took the crucifix and rosary beads into the house and set off to the police station to seek out the keeper of law and order in those parts.

Solomon looked out of the window and saw Mrs H careering down the road. All she ever did since they'd arrived was walk earnestly around the town denouncing her new neighbours to all those who would listen.

"What've you said this time, Cass?" He looked across the room.

"Nothing," she pleaded, but he knew her too well.

"Don't give me that. You never do nothing when you have a go at somebody."

Cass had started to resent Solomon's holier-than-thou attitude. "Look, she's got this guilt thing about you and me enjoying ourselves. She said that her husband doesn't know what to do when he hears us having a laugh, so I told her he can come round anytime, watch and learn and then perhaps, he could give her a few tips whenever they get it on. If they ever do?"

"Cass, you'll give the old dear a heart attack." Solomon the wise, Solomon the contrite. Cass really liked his sense of fairness and justice but was slightly bitter that on this occasion he hadn't taken her side with Mrs Hebblethwaite.

"Look, she's been having a go ever since we got here. I was just giving her back some of her own bigoted medicine."

Chapter 16

At forty-six Sergeant Baldwin had let his once-muscular frame go in pursuit of fine wines, beer and pies. He sat behind his desk indulging in his elevenses, which occurred on the hour, every hour until his shift had finished. His ruddy face broke into a smile when he saw Mrs Hebblethwaite walk into the room, all consternation and concern. She was waving a piece of paper at him and muttering. She always muttered, thought the Sergeant, usually about somebody or something that was worrying her.

"Good morning Mrs –" the sergeant said, trying to pull his ample frame to the vertical. He was cut short.

"It's not good for me, Sergeant, and I doubt if it's good for Broughton." She pulled up a chair, sat down, and handed him the piece of paper. He grabbed it, picked up his reading glasses and read. He read it again, trying to fathom out what piece of law an invitation to a house-warming party contravened. He took his glasses off and looked at a worried Mrs Hebblethwaite.

"It's inviting you to a house-warming party," stated the officer of the law.

"Lucid as ever, Sergeant," she replied sarcastically. Normally this would have earned a rebuke from the Sergeant but as Mrs Hebblethwaite was a friend of his mother and, given that she was in something of a state, he let it pass.

She carried on: "I can read, too." She paused. "Read the last line again," she implored.

" ... AND BRING A CHANGE OF CLOTHES" repeated the Sergeant in large capitals. He looked up again.

"Can't you see? Can't you see what they're up to, Sergeant?"

The Sergeant was as myopic as ever, even with his glasses.

"Right!" Mrs Hebblethwaite took the initiative, something that happened quite regularly when Sergeant Baldwin was on a case.

"It's not a house-warming as such, with beer and peanuts and the odd vol-au-vent." Vol-au-vents had been a recent upmarket addition to the local social scene, ever since a family moved to Broughton from Cheshire. They held Tupperware parties.

"Sergeant, what they intend to hold is an Orgy."

The sergeant looked dumbfounded.

"Yes, that's what I said, Sergeant, an Orgy."

The sergeant remained in his dumbfounded state, not because of the accusation just levelled against Mrs Hebblethwaite's neighbours but because he didn't know what an Orgy was. He had never been a great reader, a fact that had limited his rise in the police force.

"An Orgy!" he said with what little authority he could muster. "Well. Well. Well." He tut-tutted and shook his head from side to side. "An Orgy . . ." Mrs Hebblethwaite knew that when the Sergeant tut-tutted and shook his head from side to side he was in legal quicksand; although on another occasion she would have delighted in watching him flounder, she didn't have the time or the patience to witness it now.

"You don't know what an Orgy is, do you?" asked Mrs Hebblethwaite, luxuriating in her new-found knowledge of what the youth of the day were up to. The sergeant went a deeper shade of red.

"No," came the whimpering reply.

"An Orgy –" she crossed her arms and pushed her chest out, which she always did when Percy Filth was about to be mentioned. It was her warning sign to anybody who thought they might fancy their chances. "– is when several members of both sexes –" She looked around to check whether the walls had ears but she remembered she was in a police station. " – engage in sexual intercourse and the like."

The Sergeant was conversant with sexual intercourse, being the father of two teenage boys, but he'd never come across 'and the like' before.

"I see," he said, racking his brain to find out whether having sex voluntarily in the confines of your own home constituted a criminal act. It didn't and he winced. However, he didn't like the sound of what 'and the like' meant, so he leaned across the table and said: "I think we should visit your neighbours, Mrs Hebblethwaite and see what their game really is!"

At last somebody was doing something positive, thought Mrs

Hebblethwaite. At last somebody was standing up to all that sin and debauchery and pleasure. "Good. When are you coming round then?" she asked.

The Sergeant looked at his watch. "I've a few things to do now, but they won't take too long." He looked at Mrs Hebblethwaite. "I'll be round at, say, eleven-thirty?"

"Fine. Just fine." Mrs Hebblethwaite stood up, thanked the Sergeant and left the police station, very nearly a happy woman.

Sergeant Baldwin saw Mrs Hebblethwaite out of his office and returned to his pie, worried that he had committed himself to visiting people he didn't know, about something he didn't understand. He took solace in finishing off his meat and potato pie, and walked over to his bookshelf. He took one of the three books, a concise Oxford English Dictionary and flicked through it until he found the word 'orgy.' He read out loud: *"ORGY: a wild party, especially one involving excessive drinking and indiscriminate sexual activity."* He was concerned that there was no mention of 'and the like'. He carried on: *"Secret rites used in the worship of Bacchus, Dionysius, and other Greek deities, celebrated with dancing, drunkenness and singing."* So 'and the like' meant singing and dancing. This puzzled the Sergeant because these things happened on a regular basis in Broughton and Mrs Hebblethwaite had never complained before. He knew that she was a Catholic and that they were not averse to the odd pint or nine, so he didn't really understand why she was worried. Perhaps Mrs Hebblethwaite had joined some Fundamentalist group that abhorred such activity. Was it not true that the reason Irish Dancers do not move their arms is to keep them from holding hands with or touching members of the opposite sex? His mind was becoming nearly active when he said: "Of course, Rock and Roll is the Devil's music!" He knew what they meant, he being a Country and Western fan. "That's what it'll be," he said to the second pie of the day, which looked at him expectantly from the table, all wrapped up and eager to be eaten.

"She'll be thinking that once Mr Hebblethwaite starts dancing his natural rhythm will lead him into unnecessary contact with women at the party and who knows where *that* will lead." He smiled to himself, happy in the knowledge that once again, after training his mind on an issue, he had come up with the answer. He bit into his pie with a sense of utter gratification.

Sergeant Baldwin screwed the pie wrapper into a ball and tossed it towards the waste paper bin. It arced over the desk and once again landed a good two feet from the target. He bemoaned his inaccuracy and left the office struggling to button up his tunic.

"I'll be gone for about an hour, Perkins. If you need me I'll be at number twenty-three Prospect Street." He straightened his hat, pulled his tunic down over an ever-increasing gut and left the Police station in the capable hands of PC Perkins, whose constant battle was not fighting crime but his virulent acne.

Sergeant Baldwin very rarely walked these days. Since the advent of the Panda car, Baldwin was generally seen crammed into the front of it. He didn't drive the car, he wore it. However, even Sergeant Baldwin couldn't justify using the Panda car the two hundred and fifty yards to Prospect Street.

He finally reached his destination slightly out of breath and perspiring a little. He took his handkerchief out of his pocket and mopped his ever-reddening brow. He checked to see he was at the right address before opening the gate to number twenty-three and walked down the path. The speed at which Mrs Hebblethwaite was out of her door when she saw Broughton's law enforcement officer pass the window belied her ample frame. She was out of her house like a greyhound that'd just spotted the hare.

Solomon saw the reddening bulk of Sergeant Baldwin coming down his path and looked across at Cass. "Satisfied?" He said with an air of resignation. He went to the front door and opened it before the policeman had time to knock. "Morning, Sergeant," Solomon said, "Please come in."

"Thank you."

"Cup of tea?" inquired Solomon, realising that the unfit policeman was in dire need of rest and something to drink after his exertions.

Mrs Hebblethwaite was upset. She had expected the sergeant to give his stern lecture on the question of Orgies out in the open for all to hear, not in the relative luxury of the sitting room. The other thing that annoyed her was that now the Sergeant was inside, she wouldn't be able to hear a word of his reprimand. Although, she said to herself, that once inside he would be able to see for himself all the paraphernalia that came with being a hippy and the dissolute life they led. She went back into her house and out into her garden to see if she could hear any better from that vantage point. She couldn't. She rang Father O'Dowd instead.

Sergeant Baldwin sat down and looked at some of the posters that were on the walls and was amazed at what people thought was art. He was slightly disturbed with one picture that seemed to depict a woman of Indian origin wrapped around a man who appeared in a state of arousal. And the woman was blue. He'd heard about artists and what they got up to in the confines of their garrets. Creativity undermines morality.

"Tea would be fine. Any chance of a biscuit?" he asked.

Cass smiled and went into the kitchen. Solomon was the only other person in the room.

"So . . ." Solomon looked at Sergeant Baldwin expectantly.

"Sergeant Baldwin," he replied officiously.

"Sergeant Baldwin, how can we be of assistance?" Solomon sat down on the floor in front of the policeman.

"I had a visit this morning from your neighbour, Mrs Hebblethwaite, who was rather worried about a house-warming party you're going to have on – " He took out his notebook, looked at it and said "The thirtieth of this month. Is that correct?" The Sergeant was nothing if not thorough.

"Yes," replied Solomon.

"The invitation stated that the guests were to – " He put on his glasses and read again from his notebook. " – bring a bottle, something to smoke and a change of clothes." He took off his glasses and looked at Solomon. "Is that correct?"

"Yes." Solomon looked suspiciously at the policeman.

"Bringing a bottle I can understand. Even providing your own cigarettes, but I think it's the change of clothes that worries Mrs Hebblethwaite. What's all that in aid of?"

"Sergeant, I think my girlfriend Cass was playing a practical joke on Mrs H. You see . . ."

"Practical joke Mr – ?"

"Tump. Solomon Tump."

"You've only been here a few days and you're playing practical jokes. I thought practical jokes were played between friends who'd known each other quite a long time. Or enemies who'd known each other for longer."

The Sergeant rarely strayed into the bounds of philosophy, but today he did.

"Sergeant Baldwin," Solomon said sweeping his hair away from his eyes. "Ever since we arrived Mrs Hebblethwaite seems to have been upset about something or other. Whether it's the clothes we dress in, how we look after our son, or the van I drive. She even had the priest drop in for a word. Now, as far as we're concerned it is not unlawful to wear flared jeans, have long hair or sport multi-coloured tee shirts. Alas, Mrs Hebblethwaite thinks differently, to such an extent she is convinced I'm Beelzebub!" The Sergeant didn't have his Oxford English Dictionary to hand and couldn't therefore find out who this Beelzebub chap was. He didn't let this minor matter interrupt his questioning.

"I'm sure you're right about the clothes Mr Tump, but we live in a small town and we haven't seen the likes of you apart from on telly and in the newspapers, and that coverage hasn't been too good."

Solomon was about to respond when the tea arrived. Cass handed the Sergeant his cup and a plate of Custard Creams, his favourites.

"Thank you. Mrs Hebblethwaite has got it into her head that you are about to have an Orgy." The Sergeant bit into his biscuit. "Do you allow dunking?"

Solomon and Cass looked at each other and being the liberal kind of people they were, nodded in agreement.

"Orgy, Sergeant? Why would we be having an Orgy?"

"I don't know. It's just that she's got this word in her head and she can't seem to shift it," the Sergeant replied, just managing to get the biscuit out of his tea before it broke off. "What will be happening at this party, anyway?" he asked through a mouthful of tea-sodden Custard Cream.

"There'll be music, dancing, drinking, people just having fun, Sergeant. People who haven't seen each other for a long time meeting up at our house hoping for a good time."

" That's all that's going to happen?" the policeman asked rhetorically.

"That's all!" Solomon looked at Cass for confirmation. "Certainly, Sergeant." They both nodded emphatically.

"Well, that's what I thought, Mr Tump. I think Mrs Hebblethwaite has misinterpreted what the meaning of 'orgy' really is." Satisfied that no great orgiastic scenes were to be played out on his turf, the sergeant finished his tea and biscuits.

"Oh and she did mention the drug issue. Now I'm the last person to – " Of course, Sergeant Baldwin was the first person to be judgmental, that's why he was a policeman. "– think just because you have flared hair and smoke Afghan cigarettes –" Cass began to chuckle behind her mug of coffee and was in grave danger of spilling it. "– but where there's long hair, not far behind is somebody smoking pills." Sergeant Baldwin wasn't very good at explaining himself but he knew what he meant.

He looked at Solomon and then at Cass with his very stern 'I think you are a druggy' look. "Do you take drugs Mr Tump?"

Solomon was on his third spliff of the day. "Of course not Sergeant," he lied. "Here have a toke on this and see if there's any illegal substances in it," he asked the sergeant, whose only vices were pies and Real Ale.

"No thank you," the sergeant said. "I don't smoke." He put his cup down.

"Well, I think that's everything for now, but please try not to upset Mrs Hebblethwaite too much," the policeman said, wincing. "Once she's got something in her head she won't let it lie and we're fully stretched as it is." The policeman got up, tunic buttons straining to keep his gut from general view. "Thanks for the tea."

Solomon ushered Sergeant Baldwin out.

Cass was standing in the middle of the room, tears streaming down her face.

"What do you think you were doing, offering him a smoke?" she asked, trying to contain herself.

"Well, he hasn't got a clue so I thought we'd have a bit of fun at his expense."

They hugged each other and moved around the room to the sounds of 'The Bushmen of the Kalahari'. His Holier Than Thou halo had just slipped.

Chapter 17

Margaret walked down from the moors wiping the few bits of grass that still clung to her dress. She'd been up on the tops with Solomon and they'd chatted and had some wine and he'd stroked her hair, whilst gently kissing her on the lips. They laughed as he told her stories of what he'd done on his travels, all the scrapes he'd got into and out of. Margaret had had known beforehand what she was going to do because it felt like the right moment with the right person. Well, she was nineteen; half her friends were married with babies, and those Broughtonian males that were left, were nothing to write home about. She had been out on dates with several lads, but it was all octopus arms and drunken fumblings in the cinema. Margaret thought she was worth more than a trip to the pictures and a fish supper.

Solomon had been gentle and considerate, allowing everything to take its course. Margaret had wanted her first time to be special and it was, no grappling in the back of a Ford Anglia for her. Afterwards they'd arranged to meet up later on in the week. Margaret couldn't wait.

★★★★★

"Bless me Father for I have sinned; it has been fourteen hours since I last made love."

"What?" the parish priest asked incredulously.

"Sorry, Father, what I meant to say was it has been eight years since my last confession." Father O'Dowd wasn't convinced this is what he had heard, but let her carry on anyway. "And I ..." She couldn't bear to tell him, even though there was a wire mesh and a curtain between them.

"So what do you have to tell me after eight years?" he asked, fidgeting around on his own side.

" Well, it only happened recently, Father."

The priest moved nearer the mesh. It sounded like he was in for a riveting tale.

"I made love to a man, Father." She blushed and placed her hands in her lap.

"And ...?" He'd had five confessions so far this night and they'd all been pretty small beer. It was good to get a good juicy confession now and again.

"And I'm not married, Father."

"Oh. I see," he said slowly.

"But I love him and I don't think there's anything wrong in making love with a man you love just because you're not married," she pleaded.

"Then why are you here?" he asked.

"Because of you lot, Father." She was regretting that she'd ever come.

"Us lot ..." he paused. "By us lot you mean the Church?"

"I've just come for a bit of advice that's all."

"Well the best I can do is give absolution if you admit before God that you are genuinely sorry."

"How can I be sorry when it was the best thing that's ever happened to me?" Margaret was in full flow, confident in what she wanted to say. "I mean, I'd heard about orgasms and what they do to your body but –"

Father O'Dowd had never had Orgasms in his confessional before. He'd had manslaughters, wife beatings and lots of alcohol abuse, but this was his first orgasm.

" – this was just mind blowing Father, but then you wouldn't know, would you?" Margaret said, shocked that she had just questioned a priest on his sexual life.

"No. I suppose not."

"There's no 'suppose' in it, is there Father?"

"No." There was a pause. "Wait a minute, I'm the one asking the questions, you're the one supposed to be repenting!" He regained the theological high ground.

"I'm not going to repent, Father, because I've done nothing wrong."

"Who's the man?" the priest asked.

"Why should I tell you?"

"Because if he's married then you've got other people to consider. "

"He's not married but he has got a partner and a small child." She gave him this information freely.

"Does he have long hair?"

"Why?"

"Because if he has then you're getting yourself into a bigger mess than you realise." Father O'Dowd guessed that the man in question was Solomon Tump and he didn't want Mrs Hebblethwaite confronting him on two fronts: Hippies in general and hippies sleeping with her granddaughter.

"You know, don't you?"

"Yes!"

"You're not supposed to know," Margaret said, filling up with tears.

"Is it just an infatuation?" asked Father O'Dowd. He should have known better than to ask whether a teenage crush was 'just' infatuation. Teenage crushes are about life and death, love and hate.

"No it's not a bloody infatuation. I LOVE SOLOMON."

"OK, you don't have to shout."

"I have to if no one will listen!" she said a little less loudly. "I love him, Father," Margaret said with utter conviction.

"That may be so, but if he's already in another relationship, you shouldn't really ..."

"It's wonderful Father, it's not a one night stand."

She was off again, Broughton's answer to the Kama Sutra. My God, thought Father O'Dowd, if her mum could hear this she would tear the roof off the church and hurl it to Rome.

Father O'Dowd tried to interrupt but found that he couldn't. It wasn't that he was dumbstruck: it was the mental picture of himself thrust into Solomon's arms instead of Margaret Wainwright that left him speechless. Whilst he was having trouble re-organising his and mind, he found himself listening to an X-rated account of the seduction of Mrs Hebblethwaite's granddaughter. God only knows what would happen if she ever found out, never mind the Bishop. She was already apoplectic concerning Solomon's lifestyle. She would have his guts for garters if and when she found out, and Mrs Hebblethwaite always found out. And if the Bishop knew what he was thinking, and inside the sanctity of the Confessional, Heaven would freeze over.

"You know the teachings of the Catholic Church, that it is a sin to have sexual intercourse before you are married." Father O'Dowd trotted out the standard response. "So, unless you are truly sorry for the deed that you have committed I cannot absolve you of that sin," he said.

"I'm not sorry, Father. In fact I'm going to do it again tonight."

"Good God woman, then what are you doing in here?" Father O'Dowd was usually a calm and thoughtful man, but he was outraged that anybody could come to confession and taunt him with such things. He then realised that she wasn't taunting him, because she didn't know about his feelings for Solomon; she was there to ask advice and he should be giving it.

"I think you should think twice about seeing him tonight." Thomas said, wondering if he could arrange to see Solomon so Margaret wouldn't let herself be used again.

"It's not only your feelings that will be hurt but those of his partner and your family, especially your grandmother, Mrs Hebblethwaite." He didn't mean to mention her name, it just slipped out, and as soon as he had mentioned her name he knew he was in the wrong.

"How do you know ...?" Margaret said loudly. She tore the curtain back and yelled at the young priest. "You're not supposed to know ... You're not supposed to see ..." She was in tears now and Father O'Dowd left his side of the confessional to comfort her.

"You're supposed to listen and give advice aren't you?" She was sobbing into her handkerchief.

"That's one of my roles but I'm also supposed to instruct you on God's law," Father O'Dowd said reassuringly.

"But God doesn't listen, does he? He doesn't know how I feel about Solomon."

"He does."

"Then he should know how I feel and understand." The sobbing had stopped.

"He does understand ..." Father O'Dowd was ready to launch into his standard rendition of what the Catholic Church says on pre-marital sex.

"If God is all-loving then why can't I fall in love?"

Father O'Dowd wondered if he was talking to a Jesuit in drag. "You can ..."

"Well, why didn't you say so in the first place?"

"I mean it's wonderful to fall in love, but only with the right person."

"But you just said ..."

"I know …"

"So I can carry on sleeping with him?"

"No, you can't carry on sleeping with him," the parish priest said very loudly.

Miss Mahoney moved along her pew to get nearer the confessional box.

Margaret ran out. The crying had started again. She was out of the church before the parish priest managed to get halfway down the aisle.

"Shit!"

"What's happening?" asked Miss Mahoney, who confessed every day and twice when things were going really well. She'd already heard from her friend Mrs Hebblethwaite what kind of liberal priest Father O'Dowd was. She'd heard and read in the right-wing religious press of charismatic young priests who lead young women astray with talk of getting to heaven via wicked male ways. However, she'd never once thought that it would be happening here in Broughton. Naïve young women, she said to herself. They only have to see a pair of blue eyes, clean finger nails and well-polished teeth for all sense to fly out of their knickers. The thought that he would try to get his wicked way in a church was bad enough, but in the confines of the confessional, that was enough for Lazarus to return from whence he came. She felt all dirty and soiled, like the time Alfred Shufflebottom tried to play Doctors and Nurses behind the school sheds. She remembered that it was only when he placed his stethoscope in her hand did she realise his true intentions. The memory was scorched in her mind.

"It's OK, Miss Mahoney. She's just a little distraught." That was the understatement of the year, he thought.

"Shouldn't you go after her and see she's all right?" Of course he shouldn't, she said to herself straight away. The reason she's in that state is because of his loose morals.

"She'll be fine. She just needs time to think," Father O'Dowd said, not believing a word of it.

"Confession?" the priest asked his parishioner.

'Yours or mine?' thought Miss Mahoney, as she crossed herself and said a quick Hail Mary for her caustic thoughts. She hesitated. "Ye-es." She was a bit worried about what would happen in the confines of that small narrow box.

Miss Mahoney left the church after a statutory Our Father and four Hail Marys for lying to the Chief Librarian about a fine on one of her books. She headed straight to Mrs Hebblethwaite's.

Father O'Dowd went straight back into the presbytery to the comfort and solace of a large whisky. He poured himself out three large fingers full of some God-awful pretend Scottish malt from the Highlands of Japan, but it served its purpose and dulled the senses for a while. He knew he was drinking rather too much but hadn't yet resorted to putting real wine into the chalice just yet. He knew of several priests whose problem had resulted in this kind of action and their services were always spectacular, if less than spiritual. In fact, the last incumbent of The Church of The Immaculate Conception had fallen victim to alcoholism. At his last Mass he didn't give a gospel, he sang *'My Way'* instead and had to be forcibly carried off the altar by the Bishop's Praetorian Guard. He wasn't in that league just yet, but he'd have to be careful. Alcoholic priests were manageable, alcoholic priests with a penchant for male parishioners were a different matter altogether. He sat down at the kitchen table and hoped Margaret and Miss Mahoney were not too distressed by the evening's events. Margaret was young and impressionable; he thought he could manage to talk and rationalise with her, but Miss Mahoney was different.

"OH GOD!" he said, wanting 'Him Upstairs' to give him some advice.

"That sounds very desperate, Tom," his mother said, coming into the kitchen.

"And I don't think that's the answer!" She pointed at the tumbler of whisky. "That's fire water, Thomas, and you can't think or pray properly with fire water in your belly." His mother was from the temperance side of the family, having witnessed several members of the O'Dowd's succumb to drink.

"Mum, I'm just relaxing after a hard day with a glass of whisky. OK?" her son said defensively.

"I thought you didn't need any other stimulant than prayer Thomas," she pleaded, opening her Bible to read from Matthew 14 v 10–14. This display of spirituality irked Thomas; with anyone else he would have mentioned Pharisees and hypocrisy but it was his mother and he was too scared.

"I'm just having the one!" he retorted, trying to make light of the whole episode, but he knew it would fall on stony ground. His mother had a genuine grievance against the drink. Thomas's father and her husband for six years was a disciple of grape and grain, so much so that his mother left him. She couldn't take the constant beatings and penury enforced by his week-long bouts of boozing. It took a lot for a woman to leave her husband in those days, especially a devoted Catholic like his mother. He drained his glass and took it over to the sink. "Satisfied?"

She wasn't, but at least she was there in the presbytery to keep an eye on matters. Her son retired to bed early with a lot on his mind; she too was about to retire, but before she did so she wanted to speak to Miss Mcafferty about her son, just to reassure herself he wasn't going down the same path as his father.

Chapter 18

Mrs Hebblethwaite was by no means against the drink, even though she did give her husband a hard time when he was out on the ale and couldn't get up of a morning. She had a bottle of Guinness every night before she went to bed and a few more when they went to the club on a Saturday night. However, she never went into a Public House by herself. The only women who went into Public Houses by themselves in Broughton were 'Ladies of the Night'. However, she was there to find Tony, who couldn't be described as Margaret's official boyfriend but didn't make a secret of his desire to have the hand, or any other part of her granddaughter. Although no oil painting, he was an honest sort, if slightly dim, and he was a regular at Mass.

She walked into the Tap Room of the White Lion. Tony stood at the bar laughing and joking and smoking proper tipped cigarettes.

"Tony!" said one of his friends, tapping him on the shoulder.

"What?" he replied, drawing on his fag while lifting his pint with his other hand.

"Don't turn round now but Margaret's Nan has just walked in," his friend whispered.

"Bollocks!" laughed Tony. "She wouldn't be seen dead in here!"

"Well then, a corpse that's doing a very good impression of Mrs Hebblethwaite is on its way over." The friend moved a good few paces away from Tony in case things took a nasty turn. For a woman to walk into the Tap Room of the White Lion was very rare. For a grandmother to walk into the Tap Room was unprecedented. It meant only one thing: TROUBLE.

Tony turned around, his face half hidden by the pint of bitter he had been enjoying before Mrs Hebblethwaite's appearance.

"Tony!" bawled Mrs Hebblethwaite across the Tap Room noise.

"Yes," he said nervously, putting his glass down on the bar. The room went quiet and expectant.

"We need to talk," she said, ushering him over to her table next to the one-armed bandit. "I'll have a bottle of Guinness."

"Oh shit," said Tony under his breath. "Not only does she want to talk, she wants a drink as well." He carried the bottle over to her table and sat down.

"How much do you like our Margaret?" she asked the spotty youth whilst pouring the Guinness into her glass.

"A lot," he replied wondering where this was leading.

"Well, if you want to keep her you'd best be smart about it."

"Why?" he asked nervously.

"Because, Tony … " She finished pouring her drink and looked him straight in the eye. " … she's got her eye on this long-haired lout who's just moved in next door to me." Tony looked puzzled. Mrs Hebblethwaite continued: "And if I'm not mistaken she seems to be carrying a torch for him." The agony aunt took a swig from her drink and looked hopefully at her future grandson-in-law.

"Bloody hell!" Tony said before finishing off his pint. "I best get round there."

"Not tonight son. You've had too much ale. Now, we have to be systematic about this one, Tony. We have to be careful not to throw her into his arms."

"I'll break both his bloody arms if I get hold of him." said a flexing Tony. Mrs Hebblethwaite doubted it, but she was always amazed at the beer-fuelled bravery of the ale-house. She finished her drink, happy now that Tony and his friends would more than likely give Solomon and his friends a friendly Broughton welcome.

"You can't mistake him, Tony, he's got long hair, flared jeans and smokes fat roll-ups." Tony seemed all fired up and ready for action.

"Right," said Margaret's Nan. "I'm going upstairs for a meeting, so don't be doing anything foolish. Just yet any way." She bade him farewell. Tony walked back to the bar in a rage.

"What's up Tony?" they all said in unison on his return. Even the barman became one of his newly found confidants.

"This long haired hippy bloke's been sniffing round my Margaret." Tony said spitting anger and venom from his testosterone-fuelled body.

"Bloody hell Tony, what we're gunna do?"

"Kill the long haired freak, that's what we're gunna do!"

"Too right, smelly bastards the lot of them," intoned the smallest of his friends

"Another pint, Tony?"

"Aye."

"We'll sort him out don't you worry," said Colin from the back. "By the time we've finished with him he won't be able to put his arms around anybody, never mind your Margaret!"

They all laughed and ordered more beer from Alf the landlord who liked these fraternal gatherings. They were extremely good for business.

*****

It was with some trepidation that she climbed the stairs to the top room at the Lion to address the first meeting of the Prospect Street Action Committee. It had been hastily arranged because a third and fourth Hippymobile had arrived, leaving the bottom end of Prospect Street looking like the staff car park at Billy Smart's Circus.

"Evening, everyone," Mrs Hebblethwaite said to the assembled throng of twelve.

There was a muffled response. "I think you know why we are all here." She was not one for public speaking and it showed. "Over the last – " She was interrupted by Mr Hampson clattering into the room with a tray of drinks.

"They didn't have a Mackeson, love, so I got you a Guinness instead," he said to his wife, who sat three rows from the front. Mrs Hebblethwaite waited until he had sat down and continued. Her husband, who had been badgered into becoming the committee secretary, looked on enviously as his neighbour took a swig from his pint.

"Before I start, does anybody else want to get a drink?" There was a scraping of chairs as five thirsty neighbours ran out of the room to the bar downstairs.

"Five minutes," Mrs Hebblethwaite shouted to the thirsty revolution-aries.

"Bloody men, can't do anything without a pint in their bellies," she said to the nodding heads of the seven other women at the meeting.

The five men returned.

"Right! You know why we're here?" she said from her mock lectern.

"Yes!" came the reply.

"Well, I think it's about time WE did something," she said, pointing to the Prospect Street Twelve. "I had thought there would be many more here, and not just from our street either because this concerns everyone in the town. Everybody in Broughton will be affected by their presence. Not today perhaps or tomorrow, but sometime in the future your lives and those of your children will be blighted by these hippies. Hippies are different, they don't have morals they just have genitals and they want to use them whenever they can. They take drugs and listen to long haired music and have sex. That's all they do; I know, I looked it up in the Concise Oxford English Dictionary. You've seen them in their multi-coloured pomp, strutting around preening themselves like bloody peacocks all the time."

"And SEX !" exclaimed Miss Mahoney.

"Thank you Miss Mahoney," agreed Mrs Hebblethwaite

"Not to mention the Devil Worship and Communism." With Miss Mahoney it was a close run thing which was worse, fornication or Communism.

Bill Harris bristled at the mere mention of the word Communism. As a veteran of the Second World War he had an aversion to Communists. His real name was Laszlo Wzorowski, a Pole who'd settled in Broughton in 1948 after escaping the tyranny of Stalin's forces in what was then free Poland. He hated Communists, liberals, fascists, Trotskyites, Falangists, virtually every group that ended in ists.

"Too bloody right," Bill shouted at the top of his voice. Mrs Hebblethwaite had to ask him to sit down when he tried to sing 'God Save Our Gracious Queen. '

"WE have to mount some kind of campaign. WE have to alert the people and the authorities to what these people are really up to. WE can't have our daughters on the pill, smoking grass and listening to Jimmy Hendrix." Nobody in the hall, apart from Mrs Hebblethwaite, had a clue who Jimmy Hendrix was. Though this didn't concern them as much as the Hippies smoking their grass.

"And what about the sex?" Miss Mahoney said. It was obvious to everyone that she only had one thing on her mind. Which indeed she did. As a spinster of the parish of Broughton and now of an age to be able to voice her thoughts without attracting the attention of the medical authorities, Miss Mahoney's only quest in life was to stamp out sex outside marriage. She also wanted to stamp it out in marriage. In fact, she wanted to stamp out drinking, music, coloured clothes, laughter, TV, radio, cars, butter, sliced bread and tinned anything. She was on several other committees that discouraged making life happier.

Mrs Hebblethwaite carried on, impervious to Miss Mahoney's cries about sex.

"I have spoken to the Bishop, and he is in total agreement. He has asked if I would compile a diary of their actions." She raised the Pagan-Busting diary with both hands as though it were some lost book of the scriptures.

"And I have documented evidence of all the shenanigans that have gone on since they arrived." She began to list their atrocities and some she'd made up.

"Having long hair." This was greeted with derision and boos.

"Smoking roll-ups with illegal things in them!" Utter disbelief.

"Giving an illegal roll-up to my grandson, Gary." Medical attention was called for.

"Holding my granddaughter's hand and walking down to the newsagents!"

Miss Mahoney was on her feet. "SEX. I told you they were having SEX." She was jumping up and down, frothing at the hip.

"Having sex when not married . . ." Much blushing in the room.

" . . . making lots of noise and seemingly enjoying the act!" The room was now in utter chaos.

"Whoever heard of anybody enjoying Sex?" asked Mrs Hampson in disbelief. Mr Hampson smiled.

"So you see what we're up against. We're up against evil incarnate. In fact I would go as far as saying the Devil himself is here, living under the name of Solomon Tump!"

Mrs Hebblethwaite finished off by thrusting her hand into the air and the twelve committee members stood up screaming and chanting. It was like a Nuremberg rally. Mrs Hebblethwaite left the podium to be congratulated by all present. She was beginning to enjoy the adulation, when she realised that they hadn't decided what action they were going to take. Miss Mahoney knew what she was going to do, as did Tony Wright, her grand-daughter's sometime boyfriend who strode into the hall at the height of the celebrations, armed with a cudgel and several shaven headed friends.

Tony and five of his friends jackbooted their way across the room to where Mrs Hebblethwaite was standing. Dressed in military fatigues, they looked like an unkempt bunch of highly untrained cadets. The smell of beer reached Mrs Hebblethwaite before Tony did. They were high on testosterone and Watneys Pale Ale.

"It's OK Mrs Hebblethwaite, you don't have to worry. We'll be taking over from here," Tony said, all bluff and bluster. He stuck his pigeon chest out but nobody noticed.

"Me and me friends'll sort them out. And before you can say 'Where have all the Hippies gone?' they'll have gone." Tony started to laugh, as did his dishevelled band of followers.

"And how are you going to do that?" Mrs Hebblethwaite asked, worried that Tony's army would have trouble sorting anything out.

"Brute force, Mrs Hebblethwaite. I tell you what, once they've had a few knuckle butties they'll wish they never set foot in Broughton." Tony turned round to his mates.

"In't that right lads ?" The inebriated urban guerrillas slapped each other on the back and waved their fists unthreateningly. Mrs Hebblethwaite wasn't too convinced. However Bill Harris, war veteran and misanthrope, was up for anything that involved carving up Communists. He pulled out a ten-inch knife, walked up to one of Tony's army and said, "We'll be needing this." He thrust the knife into the air, and then ran his forefinger along its edge. "Slices through necks just fine."

Tony looked across at the exiled Pole and wondered whether they should allow him on their team. Sober he would have said no, but he wasn't, so he agreed.

Mrs Hebblethwaite's greatest desire was to rid Broughton of everything hairy but even she baulked at killing Solomon. Capture and baptise him, yes. Cut his throat and throw him in the canal, well, even she would have second thoughts.

"Mr Harris, I think we can do without the knife," she said in a rather headmistressy tone. Mr Harris looked across at the Chair of the Prospect Street Action Committee and thought that she would never have escaped the Russians with such a feeble-minded approach to warfare. He put the knife away and there was a collective sigh of relief.

Mrs Hebblethwaite turned her attentions to the drunken leader of the band, Tony.

"What if more vans and cars have arrived since this afternoon ?"

Tony hadn't thought about that, he was too busy fuelling himself up on neat aggression courtesy of the barman at the Flying Horse.

"I'll just have to get more men!" he laughed. Leading men into battle was dead easy, he thought as he marched his troops to the downstairs bar to discuss tactics.

What Tony didn't bargain on was that Solomon Tump was an internationally renowned exponent of Bushido Ru, a Korean Martial Art. He was an unarmed, long haired, fighting machine. Tony and his band of warriors were drunken youths whose main threat was numbers.

Mrs Hebblethwaite started listing again all Solomon's wayward activities, building the momentum up in the hall to a crescendo.

"We can't have none of that here can we?" said Mrs Wainwright from number thirty-eight Moortown, whose hat was quivering with indignation. Mrs Wainwright did indignation extremely well and was jabbing the town's only newspaper hack in the chest.

"What are you going to do, Norman ? What's the Bugle got to say about all this?" She directed her question at Norman Sutcliffe, or 'Scoop' to his journalistic comrades. Norman had been on the paper, The Broughton Bugle, since he was a sixteen-year-old tea boy and was renowned more for his all-year-round Boxing Day jumpers than for any journalistic prowess.

"Well . . ." This wasn't a good start, thought Mrs Wainwright. Journalists should have opinions, not sit on the fence with 'Wells' and 'If only's'. "I think there could be a headline or two in this little story," Norman said whilst scribbling down his shorthand. Norman lore was legendary in the valley. Whenever anything happened of any great magnitude, floods, fires and the one murder which happened twelve years ago, Norman was nowhere to be seen.

"Norman," shouted Mrs Hebblethwaite. "I hope we can count on your support in this. The people of Broughton and elsewhere need to be made aware of what can happen when people move into your town and smoke suspiciously fat roll-ups." This was greeted with general applause from the assembled throng.

"In fact I would go as far as to say, Norman, that Broughton is heading full throttle towards the Permissive Society. We are only a pair of flared jeans and a mini skirt away from a long-haired plague that will sweep our children off their moral feet into a soup of debauchery and sin," Mrs Hebblethwaite said poetically. She was beginning to enjoy the role of orator and chief rabble rouser. She had also inadvertently given the journalist his banner headline. It would appear the following Friday: BROUGHTON YOUTH FLOUNDERING IN SOUP OF SIN. Norman knew very well what he meant, it was just that most of his readers didn't.

Mrs Hebblethwaite again addressed her supporters.

"Does anybody have any suggestions as to how we can stop the Tumps and their like from wreaking havoc in our town?"

Several hands went up, including those of Miss Mahoney whose answers were well and truly known. Mrs Hebblethwaite asked Geoffrey Mallet, a balding man of slight stature who was known for his knowledge of almost everything. He'd been on the dole for most of his life.

"I think we should have a sit-in," he said rather quietly from his chair three rows back from the front. Mrs Hebblethwaite struggled to hear what he had said.

"Sorry Mr Mallet, could you say that again?"

"I *said*," he said gruffly – he didn't like to repeat himself – "That we should have a sit-in."

Everybody looked non-plussed.

"I'm afraid you'll have to enlighten us Mr Mallet," said Mrs Hebblethwaite rather nervously. Mr Mallet was indeed an intelligent man but often got carried away with his own knowledge of worldly and scientific events; it was with some caution you ever asked 'Mallet the Brain' to explain himself.

"Well," Mr Mallet said, shifting in his chair in an effort to get comfortable. Several of the known drinkers grew scared that last orders might be called before the Mallet had finished his explanation. One such red-nosed type, Mr Hepple, tried to make an excuse and get to the bar. Mrs Hebblethwaite gave him the eye. He sat down.

"In recent times, the students in universities all round the world have decided on this course of action to get their message across to the authorities that they're unhappy about something." He paused. "You see, you find a building and simply sit in it and don't let the people back in. It's very simple but extremely effective." He finished by crossing his arms and looking around at the other members of the action group for approval. It wasn't forthcoming straight away, although Mrs Hebblethwaite was smiling.

"You mean, when the Tumps are out of their house, we go in and just sit in there and not let them into their own house."

"Correct," replied the Mallet, happy that somebody in Broughton was bright enough to understand.

"Sounds marvelous to me," said Mrs Hebblethwaite. "Can we have a show of hands for Mr Mallet's wonderful idea?"

"Isn't trespassing illegal?" asked Mr Hebblethwaite.

"Not if there's no damage to the property," said Mr Mallet, whose knowledge of the law was second to none.

"But how do you get in if it's locked?" enquired the Chairman's husband, who was none to pleased with the way the evening's events were shaping up.

"There are several options. But don't worry; we'll be able to get in without breaking the law," smiled the Mallet, whose housebreaking activities were news to all those present, especially to Scoop Norman.

"OK. Let's have a show of hands." The chairman counted all those who'd raised their hands and the vote was unanimous.

"Right, the next thing we have to do is get a date for our sit-in," said Mrs Hebblethwaite, looking at Scoop Norman busily scribbling away. "But I would like to ask Norman to leave the proceedings at this juncture, because we don't want any unfortunate pieces getting into the Bugle that might alert our intended enemy from finding out the nature of our activities."

Scoop was none too happy and he looked round the room at those present and saw in their faces that they too would like him to leave. He left.

"Let's do it now," said Miss Mahoney impetuously. She wanted them out as soon as possible, but she also wanted to have a look at their house and see if it truly was a dwelling of evil.

"It's Works Wakes in a weeks time, can we have it after that?" said Alf King, Mine Host of the Flying Horse. "When it's over there'll be more folk around to help us out."

"Good thinking Mr King," Mrs Hebblethwaite said, annoyed that she hadn't thought of it. She didn't like Alfred King, whose capacity for alcohol was only matched by the number of mistresses he kept.

"Well, if you'll all note the week beginning the 20th of this month, we can meet up one day that week and arrange a time and a place to oust the Tumps from Broughton for good." Mrs Hebblethwaite drew the evening to a close. She went home with her husband contented that at last the whole community was now getting behind her. Her husband peeled off and went into the house worried that all hell was about to break out on Prospect Street. For once in his life he was not wrong.

Chapter 19

Having the devil in your street is bad enough, but having him sowing his seed around the town was even worse. There was one person who didn't think so and that was Margaret; she was becoming rather blatant about her own sexuality. It was beginning to worry her mother. Mrs Wainwright didn't like Mary Quant. It was nothing personal; it was just that she didn't like her designs, especially the mini skirt. Margaret came down stairs wearing the shortest of dresses, knee length boots and enough black mascara to fill a coal shed.

"Get that bloody muck off your face," said Mr Wainwright, busily eating his breakfast while reading the sports pages of the Daily Herald. "You're not going out dressed like that, young lady," her father said, putting his paper down. "You look like a bloody tart."

"Dad, I'm nineteen!"

"I don't care if you're nineteen hundred, you're not going out dressed like that." He slammed his mug of tea down onto the table like a judge with a gavel.

"Dad it's the fashion, it's what everyone's wearing," Margaret said with teenage defiance.

"It may well be the fashion, but as long as you live in my house you'll do as yer bloody told. Now come on, get up them stairs before I drag you up." Now that he'd laid the law down he continued with his second piece of toast.

"No, I won't and you can't make me!" Margaret crossed her arms, lifting her large bosom into a more prominent position.

Mr Wainwright had never witnessed such open contempt in his household and was going as red as a beetroot. He was a man of few words at the best of times, and these were not the best of times. His eyes reddened, his cheeks blew out and the lines on his forehead were furrowed with anger.

He stood up and clenched his fists. He wasn't from the spare the rod school of parenting. He was about to give her a slap across the cheek for her insolence when she said:

"You wouldn't hit a pregnant woman, would you?"

Mrs Wainwright dropped the plate she was drying.

"Who's pregnant?" he asked.

"I am," Margaret said triumphantly, pleased that her utterance had stopped him in his tracks.

"You can't be, you're not married!" her father said stupidly.

Margaret just smiled. Mrs Wainwright became more animated.

"You're joking, aren't you love? You're not really pregnant? You're just saying that because you want to wear mini-skirts," her mother said, looking at her and then her husband. "She's having us on, Dad. Aren't you, love?"

"No, I'm not."

"Well who's the bloody father then?" said her father, who'd sat down again.

"Solomon," she said with a smile so wide you could hang your washing on it.

"Who the bloody hell is Solomon?" asked her dad. Mrs Wainwright knew and her face was ashen. She looked at her husband. Mr Wainwright looked at his daughter and then at his wife, waiting for an answer.

"Well?" he implored.

"You know that couple who've just moved in ..." Mrs Wainwright didn't have to finish the sentence. Shock and horror suddenly masked Mr Wainwright's face and once again he stood up, trying to eke out an extra half inch to his five foot five frame.

"That long-haired hippy," he said with such anger and incredulity that he screeched the last word. "That good-for-nothing, drug-taking, work-shy lout?" Mr Wainwright was almost poetic in his denunciation.

"He's not. He's a very intelligent, kind human being," Margaret said, coming to the defence of Solomon.

"What you doing sleeping with him anyway? You know you're not supposed to get up to such things before you get wed," Mrs Wainwright said hypocritically. Their eldest was born three months after they tied the knot.

"I love him, Mum."

Mr Wainwright was touring the kitchen, hitting pots and pans and swearing at the sink.

"Love! Love! What do you know about love?" He moved around again like a boxer stalking his opponent. "Hippies don't love anybody but themselves. If they did they'd cut their bloody hair and have a wash every half century or so."

Mrs Wainwright had never heard such eloquence coming out of her husband's mouth.

"Did he drug you?" said Mr Wainwright, nodding his head, agreeing with himself, happier now that he'd found out why his daughter had slept with a hippy. "That's it, isn't it? Yes. He gave you some of that LTD –"

"LSD," corrected his daughter. "And no, he didn't give me any drugs. We made love and it was beautiful."

Mrs Wainwright looked on, puzzled. It was never beautiful for her. It was more of a chore, like ironing but with more sweat.

"Spare us the bloody gory details, please!" Mr Wainwright said. He didn't want his wife getting any ideas. He was a man of habit and routine. He didn't like change. Seven minutes a week was enough for anybody, he told Mrs Wainwright after their Friday Liaisons.

"You'll have to marry him," Mr Wainwright suddenly said. "And I'm not bloody paying for it, either. Solomon Whoever can dig into his bloody flared pockets and pay for it." Mr Wainwright was not one to throw his money around.

"Solomon doesn't believe in marriage," Margaret said.

"He will with a twelve bore up his arse!" Mr Wainwright didn't want a bastard born into his family, even though he was acquiring one as a son-in-law.

"He doesn't know I'm pregnant," Margaret said looking at her mother for support.

"That's bloody great that is."

"Are you sure you're pregnant, love?" enquired her mother, who'd gone over to sit next to her daughter. She placed her arm around her shoulder.

"Yes, I didn't ..."

Margaret was interrupted by her father who knew that on the subject of female plumbing women could spend hours, if not lifetimes, debating the finer points. He put his hand up.

"Look we don't need to ..."

Mrs Wainwright stopped her husband from continuing. "Yes, we bloody well do."

Mr Wainwright was shocked, not just because his daughter was pregnant, but because his wife of over thirty years had interrupted him and she swore.

"Have you been to the doctor's?" her mother asked. Margaret shook her head.

"Well, first thing in the morning we'll go down and see Doctor Brown."

"Another bloody hippy," Mr Wainwright said under his breath. The doctor had been known to wear the odd bead or two around his own neck, raising questions about his sexual preferences. The men of Broughton liked their doctors to be beadless.

As his wife and daughter were contemplating their trip to the doctor, Mr Wainwright was making plans on how to make Solomon suffer for what he had done. To have your daughter deflowered was bad enough but to have her virginity taken away by a hippy just compounded the problem. He would exact revenge; he didn't as yet have a plan, only that it would involve large amounts of pain inflicted upon the free-loving Solomon.

Chapter 20

"Your boyfriend's here," said Cass as she noticed Father O'Dowd walking down their front path.

"Who?" replied Solomon, who was bathing Leo.

"Father What's-his-name, you know, the one who came round and couldn't take his eyes off you!"

"Oh, you mean Tom," Solomon said, his answer echoing round the bathroom before it made its way down to Cass.

"Ooh, it's Tom now is it?" Cass said with a certain irritation.

"That's what he's called, isn't it?" Solomon said matter-of-factly.

Father O'Dowd knocked on the Tump's door watched by three animated sets of curtains, including those of Mrs Hebblethwaite.

"Come in, Father. What's the collection for this time?" She laughed as she said it, and so did Father O'Dowd, but his wasn't a laugh of mirth or merriment, his was a nervous first-date kind of titter.

"Cup of tea?" she asked.

"Fine."

"I'll just shout Solomon, he's bathing Leo."

"If it's inconvenient I'll ..." the priest said coyly.

"Don't worry, Father," Cass said. She shouted upstairs and then went to make a cup of tea.

Thomas smiled wanly as she left the room and he began to think why he'd come and what he wanted to say. His thoughts were violently interrupted by the front door being opened and a shouting Mr Wainwright stood in the hall alongside his very upset daughter and wife. His daughter was in tears and his wife transfixed in a state of worried expectation.

"Where's the bloody long-haired Casanova, then?" Nobody answered.

"Because by the time I've finished with him he won't have it in him to do owt to anybody." Mr Wainwright, fueled by a few pints of chemic, was raging around the hall.

Father O'Dowd was quite well versed in handling such tricky situations, having officiated at several weddings where the guests had taken a dislike to each other.

"Mr Wainwright, I think –" His attempt at mediation was cut short.

"Father, there are times when you can't stop and think and this is one of them." He paused, his anger drying his tongue. "You see Father, that hippy fella has only gone and had SEX." Mrs Wainwright blanched, crossed herself and put her hand to her mouth.

"Yes, that's right Father, sex with our Margaret and now she's having his bloody baby. It'll probably come out with hair down to its backside."

This was no time for humour and Margaret started to cry at the image her father had just created.

Cass came into the hall. "Who's pregnant?" she asked.

"My daughter, and your Solomon whoever he calls himself 'as got her in the club."

Solomon appeared at the top of the stairs. "Do you mind, I'm trying to get Leo to sleep!"

"I'll be putting you to bloody sleep, you dirty – " Mr Wainwright tried to make a break for the stairs but Father O'Dowd, who in his younger days had enjoyed some success in Judo, held the angry Mr Wainwright firmly in his place.

"Father, if you don't let go I won't be responsible for my actions!"

Father O'Dowd decided that the best policy was to throw Mr Wainwright to the floor and secure him in a headlock until he'd calmed down.

Mrs Wainwright didn't take kindly to this course of action, especially as her husband was related to the injured party. "It's not the bloody Spanish Inquisition, Father!" She put her hands to her face. She'd never sworn at a priest before.

Solomon descended the stairs. Mr Wainwright tried one last time to get free. Alas, his attempt was in vain and he sat there, defeated. His daughter was pregnant and he couldn't do anything. He was in a headlock, impotent, and Solomon the Seed Sprayer was walking free to indulge in whatever dark practices hippies got up to. He needn't have worried.

Cass was seething, not from the fact that yet another woman was pregnant by Solomon, but because he hadn't told her. Theirs was an open relationship and they were both free to do what they wanted. The rule, and there was only one, was that they must be open and honest, and he hadn't been. She hit him across the face as he reached the hall. Martial arts expert or not, hell hath no fury like a woman scorned. It was quite strange, but for the first time since they'd moved to Broughton she felt an affinity with the women of the town. She, like them had been cheated.

"Yes!" said Mr Wainwright victoriously. "Give him one from me!"

Cass tried to, but he now had his defensive guard up.

"Is it true? " Cass asked.

"I don't know if she's pregnant, but we *have* slept together," Solomon said very matter-of-factly. Mrs Wainwright burst into tears. Margaret smiled and Mr Wainwright tried to wriggle free.

"The dirty –! Father, will you let me go? I won't hit him!" Mr Wainwright pleaded.

"You might not hit him but I certainly will!" Cass again launched herself at the father of her child. She was angry, Buddhist or not, and she wanted her pound of flesh.

Margaret, incensed that her lover was under attack from all sides, said "Stop it, everyone. Can't we all just sit down and talk about what's happened?"

"It's a pity that you didn't just talk the last time," Mr Wainwright said, rubbing his neck.

"Bloody strong grip you've got there, Father. Where did you learn that, the Vatican?" There was nearly a ripple of laughter but the occasion forbade any such hilarity.

"Right, shall we all go into the front room and discuss this like mature adults?" Father O'Dowd pleaded. He'd originally come down just to speak to Solomon and see what reaction, or indeed erections, occurred. Now he was embroiled in a huge Domestic. He prayed that Mrs Hebblethwaite hadn't heard what had happened. If she had, even his Judo skills would be useless against an enraged senior member of the church.

"Now then." Father O'Dowd took it upon himself to referee the proceedings. He'd placed the main combatants at either end of the room for fear of bloodshed. Mr Wainwright sat at the back of the room, arms folded, all heavy breathing and testosterone. Solomon sat near the door on the floor, all patience and control. He was rolling a cigarette.

"See, Father, he's doing drugs right in front of the Lord." Mr Wainwright pointed at the accused. He wasn't a pious man but he thought to call upon the Almighty at such a time might not be such a bad idea.

"It's only tobacco!" Solomon said.

Margaret just gazed at Solomon whilst Cass seethed, her beautiful eyes incandescent with rage and betrayal. Mrs Wainwright sat dutifully next to her husband.

Father O'Dowd looked across at Margaret.

"Margaret, is what your father says true?"

"Well, we have ..." She looked around the room but couldn't look at Cass. "You know, we ..." She looked down to the floor and whispered, "We made love."

Mrs Wainwright squeezed her husband's hand. She cried, not in anger, but in loss. She knew she'd lost her daughter. Forever.

Father O'Dowd looked across at Solomon who'd finished constructing his cigarette.

"Solomon?"

"I don't deny making love to Margaret, but what I do object to is being subjected to this kangaroo court. What have two people who make love to each other done wrong?" Father O'Dowd was about to launch into a lecture but was stopped by Solomon raising a hand. Mr Wainwright was also about to launch into something and that somebody was Solomon. Father O'Dowd looked across at Margaret's father with a look that told him to stay seated.

"I know that some people think that having sex before getting married is the most heinous sin imaginable ..." Having any kind of sex is unimagineable, thought Mrs Wainwright as she looked across at her drunken husband. " ... but when something is as pure as that which binds Margaret and me, then I can't see what the problem is. It was consensual, nobody got hurt and it was a beautiful experience for both of us."

"Pass me the sick bucket!" said Mr Wainwright. "I'll tell you one thing, you've got the gift of the gab ..." He was trying to think what consensual meant, but carried on regardless.

"Look matey, in your world it might be OK to sleep around and have wonderful bloody experiences, but here in Broughton we have standards and morals that keep us all on the straight and narrow. If we don't, then everything goes to pot. You can't go siring children all over the place. A man has responsibilities for his children, he has to provide, not just wander round the countryside listening to dodgy music in a souped-up bloody ice-cream van."

Father O'Dowd put his hands up.

"I think it would be best if we all go to our own homes and have a good night's rest. It's all highly charged and I don't think we're going to get anywhere now."

"Come on, love." Mrs Wainwright stood up and walked over to where her daughter was sitting. She put her arm around her shoulder. "Come on, you'll feel better after a night's rest." They left the house followed by Mr Wainwright, who never took his eyes of Solomon. The door slammed.

"Think I'll get going too," Father said, erectionless, which would have pleased the Bishop but just confused Thomas O'Dowd.

"You never did say what you wanted?" Solomon said.

"It'll wait. I think you and Cass have a few things to sort out." Father O'Dowd got up from the umpire's chair and left.

Cass looked at Solomon like parents do when they've been let down.

"Why?"

"What do you mean, why?" Solomon shifted uneasily in his chair.

"Don't get smart, Solomon Tump. I've known you long enough and you know the rules."

"Rules, what rules? I thought we railed against rules, I thought that's what all this was about, not being constrained by rules."

"You know damn well what I mean, Solomon. Our rules, the rules that we live by." Cass was livid but she was managing to keep her cool. Just.

"Don't get all heavy on me, Cass, I thought you were above all that."

"Don't turn it round Sol; don't make me out as the bad guy ..." Cass managed to light a cigarette without shaking. "You know that if you sleep with someone you tell me. You tell me because we have no secrets and when we have no secrets we are one. When we have secrets we're not – and that stinks." She walked over to the other side of the room and turned off the stereo. Music and retribution do not go together.

"I was going to – " Solomon started.

"No you weren't. You weren't going to tell me at all. You were going to have your fun with some teenager and ditch me and Leo. Am I right?"

"I'd never leave you and Leo," he lied. Solomon lied well, he had the eyes for lying, but Cass wasn't convinced.

"I knew you were up to something because you couldn't get a hard-on. The penis doesn't lie, Solomon."

"Look Cass, I'm sorry, I didn't mean to lie but what with all this shit from next door and then I find out that Margaret's Mrs Hebblethwaite's granddaughter, I thought it was best to keep it under wraps for a bit. You know, lie low for a while." Solomon was desperately trying to dig himself out of a hole.

"Were you going to sleep with her again?" Cass asked, more in hope.

"I doubt it." Solomon replied.

"If I see you with that girl or anyone else without you telling me what's going on, I'll feed your balls to Mrs Hebblethwaite. OK?"

"Yes," said Solomon The Only Slightly Contrite.

Chapter 21

The police arrived at Solomon's house at about 11.30pm.

"Probably just a domestic," said PC Sutcliffe as they ambled round to the house.

It was a disturbance, but not a domestic. There was violence involved but not attributable to either Solomon or Cass. The two policeman were greeted with a scene which was not one you would typically associate with Broughton. The Bronx maybe, but not Broughton. PC Hartington was flicking through his police handbook trying to find the chapter on urban terrorism.

There in the middle of Prospect Street was Miss Mahoney in full battle fatigues walking around a blazing crucifix. Broughton was home to many religious sects: Methodists played Bridge with members of the Church of England who happily had Christmas dinner with the Russian Orthodox Church of Andrew the Pilloried. Catholics played bingo with those that followed the Jewish faith and a lone Rastafarian smoked by himself in the hills above the town. The Jehovah's Witnesses played Postman's Knock with the Presbyterians and the Salvation Army competed with anybody to increase their numbers by doing the rounds of all the public houses. Up until now the Broughton section of the Ku Klux Klan had played their cards very close to their chests and hadn't as yet revealed themselves to the general public.

Everyone knew Miss Mahoney was from the Catholic School of Zealotry but with the advent of Vatican Two, the introduction of the female Pill, and David Steele's Abortion Act, she had shifted even further to the right. Most people in Broughton knew she was one Commandment short of the full ten and here in Prospect Street their assumptions were confirmed.

She raised her crucifix to the stars and proclaimed: "And I stood upon the sand of the sea, and saw a beast rise out of the sea, having seven heads and ten horns, and upon his horns and ten crowns, and upon his heads the name of Blasphemy. And the beast which I saw was like unto a leopard, and his feet were as the feet of a bear ..." There were those in the crowd who didn't know their Scripture and were desperate to place the beast with ten horns. The Prime Minister, Harold Wilson, was favourite.

" ... and his mouth as the mouth of the lion: and the dragon gave him his power, and his seat, and great authority." Those who didn't know Miss Mahoney were convinced she was speaking from The Old Testament Book Of Sherry. However, she was as sober as a Born Again Christian driving home from his Baptism. She was fired up and shooting from the lip.

"And I saw one of his heads and it were wounded to death ... And they worshipped the dragon which gave the power unto the beast: and they worshipped the beast, saying Who is like unto the beast? Who is able to make war with him? And there was given unto him a mouth speaking great things and blasphemies ..."

There was one bright spark who shouted out that he knew who she was speaking about:

"Ian bloody Paisley!" Much laughter ensued. Undeterred she carried on.

" ... and it was given unto him to make war with the saints, and to overcome them: and power was given him over all kindreds and tongues and nations. And all that dwell upon the earth shall worship him ..." Miss Mahoney certainly knew her Revelations. She finished with an emotional and motivational plea to Solomon and all those around.

"If any man have an ear, let him hear!"

Miss Mahoney was really pumped up, ready to let fly with even more scripture when she suddenly deviated from the good book and said "You heathen bastards!" She spat towards number twenty-three. "Hell fire is too good for the likes of you. When the Good Lord sees fit you will rot in the bile of a maggot-infested goat, you son of Lucifer." She was getting up steam when PC Sutcliffe walked towards her rather nervously. He had no problems with baying football fans, or tipping-out time on a Friday night, but this was a first.

"Evening, Miss Mahoney," he said carefully.

"And I beheld another beast."

The assembled throng were quite impressed with the first bit of Revelations but were rather dismayed that she hadn't continued with her own personal and vitriolic attack. "And he causeth all, both small and great, rich and poor, to receive a mark in their right hand, or on their foreheads: Here is the wisdom. Let him that have understanding count the number of the beast: for it is the number of a man; and his number is six hundred three score and six!"

Her head fell to her chest and her crucifix came down to rest by her side. Only when she raised her head did she see what lay on PC Sutcliffe's epaulette. His number was 666. She let out an almighty wail and pointed furiously at his shoulder and ran into Mrs Hebblethwaite's garden, screaming.

"It's him, it's him." She looked up at her Catholic friend and said "He worships at the foot of the cloven hoofed one, too!"

"Now we don't want any trouble, do we?" he said rather more forcefully.

"Trouble? I'm trying to stop trouble, to expunge sin and fornication from the streets of our town," Miss Mahoney replied, pointing to Solomon's window and then at the policeman.

"That may be so." He knew he shouldn't have said that because the bile-ridden cross-burner went into such a rage that her mouth started firing gobbets of spittle and her eyes seared through his tunic and into his soul. She launched herself at the Tump's house, a blazing harridan determined to rid the town of evil. PC Sutcliffe, in a moment of heroism that would later result in a commendation from the Chief Inspector, caught the Whirling Dervish before she got to the front gate. His unselfish act had at first stopped Miss Mahoney in her tracks but, when she saw the door of number twenty-three open and Solomon appear on the front door step, she garnered strength from the heavens. Peeling herself from the policeman's grip, she managed to hurdle the front gate before PC Sutcliffe rugby-tackled her to the ground fifteen feet from the front door.

"B-A-S-T-A-R-D!!!!!!!!" was the last word heard from Miss Mahoney as the full weight of the policeman expelled the last ounce of hate from her lungs.

Solomon leapt forward. "Is she alright?" he asked.

"What would you care?" said Mrs Hebblethwaite, gleefully enjoying the evening's activities.

"I care about anybody who's been injured!" Solomon replied sincerely.

"Huh!" came the succinct response from his girlfriend. Solomon was glad she didn't say anything else.

PC Sutcliffe got to his feet while his colleague doused the flames on the cross. A small crowd gathered and formed an arc around Solomon's garden. Miss Mahoney was placed in the recovery position and mouth-to-mouth was administered. She coughed and spluttered, and sat up slowly. She glanced around and everyone knew she was returning to normality when she started to rant and rave about this and that, but mostly fornication. A Panda car arrived at the scene and Miss Mahoney made her first and last visit to the police station. They would pick the cross up later.

"See!" said Mrs Hebblethwaite, pointing to the Panda car that was leaving Prospect Street. "You're turning this place into Sodom and Gomorra. What with your fancy clothes and cigarettes and all night fandangling, poor Miss Mahoney has gone and lost it completely." For those who knew Miss Mahoney this was slightly disingenuous. She had lost the plot many years ago when Alfred Shufflebottom placed his stethoscope in her hand.

"We've done nothing wrong, Mrs Hebblethwaite," Solomon replied.

"Will you shut that bloody door, woman!" Mr Hebblethwaite shouted from the upstairs window. "I'm at work in four hours and I want a bit of shut-eye."

"The Lord's work is more important than sleep, Mr Hebblethwaite, and isn't that the truth Mr Tump!"

The late night rumpus had woken several neighbours, but the last to emerge from his front door was Mr Wainwright, whose drinking session meant he slept through the earlier moments of Miss Mahoney's crusade. He ambled across the road, pulling first his right brace and then his left brace over his shoulder. With belt and braces fixed in position he approached his mother-in-law's house.

Mr Wainwright and Mrs Hebblethwaite did not have the best of relationships. In fact, for the first four years of his marriage to her daughter, Mrs Hebblethwaite didn't step into her daughter's house. Mrs Hebblethwaite would be the first to acknowledge that her son-in-law was a hard worker, provided for his family, didn't let his eyes stray and was for all intent and purposes a fine husband. However, and it was a big however, he did not attend Mass on a regular basis. They were civil to each other, but that was it.

"Evening, Mother," Mr Wainwright said, doffing an imaginary hat.

For once Mrs Hebblethwaite was lost for words. The last time he'd called her Mother was at the wedding, after he'd drunk the best part of ten pints of bitter and three glasses of Asti Spumanti. She didn't like it.

Neither did Solomon, who was trying to make a tactical retreat.

"And you can stop where you are an' all!" Mr Wainwright said, adjusting his belt.

"What's up, Brian?" Mrs Hebblethwaite asked tentatively.

"I'll tell you what's up. He's only gone and got our Margaret up the bloody duff!"

Mrs Hebblethwaite blessed herself and frantically tried to find her rosary beads, but she'd left them in the house. She looked across at Solomon. There were tears in her eyes.

"Jesus, Mary and Joseph," she cried through a mouth that was tightening with anger.

"Heaven help us, she's only nineteen!" She pointed her legendary digit at Solomon and cleared her eyes. The sorrow soon turned to anger. "Did you soil my granddaughter?"

"We're not sure yet," Solomon said.

"But you don't deny you did it?" Ethel Hebblethwaite was warming to her task.

"Why should I? We've done nothing wrong," Solomon replied with an air of injustice.

Mrs Hebblethwaite had never been to the Garden of Gethsemane, but she felt she now knew how Jesus must have felt. Totally deflated and destroyed.

"Sam, get yourself down here now. Yer long-haired man here has just made you a great-grandfather," Mrs Hebblethwaite shouted with some resignation. Sam turned over and placed the pillow over his head, a practice he'd mastered over the course of his marriage.

After half a minute with no sign of her husband, she again shouted "Will yer get yourself down here, now!" Sam knew that tone of voice and it was one that had to be obeyed.

"I'm coming."

Sam arrived in his blue-and-white striped pyjamas and a tatty dressing gown, bought by his wife twelve years ago. He saw his son-in-law and Solomon plus the assembled crowd and knew all was not well. "What's up that can't wait until the morning?" he said, desperately wanting to return to his warm bed.

"He," Mrs Hebblethwaite said, pointing to Solomon, "Has got our Margaret pregnant."

"Bloody hell, you haven't have you?" pleaded a concerned grandfather.

"Look Sam –" Solomon started to say.

"We're not family yet! Mr Hebblethwaite will do fine," Sam said, trying to restore some etiquette to the proceedings.

Solomon sighed. He'd a full day of explanations and was tired. Nothing could be sorted out in the middle of the street. He was confronted by two men wearing pyjamas, one with a pair of trousers over them and the other a dressing gown. Mrs Hebblethwaite was adorned in nightly hair curlers and revenge. Solomon was tiring of flaming crosses and judgmental neighbours. "Right, I'm tired. We've had this all day and we're not getting very far. I suggest we talk about this tomorrow when Margaret's been to the doctor's." With that Solomon shut the door.

"Well! The bloody cheek of the man!" Ethel Hebblethwaite tut-tutted.

"You got me out of bed for that?" Sam turned round and went back to bed. His son-in-law did likewise.

"Men," said Mrs Hebblethwaite under her breath. "Show's over, everybody, you can go to your beds now." She walked into her house and shut the door.

She tried to shut her eyes once she'd got to bed but she couldn't. She couldn't stop thinking about Margaret and what would happen at the doctors tomorrow. Sam was snoring.

Solomon told Cass he was going to see the priest.

"What for? You don't believe in God!" Cass said as she lay naked on the bed, trying to see if she could entice him. This was her last act to try and get Solomon's eye away from the younger females in Broughton.

"You're right, I don't believe in God."

"So is there another reason?" Cass began stroking her naked body

"I'm going to have a chat with him." Solomon was tiring of Cass's imaginative mind and innuendos.

"Isn't my decaying body good enough for Solomon these days?" Cass asked, revealing herself to Solomon. "Or does the great Solomon Tump only like the lily white skin of amateurs?" Cass roared with laughter. It was a dirty and revealing laugh.

"You're stoned!" Solomon accused.

"Judgmental as well as a liar," she retorted.

"You're becoming a bore, Cass. Grow up."

"Me, boring? You're the one who wants to buy a shop and be Mr Good Morning. Jesus H. Buddha, I never thought I'd see the day that Solomon Tump would rather sell half a pound of tuppenny rice than smoke a 'teenth and have a roll with his old lady!"

"It's called getting a life!" Solomon said through gritted teeth. He tried to believe what he was saying.

"It's called selling out." Cass turned her back on him. "Come back in ten years' time when you've stopped giving up giving up." She laughed and Solomon left the house angry.

Chapter 22

He was annoyed that he'd got angry, and angry that he couldn't have talked to Cass without raising his voice.

"Shit!" he said as he walked out into the midnight air. He'd not been angry since his fifteenth birthday. He put both hands into his pockets and marched purposefully to the presbytery. He was annoyed that all the chakra-rubbing and incense-burning had come to nothing. He'd eaten enough brown rice to cure the Third World of most diseases and prayed to that many eastern deities he was convinced evil was on its way out.

Who does he turn to when all things become befuddled?

Buddha.

Leave it out.

Confucius.

You're having a laugh.

The great gods of Hinduism.

Mine's a pint.

He turns for succour not to Muhammad or Lao Tse; he'd even given Winnie the Pooh the push. No, he was turning to a thirty-three-year-old priest who'd studied in Rome and was having a crisis of conscience about his sexuality.

Solomon marched up Millgate fuelled by anger and not a little self-doubt.

He knocked on the presbytery door. It was just after midnight and he hoped the priest was up. He was. Solomon saw the hall light go on. The front door opened slightly. The chain on the door obscured Solomon's view, but he was sure it was Thomas who was standing there in striped pyjamas.

"Who is it?" yawned Father O'Dowd.

"Solomon Tump and I need to talk."

"Holy ecclesiastical erections!" thought Father O'Dowd.

"Do you know what time it is?" the priest asked. He was stalling so he could assess the situation. Being aroused in your soutane was one thing, but when you were in your jim-jams exposure was just an open fly-hole away. He blessed himself and had a quick look below the equator. Everything was in its place. Just. He sighed and took the chain off the door.

"I know it's late, Thomas, but I do need to talk," said Solomon with some conviction.

"OK." Thomas O'Dowd opened the door and let him into the presbytery. It was after midnight and he hoped beyond hope that no one was around to witness this clandestine meeting.

Father O'Dowd grabbed his dressing gown. He didn't want any apparitions to appear. Saintly or mortal. They both walked into the kitchen. The cleric headed straight for the kettle. Solomon sat down.

"So what's the problem?" the priest said, wiping the sleep from his eyes.

"I think I've fallen in love."

"At least you can!" replied the priest, pouring out the boiling water into two cups.

"I suppose there is that, but this has never happened before and I'm scared." Solomon Tump scared, this was a first. It was an admission of vulnerability. Father O'Dowd was shocked. Not at this statement but at the fact his nether regions were dormant. A smile appeared on his face.

"Why are you smiling?" asked Solomon.

"Oh, it's nothing, " Thomas lied.

"If you can smile at nothing, Father, then I think you've found the answer."

"No. Its just that when I first met you I had –" He handed Solomon his coffee. "I had, shall we say, certain feelings."

"Cass did say she thought you fancied me," Solomon said, taking his cup from the priest.

Fancied wasn't exactly the right word. He had wanted to run naked through the cornfields and put kisses on every inch of his toned body, including the bit all priests have to airbrush out. "It was more than fancied," Thomas admitted for the first time. "I wanted to sleep with you!" Good Lord, thought Thomas, where did all this honesty suddenly come from?

Solomon nearly spat his coffee across the kitchen floor. He could handle the priest having fancied him, but full frontal nudity and penetration, well, he thought he had problems. Solomon blushed. It was he that had come to the presbytery for a talk and a chat and yet here he was listening to the priest's own confession.

"But I don't think so any more," Thomas O'Dowd said with a sense of achievement.

"Are you aroused now?" asked the man who thought he had recently fallen in love with a nineteen-year-old girl.

"No," he said, putting some more water into the kettle. "Not yet."

Solomon laughed.

"Anyway, enough about clerical erections. What can I do to help?" Father O'Dowd said, coming out of the cupboard and trying to embrace hetero-sexuality with both hands. The Agony Aunt in him was acting out of pure generosity.

"I just need to talk to somebody, you know. I mean, all this business with Mrs Hebblethwaite, calling me the spawn of the Devil," Solomon said, throwing his hands in the air. "I mean, it's not what we came here for. We came to start afresh, you know, but Cass is saying I'm copping out and all and well ..." Solomon didn't finish the sentence, he just sighed. There was a pause. Thomas didn't say anything. He'd decided he'd said enough already and was going to be the Big Ear and just listen.

"And Leo will be two soon and I want to settle down and for him to go to school. I mean it was fine, all that alternative lifestyle thing, because we all had alternative minds due to mind-altering drugs. And don't get me wrong, it was great, no responsibility, you know, tune in, turn on and drop out. Fine. But when you've got a kid, you can't keep dropping a load of acid 'cos he needs things, you know. Not only food and the like, but he needs someone to talk to and you can't do that if your heads orbiting a parallel universe."

The permissive society at prayer, thought Father O'Dowd. Even Mrs Hebblethwaite would be impressed. Probably.

"And there's Margaret, she may be pregnant which changes the whole picture with me and Cass." Solomon looked up. It wasn't exactly a Damascene conversion, but it was bloody close. Three weeks before and this man, this totem of everything alternative, would have laughed in the face of such comments. He would have just got on.

"Why did you come here?" asked Father O'Dowd.

"I've told you already, to settle –" Solomon was interrupted by the priest.

"No. The true story."

Solomon wasn't sure where this was leading. "I don't follow."

"Well, look. I came here because I had to. You know, when the Bishop tells me what to do I have to do it. You don't."

"To be honest, Thomas, I think Cass and I both came here thinking this would be the last chance we have of seeing whether we'd stay together."

"But you've been together for a long time."

"I know, but it's easier when you're younger." Solomon looked towards the ceiling for help. "Have you ever thought that what you're doing is false? I mean, you go through the motions and do what everyone expects you to do, but it doesn't mean anything."

"What, like catching a fish and then throwing it back into the river?"

"What?"

"Never mind." Father Thomas handed him another coffee and sat down. "Why did you become a priest?"

"I thought I had a vocation."

"Thought?"

"Well, I know I have a vocation, it's just that it slips every once in a while."

"Did your parents want you to become a priest ?"

"My mother did. She was in tears when I was ordained."

"Your father?"

"Don't know. I've not seen him since I was eighteen months ..." Thomas paused, looked ruefully across the kitchen and smiled wanly. "He's probably in some boozer, pissed out of his tiny mind." He took his cup to the sink, rinsed it and said "What about your folks?"

The prying had started, thought Solomon. Over the years he'd perfected the skill of deflecting conversation that might reveal something of his past or indeed of himself. He remained tight lipped.

"Well, I don't know if I'm cut out for all this hippy shit any more. I don't know whether it's me or not."

"I thought that was the whole thing, to find yourself," replied the priest, still intrigued that Solomon had not told him anything about his past.

"But what if you found yourself a long time ago and now you're just playing out a role?"

"Oh."

"Is that it? Oh?" Solomon replied rather tersely. "Ten years theological study in Rome and the best you can give me is 'Oh'?"

"Have you spoken to Cass?"

"She just thinks I'm copping out."

"I thought you had an honest open relationship."

"Well we did, but to tell the truth over the past couple of years I've been playing the role."

"And the field. "

"Thomas, I may have lost the whole alternative thing but a good-looking woman is still a good looking woman," Solomon said, reading straight from the script of a B-Movie. "But you see, Thomas, I thought this would be a good idea, you know"

"Opening the shop and settling down?" Thomas said.

"Yes. I thought a new start for Leo's and our sake would be the way forward, but I don't know whether it is." Solomon drank some coffee.

"It's called responsibility." The priest walked over to the table and sat down

"I know." Solomon's brow became furrowed and his eyes narrowed. "It's just that I don't know whether I can settle down with one woman. With any woman."

"You've got two, remember."

"I know."

"So what are you going to do? Run off with Margaret?"

"What, and have the whole Wainwright and Hebblethwaite clans right behind me?"

"Coward!" the Priest said mockingly.

"I'll take the thirty pieces of silver every time," said Judas Tump.

"A capitalist to boot."

"No. Just an out-and-out coward." They both laughed

"Anyway," Thomas said with a giveaway yawn. "I think it's time I turned in."

"Yes. Me too." Solomon walked over to the sink and washed his cup. "Thanks for listening, Thomas." He walked over and gave him a hug. The last time Thomas had been a tree was at Primary school.

"And no more erections," Solomon laughed. "See you later."

"Yes. 'Bye."

He sighed in relief and felt rather sorry for Solomon's predicament. If he had his religious cap on then he would have to say Solomon should commit to his responsibilities and look after Margaret and Cass. On a purely personal level he was just hoping that things would settle down. Thomas was thankful that his feelings for Solomon weren't as strong as they used to be, but there were aberrations.

He had missed the Prospect Street debacle because he'd tried for an early night, which he didn't get because he was talking to and then hugged by Solomon.

These midnight erections were getting him down. He was in his office with his glass of whisky and this week's copy of The Catholic Herald when the phone rang.

"Damn." Father hated anything that distracted him from reading the weekly Catholic news, especially the section on those colleagues who'd been defrocked.

"It can't be the Bishop," he muttered, "Because he always has an early night." He put the glass down and picked up the receiver. "Hello?"

"Sorry to trouble you at this time of night, Father, but we've got a slight problem," Sergeant Baldwin said with an efficiency that had eluded him on numerous other occasions.

Father O'Dowd was struggling to hear what the policeman was saying because there seemed to be somebody singing in the background.

"WE SHALL NOT, WE SHALL NOT BE MOVED ..." It didn't matter to Miss Mahoney that one minute she was using the totem of the Ku Klux Klan and the next minute espousing the oratory of Martin Luther King. Sergeant Baldwin didn't know about either and he didn't care. All he wanted was a quiet station so he could get back to his elevenses.

"I can hardly hear you, Sergeant, can you repeat that?"

"GO TELL IT ON THE MOUNTAIN ..."

"I'm sorry, Father." Sergeant Baldwin put his hand over the mouthpiece.

"If you don't shut up NOW you're in the cells for the night," Sergeant Baldwin shouted at the prisoner before carrying on his conversation with the priest .

"Sorry, Father, this one's a bit livelier than most. What it is, we've got someone down here who won't co-operate until they see you."

Father O'Dowd looked at his watch. It was nearing one o'clock. The pubs had closed so he assumed it was either some drunk who'd found the Lord in the bottom of his glass or a parishioner hoping that the priest could help him get off with a caution.

"Who is it?" he asked.

Sergeant Baldwin looked at the arrest report. "Miss Winifred Mahoney."

"Shit!" Father O'Dowd said under his breath.

"What was that?" asked the policeman.

"I said I'll come down in about ten minutes."

Chapter 23

Cass and Solomon were just about on speaking terms. Just. They walked round each other like big cats in a cage wondering who would strike first.

"It's all right, this free love thing, if we play by the rules ..." Cass said to Che Guevara who was hanging on the wall. Once again he remained tight lipped. " ... there's no such thing as a free fuck!" She looked out of the window and saw three generations of the Hebblethwaite clan walking down the road.

"Children playing as adults," Mrs Hebblethwaite said to her daughter, but she wasn't listening. She was too busy worrying about Margaret's pregnancy test.

"You can't sleep around and not hurt somebody, however many trees you hug," Mrs Hebblethwaite said, trying not to notice all the curtain twitching that was going on. The word was out that Margaret was pregnant and the guilty party was the hippy. Pride had to be swallowed and, oh, how it hurt. Mrs Hebblethwaite was suffering. No matter how many candles you light and prayers you say, pride, when swallowed always tastes awful.

As head of the family, a title that Mr Hebblethwaite always disputed, Mrs Hebblethwaite took it upon herself to accompany her daughter and granddaughter to the doctor's surgery. They couldn't possibly hide the fact that something was wrong, because three generations of Hebblethwaite's going anywhere meant trouble. Mrs Hebblethwaite had been under Doctor Brown for as long as she could remember and an appointment had been made for ten o'clock. The three ladies walked sombrely to the surgery with barely a word spoken. Margaret's eyes were puffy from constantly sniffing and sobbing. Occasionally she would dab the odd tear away with the corner of her handkerchief. Her Nan didn't say much, just tut-tutted and made the sign of the cross. Her mother held her hand and gently squeezed it every now and again.

They arrived at the surgery in good time. Margaret went up to the reception where she was greeted by a stern spinster of the parish whose intimate knowledge of everyone's medical history was used with judicious spite.

"Morning," she said her eyes still transfixed by some meaningless post. She finally raised her head. Her hair was pure white and resembled a two-scooped ice-cream. Half moon glasses revealed eyes that were cold and austere. To everyone in Broughton she was Cruella De Ville; she may not have had the 101 Dalmatians and The Panther De Ville car, but she was The Ice Maiden.

"Yes?" she said to Margaret. "Haven't got all day, M'Dear. What is it, time of the month or do you want some contraceptive pills?"

Mrs Hebblethwaite was the first to react. "It's none of your business!"

"Oh, but I'm afraid it is, Mrs Hebblethwaite. The doctor is a very busy man and we don't have time for monthly illnesses." The doctor's Praetorian Guard was defending her line.

"Margaret has a ten o'clock appointment with Doctor Brown. That's all you need to know" said Margaret's mother, outraged that her daughter's credibility was being impugned.

Miss Buckley smiled to herself. "Yet another unwanted pregnancy," she said under her breath, with just enough volume that the three women heard. "And them doyennes of the Catholic Church too." She raised her head and smiled. "Doctor's ready for you now. Room Two."

"Thank you, *Miss* Buckley," said Mrs Hebblethwaite with just enough emphasis on the Miss. To be unmarried in Broughton was grave indeed, with the finger of suspicion pointing to one thing only. Miss Buckley was a Lesbian. It didn't need Hercule Poirot to work it out as she never wore a dress, always wore a shirt and tie and smoked untipped cigarettes from a long silver holder.

Miss Buckley was used to such comments and smiled. "Don't knock what you've never tried," she said to Mrs Hebblethwaite. "You never know, you might like it."

Mrs Hebblethwaite winced as she walked past the receptionist and followed her daughter and granddaughter into the doctor's surgery.

Dr Brown was from the tweedy branch of medicine. He didn't practice what he preached because he knew better. He smoked like a chimney, drank like a fish and didn't have time for female ailments. He studied at Edinburgh where he graduated with a First. His hobby was the growing and tending of his moustache which hung down over his top lip like a dirty shower curtain. It was greys, mucky browns and nicotine yellows, and just long enough to conceal his one tooth which hung on to his gums like a mountaineer desperately clinging onto a rock.

"YES?" He didn't look up from whatever it was he was reading.

"It's my daughter, Doctor Brown," Mrs Wainwright said nervously. "She's –"

"Lost her tongue has she, or has she lost the facility of perambulation?" The doctor liked to impress his patients with his command of the English language. When he spoke his moustache left his top lip like a kite about to take off.

"I don't know what …" muttered Margaret's mother, confused.

"Well, if you did know, you wouldn't be here would you?" He harrumphed at his own joke and finally looked up.

"Good God, there's three of you!"

"Morning, Doctor Brown," Mrs Hebblethwaite said.

"Morning," said Margaret.

"Morning. Come on girl, haven't got all day. What's up?"

"I think I'm …" she paused and looked at her mum. " … Pregnant."

"OK. Well I'll have to examine you," the Doctor said matter of factly.

Margaret had only let one person see her naked body as a woman and that was Solomon.

"Do I have to ?" She asked.

"Well you can't have a baby fully clothed, can you?" The doctor laughed. "And you two ladies, if you wouldn't mind, would you please leave the room." It was more of a bark than a request but they acquiesced. Margaret was mortified and told herself she would never get pregnant again if it meant taking her clothes off in front of this Medical Sergeant Major.

Doctor Brown walked over to a bed and drew a curtain around it.

"Right, if you take your dress off we can get started." He went over to the basin and washed his hands.

Margaret swallowed hard but did as she was told. For the first time in many years she started saying a prayer.

The examination over, he passed her a small glass bottle.

"Right, if you could fill this."

"What with?" she asked nervously.

"Urine, woman. Can't tell if you're properly pregnant without urine." He muttered something disparaging about the female race and washed his hands again.

"And you'll have to do it first thing in the morning." The Doctor dried his hands and walked back behind his desk. "Bring it back tomorrow, and we'll have the results for you in two weeks time."

"Thanks," she said. She didn't know why she'd thanked him for what was a truly embarrassing and horrible experience. She walked out into the main reception area where her mother and Nan waited. They both stood up.

Chapter 24

Thomas O'Dowd hadn't been to Manchester since he was fifteen. He'd left his mother and friends in 1948 to join a Seminary in Rome. He left a boy, returned a priest and was desperately trying to find out where the man had got to. Manchester itself had managed to remain remarkably intact, despite the best attentions of the Luftwaffe. It was still as dirty as he'd remembered and the sky had been sewn with new concrete skyscrapers which lit up the night like candles on a cake. The entrances to the tall office buildings were the new homes to tramps who were wrapped up in brown coats, tied up with string like damaged parcels. It was austere, cold and new.

It was eight o'clock on Friday night and he was petrified. He wasn't petrified by the city or those that scurried around, mean-faced and bitter. He was worried what he might do. Father O'Dowd had never done what he was about to do and he was all of a shake. His mother would be horrified, the Bishop apoplectic and Mrs Hebblethwaite would suffer the holiest of heart attacks if she knew. He was going to visit a gay pub. The last time he had seen Solomon he hadn't become aroused straight away, but it did happen when he was hugged. This pseudo-scientific experiment was being conducted to see if he was truly over his sexual aberration.

He didn't know what a gay pub was or how it was different, but he knew there were some and he was going to try and find one. So, he set himself the task to see if he really was homosexual. He'd thought about it endlessly, what he would say or do if challenged, asked, or picked up. He didn't know. His mind was racing, thoughts colliding with each other, and none of them helpful. Of course he didn't have the dog collar on, or any Catholic paraphernalia, except a life's worth of guilt.

He walked first of all to Chorlton Street Bus Station. He didn't have any reason for this other than it seemed a damned good place to start. He walked into the pub opposite. It was called Paddy's Goose.

"Pint of bitter please," Father Tom said to the aging barman, who had a face like a gnarled conker. The barman pulled the pint. He didn't speak, just finished off his job and said "One and six." He had the demeanour and gait of an animal awaiting the delights of the abattoir.

Father Tom gave him the correct change and, sated with the barman's happy-go-lucky nature, took a seat near the one-armed bandit.

He looked around. He couldn't see any homosexuals, but then he didn't know what he was looking for. There were a few city types and their secretaries mulling over the week's events and office gossip. Two under-aged boys were nursing their pints whilst furtively looking around, waiting for the ambush to come from the unhappy people. The police. A lady of the night who'd obviously started early stood at the corner of the bar, all patent leather, mini-skirt and wrap-around lipstick. She teetered on high rise stilettos and wistfully flashed her eye lashes at whoever caught her gaze. Father Tom caught her eye, more out of nosiness than design. She came over. He said a quick prayer to Mary Magdalene and buried his head in his pint.

"Is it all right if Ah sit next to you, love?" she asked, taking a drag from her cigarette. She blew the smoke triumphantly over her right shoulder and placed the cigarette between her long slender fingers.

"Er, yes," stammered the priest.

"All on your lonesome?" she inquired. Tom tried to think of some suitable reply but couldn't lie.

"Yes. Just popped in for a pint before I go home," he said, reddening.

"And where's that then?" She pulled on her cigarette as though it was her last breath.

"Sorry?" Tom asked, trying to breathe through the vats of cologne she was wearing.

"Home, love. Where do you live?" she asked.

"Well, I'm living in Broughton."

"Get away! That's where I'm from," she laughed.

Father Tom didn't. He nearly choked and took a quick swig of his pint, to dampen the shock.

"Don't live there now, mind."

"Thank God for that," he said quietly.

"What did you say?"

"Nothing," Tom lied.

"No. I left years ago, bloody hated the place. Small-minded people all crushed together in a small-minded town hemmed in by those bloody Pennines. Pissed it down most of the year. I got out before I started to rust." She laughed at her own joke, but the years of nicotine and alcohol cut short the laughter and she started to cough, a rasping, lung-wrenching cough that drowned out the one-armed bandit.

"I'll be all right in a minute, I just need a quick top up." She grabbed a new packet from her handbag and took out a cigarette with all the dexterity and speed of the finest pick pocket. She lit it, drew on it and sighed. The coughing stopped, her eyes regained some semblance of normality and her chest stopped thrashing around and merely bobbed up and down like a toy yacht on a park lake.

"I'll have to stop," she said. "Mind you, I've been trying to stop for twenty year and I still can't manage it." She coughed delicately into her handkerchief. "Do you smoke, love?"

"No," Tom replied, his face returning to its normal colour. The barman winked at him and put five fingers into the air. Tom looked puzzled. His female companion looked around and saw what was going on.

"What does five mean?" Tom said naively

"Oh take no notice of him, he's just stirring it," came the reply.

"No, tell me?"

"Look love everything's negotiable," she said and leant a little closer to him She cupped her hand over her mouth and whispered into his ear. "A fiver for a fuck, three for a blow, and a couple of quid for a hand job," she said matter-of-factly.

Thomas knew what a fuck was, hadn't a clue about a blow and had first hand knowledge of the latter.

"Well, must go, got to catch the 8.35." He finished off his pint. "Nice speaking to you." Thomas walked out of the pub concerned that he wasn't up to all this night-time lark and speaking to strangers.

The barman heard the clicking of heels coming towards the bar. He finished drying a glass and greeted the customer with his usual panache.

"Bastard. I had him eating out of me hand, and you go and ruin it. Means I'll have to work longer tonight to make up me money." She slammed her glass on the counter and teetered into the spring sunshine looking for lonely customers.

One lonely tourist walked around the streets next to the canal, hands in pockets, wondering what to do next. The decision was made for him. He heard music and laughter coming from a pub adjacent to the canal. The pub looked dissolute and unwanted, it was rather scruffy and looked as though it could do with a good Dettolling. It was next to Canal Street. He walked in nervously. The interior was in stark contrast to the outside. A mirrored ball hung from the centre of the room reflecting the garish lights that spun frantically around. A small stage was in one corner which held a double decked record player where a transvestite Marilyn Monroe was singing along to a Judy Garland record. He must have been in his seventies, but was still proud of his twenty eight inch waist. Marilyn would have too, although Judy would have had a word with him about his make up. Nobody was dancing but this didn't seem to matter to the DJ who was merrily singing away.

"A pint of Guinness please," Tom said to the bar person who was all tutued up.

The pint was brought across and the bar person flashed her false eyelashes at Tom. They were as elegant as funereal blinds.

"I like my men to drink pints. A girl needs a bit of rough to keep her on her toes," he said pouting. He'd never been to pouting school and his rouged pursed lips looked like a sore cat's arse. Tom was not aroused. He handed over a ten shilling note and grimaced.

"No need to be like that. A girl's got to try, you know." He brought the change back and teetered off.

The bar was full with those men who liked to dress up and those that didn't. He saw at least four Marilyns, one Shirley Bassey and another Judy Garland who didn't really pull it off. A large Irishman, probably a builder, stood at the end of the bar. He'd obviously been poured into his twin set and pearls by his own trowel.

"Oh, God give me strength," Tom said to the bar towel, realising that he shouldn't be there. He imagined what the fall-out would be if anyone saw him. His pensive and furtive face told the regulars that this was a first-timer.

"First time is it, love?" asked a shortish man in jeans and a leather jacket.

Tom thought he was trying to look like Marlon Brando, but he had neither the stature, the looks nor the presence.

"Yes," Tom said truthfully. You can take a priest to Hull, Hell and back, but you can't make him lie. Yet.

"You'll get used to it. It all feels a bit strange at first." Marlon said sipping his Campari and lemonade. "The thing is, it doesn't matter who you are here because we all have such a giggle." And Marlon did just that. He giggled. "And then afterwards, well." He raised his eyebrows up to the mirrored ball and said. "WE ALL WASH OUR DIRTY DISHES, if you catch my drift!" Tom didn't and his flaccid penis retreated even further at the thought of having any kind of fun with Half Man Half Brando.

"I bet you've been kept awake at night wanting fun. I can see it in your eyes." Marlon winked a stage wink that was neither seductive nor convincing. "You're dying to try, and I'm kind of experienced in that way." He smirked. "If you know what I mean." He grabbed his crotch and smiled.

Thomas nearly threw up. He looked again at Half Man Half Brando and realised that he knew the man hiding underneath the leather jacket. It was Monsignor Pissalero from St. Cuthbert's. "Oh my God!" he said under his breath and put his pint down and walked away.

"Where are you going?" the jeaned one said.

"I've just got to pay a visit," Tom replied. The jeaned one smiled and once Tom had reached the toilets, he followed.

It was all getting too much for Tom and he went inside a cubicle. He was suddenly aware that the cubicle next to him was occupied. And from inside a voice said.

"Are you a true friend of Dorothy's?"

"No, I'm a Catholic!" said Tom.

"That's funny, so am I. Well, you know what they say about priests don't you?"

"No!"

"Well, all that dressing up in robes, candles, wine and altar boys. Bit strange don't you think ?"

"No, not really." Tom said sternly defending his faith.

"This is funny isn't it?" Marlon chuckled.

"What is?"

"Two Catholics sat in adjacent cubicles in a gay pub."

It wasn't bloody funny thought Father Tom, it was a bloody nightmare. All it needed now was for the Bishop to go into the cubicle on the other side and ask him if he wouldn't mind rubbing his bunions

"I suppose it is," Tom lied.

"Bit like confessional really."

Tom heard a rustling and didn't like it. It sounded like a belt buckle being undone. He could hear the sound of deep breathing and it wasn't his.

"I know!" said Monsignor Brando. "I'll be the priest and you can be the naughty parishioner." The heavy breathing started to get faster.

There was silence. Tom O'Dowd's worst nightmare was about to happen.

"Go on, I'll start you off. Bless me Father ..." Before he could get to, 'for I have sinned' Father O'Dowd was out of that cubicle faster than Lazarus rising from the dead.

"Where are you going?" Tom heard the cubicle say. He also heard the sound of somebody enjoying himself. "Don't go! I've got something to show you, and besides I haven't given you absolution." HALF MAN HALF BRANDO WAS IN TUMESCENT HEAVEN.

Tom walked as quickly and calmly as he could, leaving the singing Marilyn and her friends to enjoy their own company.

He was mortified, sullied and dirty, and more importantly for the Catholic Church, unaroused. He was pleased about that but still didn't know whether he could set foot in Solomon's house. He would have to put it to the test, but at a much later date.

Father O'Dowd walked slowly back up to the station still wondering what a 'blow' was.

"Hello Father, night on the town is it?" said Gary.

Father O'Dowd looked round nervously and saw Mrs Hebblethwaite's grandson at the railway bar with a group of five other teenagers.

"Hello, Gary. Not really, just had to see somebody in town," he said guiltily and wondered if it looked like he had been talking to a prostitute. He didn't know what the signs were, but was worried just the same.

"Do you want a beer, Father?" Gary asked. His friends turned away, worried that their chances of pulling anything in a dress would be seriously hampered by having a priest sitting with them.

Father O'Dowd looked round and, noting that his train wouldn't be arriving for at least twenty-five minutes, accepted. He tried to get the thought of the Monsignor out of his mind but he couldn't. He hoped Gary wasn't a mind reader. Mind you, Gary had trouble dealing with his own mind, never mind anyone else's.

"So what are you lads up to, or need I ask?"

"We're going to that new club, Father. You know, the one that plays all that Northern Soul," Gary enthused.

"Oh." The priest was none the wiser.

"You must have heard of it. The Twisted Wheel."

"Dance till you drop. Sweat, blueys, birds, and music. Doesn't come any better than that!" announced the largest of the group. He got off his stool and spun round to much applause from the rest.

"No Elvis, then," said Tom O'Dowd ironically.

Derisive laughter followed and a few curled-up lips later, Father O'Dowd was deep in conversation with Gary and his mates about the finer points of Northern Soul.

"Time to go." The priest looked at his watch. "Thanks for the drink Gary, and have a good night." He left them at the bar and caught his train home.

"I wonder if they knew I had been in a gay bar," he said quietly as he got on the train.

Chapter 25

He arrived home at about ten past ten and Broughton was in full swing. The window in the Flying Horse had been put through, but then the windows in that pub had a life expectancy of a week at the most. He walked as quickly as he could without drawing too much attention to himself. He hoped that nobody had died or had wanted the last rites while he was sitting next to Monsignor Brando. He got to the presbytery to find his mother still up.

"Where've you been?" she asked, concerned that he hadn't told her where he was going.

"I had to go to Manchester, to a Catholic Mission," he lied. He was becoming worryingly good at lying. "Everything OK?" he asked.

"Yes, apart from Miss Mcafferty," his mother said.

"What's wrong?"

"I don't know, but she's coming out with all sorts of stuff about you, the Bishop and Mrs Hebblethwaite." His mother had that look that he had seen many times before. It was a look that said 'SEX' was on the conversational menu.

Thomas sat on a chair. His mother just kept pacing up and down the kitchen.

"I don't know how to put this, Tom, but I'm worried. I'm worried that either she's mad or something's happening in this presbytery that's not right." She walked over to the drinks cabinet and, unusually for her, poured herself a large whisky.

"Tom, she mentioned something about ..." She took a nip of the firewater and continued. "She was talking about ..." She girded her loins and everything else that needed girding. "Thomas, I know Catholic priests are celibate, and I know you are and that you never would because of your vocation and God and everything, and besides I know you wouldn't because you've done your vows and things, but if you did want to do things, you know, if you had thoughts about below the belt happenings, would they be thoughts about women or men?" She sat down quickly and closed her eyes.

"Why do you ask?" Thomas knew his mother was perceptive but she was no mind reader.

"It's just something Miss Mcafferty said in her sleep about arousal."

"What kind of arousal?" As soon as he said it he knew. God, he was being as naïve as the Bishop.

"Thomas, this is hard for me to say." She paused. "Now I know you've not had many girlfriends, in fact you haven't had any, but then you're married to God." His mother was moving from chair to chair. "And being married to God is no bad thing and he loves men and woman in equal amounts." She wasn't just going round the houses she was putting in detours round the whole town. "But what I mean to say, are you aroused by other men?" She finally sat down and drank her whisky. "I know what with all the fancy dresses you wear and the wine and incense and young boys an all, it wouldn't be the first time somebody has strayed." She got up again and stood next to him. "Whatever you did, you know I'd still love you." She went back to get another drink.

"It's just that Miss Mcafferty says you have homosexual arousals while the Bishop's around." Mrs O'Dowd took a deep breath and then launched into part two of her treatise on The Catholic Church and Erections. "Thomas, she said that after you get a downstairs steeple . . ." She blushed and covered her eyes with a shaky hand. " . . . the Bishop then communes with Mrs Hebblethwaite and you look on." She sat down exhausted. "Is that right?"

Father O'Dowd was exhausted just listening to his mother's garbled talk.

"Where did all that come from?" he asked.

"Well, I told you I was worried."

"The answer is NO mother, I don't have homosexual erections," he said confidently, because he'd been to a gay pub and hovered over a gay toilet seat listening to a gay Marlon Brando trying to excite him, and he didn't have one flicker of an erection. He smiled.

"Thank God for that," his mother said, smothering him in kisses. She blessed herself. She asked him if he wanted a cup of tea. He said yes, but what he really wanted was to see Solomon and find out if his soutane would still rise when he saw the hippy.

Chapter 26

Cass decided to have a wander around town. Well, if the truth be known she wanted to bump into Teen Blonde and Cherry on a Stick and it being Friday night she thought this was the best chance she had of seeing them. Solomon said he didn't mind but she knew he did. Cass reckoned he'd planned some kind of tryst but he never let on. He was slightly annoyed because she was going into Broughton with some solid lippy plastered on.

She walked briskly through the town peering into three pubs before she spotted Martha and three chums. They were sitting round a table laughing and giggling into their Babychams. Cass took a deep breath and walked into the pub they called Ruby Tuesdays. The clientele were teenagers and the bar staff looked even younger.

"Mine's a Guinness," Cass said, brandishing a pound note. The spotty youth looked non-plussed. He'd heard there were hippies in the vicinity but he never thought he would see one. He knew there were tigers in India but you didn't expect them to wander into your pub and ask for a drink.

"What?" he said

"You do sell Guinness?" she said slowly.

"Yes," came the courteous reply.

"I'd like one then, if that's not too much trouble." The barman did as he was told.

"Isn't that the hippy chick you were talking about in the park?" one of Martha's friends said as she negotiated the cherry on top of her drink. Martha turned round.

"Oh yes," she replied and returned to her conversation.

"Looks a bit of a slapper if you ask me," Cherry on a Stick said, curling her top lip in disgust.

"Nobody's asking you," Martha said in Cass's defence. "And anyway you don't even know her."

"Whenever has knowing anybody stopped us from calling them slappers!" Miss Judgmental left the table with her pride between her legs. Something else would fall before her night was over. Another Babycham was required.

The barman returned with Cass's drink.

"This is a half!" Cass looked at the barman in disbelief.

"I know. You're a woman," he said knowledgeably.

"What's that got to do with the price of fish?" Cass was beginning to get irritable.

Hippies. And now Fish. The young barman was having a surreal baptism into the delights of serving the public.

"You asked for a Guinness and I brought you one. A half."

"I don't drink halves. I drink pints." Cass looked around and shook her head.

"Women can only have halves!" came the retort from a large-bellied man she took to be the landlord. The barman smiled. She wouldn't be talking about fish to him he thought.

"OK, if you don't sell pints to women I'll have ten halves, please." There was muted laughter from an elderly gent sitting at the corner of the bar. The landlord gave him the eye and the old fella knew his days as a regular were numbered.

"That's five pints!" the landlord said, reddening.

"Give that man a cigar," Cass said.

Hippies. Fish. Cigars. The young barman was confused. He thought selling beer was simple. He know knew different.

"I know it's five pints."

"We don't allow women to drink five pints at one go in here."

"I'm not drinking them all," Cass said smiling. "They're for my friends over there." Cass pointed to Martha's table.

"Oh," the landlord said quietly, the wind having left his sails.

"Well just think on then." The landlord returned to his table chastened. A man in his position was not used to public ridicule and someone would have to pay. Probably his wife.

"Can you bring them over?" Cass asked the barman. He nodded. She paid for the drinks and went over to where Martha was sitting.

"Is it OK if I join you?" Cass pulled a chair from the table. "I had to get out or I would have killed him."

"Course," Martha said, winking to the other girls. This was female semaphore for not saying anything.

"You certainly handled Geoff," Sharon said.

"Who's that, the landlord?" Cass replied.

"Yes. He's a right bastard. Always throwing his weight around and trying to touch you up"

"Yuck!" Cass said.

"It's worse than that." Martha threw the debate open.

"Can't be." Cass was thinking nothing could be worse than Solomon lying and getting Margaret pregnant. Well there was, but not at this precise moment.

"Yes. Fat bastard's a bit free with his hands."

"You mean he hits women?"

"Yeah. His missus." Silence fell.

There was a long pause as The Landlord's Punch bag walked past the table, emptied the ashtray, smiled and tried to hide the large bruise that stuck to her eye like a badge of dishonour.

"Anyway, sorry to barge in on you but I needed a girls' night out," Cass said apologetically as the drinks arrived.

"As bad as that?" Martha said, screwing her nose up. Her friends didn't say a word.

"Worse ..." Cass said, demolishing her half of Guinness.

"Well ?" Martha shuffled her chair nearer to the table. They were all ears.

"It's Solomon ..."

One of Martha's friends mouthed "Who's Solomon?"

"I've just found out that he's got a local girl pregnant."

Bombshell.

Two more chairs screeched closer to the news that was breaking.

"Who?" Martha asked, dying to know.

"Oh some nineteen-year-old who lives across the ..."

"Not Margaret Wainwright?" Martha said in disbelief.

"Yes. That's her," Cass confirmed.

Martha's mouth remained open for some time but Broughton flies were wary of such tactics and left her alone. "Bloody hell Cass, what you gunna do?" Martha was agog.

"Her gran'll have his balls for this."

"The way I feel at the moment she can have them," Cass laughed.

"I'll get another round in, we may be here for some time," Martha's friend said.

"God, I don't even know you that well and I'm pouring out all me troubles!" Cass looked across at Martha. "You must think I'm a right drongo."

"Hey, we've all been there," Martha said reassuringly and she patted Cass's shoulders.

"You mean you've slept with the bastard too?" Tears coursed down Cass's face. She didn't know whether these were tears of anger, joy or madness. She was just glad she was with other women.

"OOO I don't know about that but he looks as though he'd be pretty good in bed to me!" Martha put her hand to her mouth. "I'm sorry it just kinda slipped out."

"That's never been a problem with Solomon," Cass said moving her hands apart.

"You mean he's well hung?" Martha asked.

"Like a donkey." It was Martha's turn to laugh. "Mind you, his brain is in inverse proportion to his dick." Cass wiped the tears from her eyes. More Guinness arrived.

"What do you mean?" Martha asked.

"Well," Cass said, "He has a massive dick but you could fit his brain into a matchbox."

"That intelligent!" Martha laughed. The Landlord didn't.

Chapter 27

The Estate Agent showed Solomon around the Old Co-op. He had a superior air about him that had been acquired. His aquiline nose was permanently raised. He had top floor arrogance and basement manners. Armed with a clipboard and a silver Parker pen, he scribbled away frantically whilst Solomon followed. Solomon wasn't listening to a word he was saying because he'd already decided that this was the place for them. It was a huge step but they'd come this far and they had Leo to think about.

" And I'm sure with a little bit of paint here and there, and not forgetting the woman of the house's touch –" Mrs Grigg's bra stayed firmly in place, there was no chance she would burn it for the rights of her sisters. "This place could look wonderful," said Mrs Estate Agent. They came as a team, joined at the wallet. The estate agent sold and rented out properties, whilst his wife, the interior designer, charged a fortune for helping those unfortunates who can't make decisions on how to choose their colours and furniture. She was also a master of Feng Shui. Feng means 'should know' and Shui means 'better'.

She was in her late thirties, slim, with monkey brown hair, and a supercilious accent. She was all pretence and posture, prone to platitudes and clichés, the master of stating the bloody obvious, which is what clients wanted, thought Solomon. Interior designers hold the hands of their clients while fleecing them of their money. She was called Julie Griggs. Her husband didn't listen to her, but did stop when his client spoke.

"This is fine, I'll take it." Solomon smiled, trying to convince himself this was the best thing to do. The interior designer was still prattling on about Carnaby Street.

"Excellent," the estate agent said, mentally counting how much he would be making on this particular deal.

"And if you had some fur on the walls over there . . ."

As a vegetarian he didn't take kindly to this particular design concept.

"I don't believe in killing animals for the sake of art," Solomon said, taking the moral high ground, which wasn't too difficult when dealing with an estate agent and an interior designer.

Mrs Griggs was worried that her commission to re-design the old Co-op could be affected by her comments. "I'm sure fake fur would do," she said, trying to regain the commercial ground she'd just lost.

"That's just as bad. Sends out the wrong message. Animals were never meant to be wallpaper."

The estate agent stepped in. "Hear, hear," he said, worried that his wife might be talking the client out of renting the property he'd been trying to get rid of for nearly twelve months. His wife was most bemused, a state she often found herself in.

"But we have a ..." She tried to tell Solomon that they had a fake fur wall and all their friends liked it. Or so they said.

"Right, I think that's all we need to talk about. I'll send all the relevant documentation to you and as soon as you sign, you can have the keys." He shook Solomon's hand with all the integrity of a seasoned politician.

He looked around their new adventure, still unsure if it was the right thing for both of them to get involved in. "In for a penny in, for a pound." And he didn't borrow that phrase from any Sanskrit teachings.

Solomon left the shop and said goodbye to the woman who wanted animal wallpaper.

He walked through Broughton slightly bemused by it all. It was as if he'd won the Pools but had been told he had only three months to live. He walked over the canal bridge and spotted Gary and a mate trying to roll a cigarette. Solomon laughed. Gary was rolling a 'Broughton,' as it was to be called, an uneven roll-up that failed to burn and left the smoker with tobacco everywhere other than where it should be.

"Yo, Sol!" Gary said, raising his fist in a salute of solidarity. "How does it hang?"

"It hangs well, Brother." And Solomon returned the salute.

Solomon smiled at Miss Mahoney but she put her head down and busied herself along the main street. He passed the café where heads turned and laughter followed. Even after three weeks the sight of Solomon and his clothes caused much entertainment.

"Is it a girl, is it a bird, no it's a hippy" was the latest topical refrain. Solomon smirked, shook his head in disbelief and went home to tell the Cass the 'good' news.

Chapter 28

The following morning Solomon signed the papers with Cass and Leo at the Estate Agents and collected the keys from Doreen. Mr Griggs and his wife were out charming the pounds from the pockets of clients.

"This is It, Cass," Solomon said.

"Yes." Cass was underwhelmed by the whole thing. She smiled and tried to look enthusiastic but it just wasn't there. They walked round to their new shop in silence.

"Are you worried?" Solomon asked.

"Yes. You?"

"Yes." They sounded like two teenagers on their first date both wanting to say something profound but scared of the reply they might get.

"It's a big step, Cass," Solomon said as they turned the corner into Water Street.

"The biggest."

"What if it doesn't work out?" Solomon said quietly in case the gods of things that don't work out were listening.

Cass didn't reply. She was trying to work out if their conversation was a giant metaphor for their relationship or whether Solomon, the born-again Capitalist, was having second thoughts.

"I'll make it work."

"Yes," The Tump replied placing the key in the door and opening their brand new adventure. Cass put Leo, who had fallen asleep, on a giant bean bag in the corner of the shop.

It was a huge space and would take some filling.

"It's bloody GI-NORMOUS!" she said. "Have we got enough gear to fill all this?" she said spinning around and pointing at all the shelf space.

"Hope so," Solomon replied, running his finger over one of the shelves. "Bloody years of dust here." The windows hadn't seen a cloth since the last pork pie left the premises twelve months since.

"We'll need an army to clean this place up." She looked dismayed. Although very particular with her own appearance she wasn't one for Marigolds and dusters.

"Three van loads coming up tonight," Solomon said. "And I reckon if we work all through the weekend, everything'll be sorted come Monday."

Cass wasn't too sure but she didn't say anything, she just went over to check on her son who was sound asleep.

Cass knew what she was going to do next, she was going to test Solomon and herself for that matter. She took off all her clothes and walked over to where Solomon was standing.

"Solomon."

He turned round but didn't say anything.

"I thought we might consummate our new partnership with some fun."

"Cass, somebody might see!" The response said everything. He didn't want to have sex with Cass any more. They hadn't done anything for days. He'd even resorted to the 'I'm too tired' line. She too wasn't that keen. It was a last chance to see if they could keep whatever they had going.

"Solomon, it's called spontaneity." Annoyed at his response, she walked over to where he was standing. She wanted some control and she was going to have it. If he could impregnate impressionable teenage girls then he could damn well have sex with her, wherever she wanted it and when she wanted it.

"We've got loads to do," Solomon said.

"I know." Cass started to undress him. "And if we don't start now Leo will wake and that'll be that." His trousers were off and she just pushed him on his back.

"No chance," Solomon said as he turned her over. There was no foreplay they just started hammering away at each other like mad. They were scratching and biting and pulling each other's hair, not because it added to their sexual pleasure, but because they realised they didn't really like each other that much. It was over in minutes and Solomon got off and started pacing around. He was glistening with perspiration and indifference. At least with hate you can direct your anger but indifference is the worst kind of response. Cass was livid.

"Two minutes of uncontrollable passion!" Solomon said to himself sarcastically as he walked away. He didn't get dressed straight away but paced the wooden floor of the old Co-op, muttering to himself.

Unconcerned about each other, they were a bit like a married couple reaching their fifteenth year of 'marital bliss.' They stood at opposite sides of the shop like boxers trying to decide what to do next.

Mrs Platt had just bought a pound of mince from Tommy Jones the butcher and was bemoaning the cost of good quality mince, when she happened to see what she thought were two mannequin dolls on the floor of the old co-op. She hadn't seen these dolls before which seemed strange as she passed these premises regularly. Her eyesight had never been that good and so she took the opportunity to have a closer look. She pressed her face up to the shop window, wiped it with her handkerchief and peered in. She thought she saw two dolls writhing around on the floor but then dolls can't do that, they're inanimate objects she told herself. She then noticed a naked bottom and if her memory wasn't playing tricks on her, it was a male bottom which was rapidly moving up and down like a sewing machine. She heard some moans and a scream and then the fleshy sewing machine stood up, turned round and gave the onlooker a view of Solomon's pride and joy. It wasn't yet deflated but still large enough for Mrs Platt to put her hand over her mouth and quickly work out how big Solomon Tump was.

"Shit !"

"What?"

"A woman!"

"Where?"

"At the window."

"Shit."

"That's what I said."

"Did she see us?"

"I think so."

"Is she still there?"

"Yes. I don't think she can move," Solomon said, pulling up his trousers. Cass rolled over and managed to put her top on without giving too much away. Mrs Platt hadn't moved since she first encountered the sewing machine and the moving mannequins.

Solomon swept his hair from his face and unlocked the front door.

"Are you OK?" he said to the statue that was Mrs Platt. She was holding her mince with one hand and her mouth with the other. There was no reply.

"Can I get you something, a cup of tea or ..." Solomon said in his best funereal guise.

Mrs Platt moved her hand and turned her head slightly to look at Solomon. She slowly moved her eyes down to where all the action had taken place. She wanted to see whether he was decent. He was.

"A cup of tea would be fine," she said surprisingly. One of Broughton's more liberated citizens, thought Solomon as he escorted the still slightly distraught Mrs Platt into the shop. Cass was now fully clothed and had gained her composure. She picked up Leo.

"Lovely morning," Cass said, trying to distract Mrs Platt from mentioning what had just gone on.

"Yes," Mrs Platt said. "I've just bought some mince and ..."

"Shepherds pie?" queried Cass.

"We always have Shepherds pie of a Wednesday," Mrs Platt said.

The realization of what she had seen began to percolate its way through. She looked at Solomon, then at Cass and finally at Leo before she let out an almighty shriek.

" AAAAAAGGGGGGGGHHHHHHHHHHHHHH."

Leo began to cry as Mrs Platt and her pound of mince exited left into the abyss that Broughton had just become.

Mrs Platt wasn't known for demonic behaviour. She was from the more reserved side of Broughton. Only the best china served in her dining room, plus the odd Garibaldi. She had never made a spectacle of herself and hadn't intended to that Monday morning. Running down the high street like a whirling dervish, Mrs Platt was finally stopped by a concerned policeman.

"Is everything OK Mrs Platt?" said Sergeant Baldwin.

She tried to answer the policeman but everything came out garbled. It was as though she had eaten too many words and couldn't digest them fast enough to make sense. Sense was the last thing she made.

"Naked sewing machines," said Mrs Platt, moving her arms up and down as though about to take off. "Hairy naked bottoms, and there was a child there too."

This was a first, thought Sergeant Baldwin who had recently read a pamphlet on Satanic worship making inroads into Britain. If naked bottoms, sewing machines, mannequin dolls and children weren't testimony to satanic worship, then he didn't know what was. Which wasn't surprising because he *didn't* know what was. He led the distraught Mrs Platt over to a bench where they sat down.

"Would you like a cup of tea?" The Sergeant asked whilst rifling through his pockets for some change.

"Bottoms and breasts and a two-foot penis." Mrs Platt was becoming more coherent. The sergeant however was becoming more distressed with every new piece of information.

"I'll just go and get us a cup of tea. Don't move!" he ordered. Mrs Platt wasn't going anywhere.

"It's not safe. You allow one pair of flared trousers into the town and the next thing you know, you've got nakedness and bottoms in full view," she said to no one in particular.

Sergeant Baldwin walked swiftly to Everything but the Squeak.

"Could I have two teas please, Mrs Butterworth," the sergeant said, handing over the correct change.

"Is she all right?" asked the proprietress. "She seems upset about something." Mrs Butterworth turned towards the giant tea pot that looked like an overfed chicken and poured out two teas.

"She says she's seen a hairy bottom and a two-foot penis," the Sergeant mouthed. He didn't want to alert the rest of Broughton to these Satanic happenings.

"She should be so lucky. There's some round here who'd die for something like that," Mrs Butterworth said.

"No, I don't think she was a party to the goings on. I think she's witnessed some satanic worship." The Sergeant nodded in disbelief as did Mrs Butterworth.

"It'll be them hippies. Mrs Hebblethwaite told me all about them. Dodgy roll-ups, flares, music and orgies. That's all they do, Sergeant. Sleep with anything that moves and some that don't, I bet." Mrs Butterworth handed over the teas.

"Why don't you bring her in here, you know, a woman's touch and all that." Mrs Butterworth was genuinely concerned for the welfare of Mrs

Platt, but there could be a lot of mileage in what the distraught Mrs Platt would have to say. It was a well known maxim in the catering trade that gossip kept your customers tied to their tables. She took the teas from the policeman and went over to a table in the corner of the café, away from prying ears. The Sergeant went outside and escorted Mrs Platt into the café.

"Now you sit down here with a nice warm cuppa tea, love." Mrs Butterworth put a protective arm around her.

"Now you tell the Sergeant and me all about it." Mrs Butterworth sat down, straightened out her pinny, checked her earrings and crossed her arms, eager to hear about this morning's exploits.

Mrs Platt took a sip of tea, coughed and then launched into her tale.

"Well, I'd just bought a pound of mince from the butcher's and was walking past the old Co-op, when I happened to be looking in the window. At first I thought I saw two mannequin dolls on the floor, but as I got a bit nearer I could see them moving." Mrs Butterworth pulled her chair nearer the table. "I put my face to the window and I saw a man's bottom going up and down like a sewing machine, and there was ever so much noise. Screaming and moaning, I thought he were going to kill her. And then he stood up, turned round and I could see it there right in front of me. I'd never seen anything like it. It was –"

For the sake of decency and decorum Sergeant Baldwin intervened. Mrs Butterworth was most disappointed.

"Yes, I think we get the picture Mrs Platt," he said, blushing slightly.

"But it was this big!" She could tell a few anglers a tale or two.

Mrs Butterworth smiled. "Really?" she said trying to think which of Broughton's male citizens possessed such an asset.

"And then he came outside and asked if I wanted a cup of tea. I didn't know where to put me face."

"I would," laughed Mrs Butterworth.

Mrs Platt gave her one of her sanctimonious looks.

"Sorry."

"It was only when I went inside the shop did I see the baby in the corner." She took a sip of tea and carried on. "And them having full-frontals as well. It's against the law." She looked at the Sergeant. "Isn't it?"

The Sergeant wasn't sure.

"Yes it is. Especially in a public place."

"But it was in a shop," Mrs Platt said. "And the windows were quite dirty." This new piece of information threw a new light on the proceedings.

"How dirty?" inquired the sergeant.

"Pretty dirty. I had to use my hanky to wipe the window so I could get a proper look."

"I thought you said you could see them through the window while you were walking past?" The sergeant was in inquisitorial form.

"Well, not really. It was the noise I heard first."

"Oh!" said the policeman.

"What do you mean 'Oh'?" asked Mrs Butterworth. "They were still having how's-your-father in broad daylight in a shop in the middle of town."

"Yes, but if nobody can see in unless they wipe the muck away from the window, then I can't see them doing anything wrong."

"Bloody hell! It's coming to something if you can't prosecute somebody for having whatever in the window." Mrs Butterworth grabbed Mrs Platt's hand and gently squeezed it. "If the police won't do anything, love, then I'm sure Mrs Hebblethwaite will."

"I won't have any talk of vigilantes in this town," said the policeman.

"You'll have no choice, will yer! If you don't do anything then we'll have to. Sex, drugs and rock and roll is not what this town is all about, Sergeant. If they want to show their naked bodies and smoke rolled-up orgies, then they can, but not here. Not here in Broughton." Mrs Butterworth was adamant.

"Another cuppa, love?" she asked Mrs Platt, who was still trying to come to terms with what she'd seen and what little the police could do.

"Thanks."

"Well I'd better go round and just have a word." The sergeant stood up, said good day, which on no account it was, and left the café.

"Bloody useless," Mrs Butterworth said. Mrs Platt agreed and the two sat down and went through the story again, only this time there were even more embellishments.

If Sergeant Baldwin wasn't going to help the good citizens of Broughton in their hour of need then Mrs Butterworth, with the help of her friend

Mrs Hebblethwaite, would.

"Is that you Ethel?" Mrs Butterworth screamed down the phone that was housed in the corner of the café, next to the door and the jukebox.

"Yes."

"I've some bad news, Ethel!"

"Speak up, I can't hear."

"It's this bloody bandit. One of these days I'll take a hammer to it," said Mrs Butterworth. "No, what I said was that your worst nightmare has happened."

"You don't mean . . .?" asked Mrs Hebblethwaite.

"I certainly do," said the café owner with a certain amount of gravitas. "The Devil himself rides with us in Broughton, Ethel, and they've just been doing it in the old Cooperative building in Market Street."

"In broad daylight?"

"Not only in broad daylight, Ethel, but in front of Mrs Platt!" This was cause for concern, thought Ethel and duly gave it as much by pausing. The effect worked.

"I was thinking, Ethel. Do you know Mr Greenwood?"

"The magistrate?"

"Yes. You know the one, he used to be a doctor."

"Oh yes, that one. Nice chap."

"Well, I thought that considering the police want to wash their hands of Solomon 'the Devil' Tump, what if we asked Mr Greenwood if he could prosecute?"

"Worth thinking about," replied Mrs Hebblethwaite.

"Better than doing nothing." Mrs Butterworth was warming to the task.

"I don't see what harm it will do. Right, I'll meet you in the café in ten minutes and we'll go round and see him." Mrs Hebblethwaite put the phone down, picked up her shawl, rosary beads and the Pagan-Busting Diary and made her way round to the café.

Sergeant Baldwin turned the corner of the street and found Solomon, Cass and Leo leaving the premises of the old Cooperative building.

"Morning Sir, morning Madam. Is it possible to have a word? It's just that I've heard rumours that some sort of hanky-panky has been going on in this shop," the policeman said, taking out his notebook. "And I can tell you we have one very upset pensioner who says she saw things that ladies of her age shouldn't be seeing."

Cass looked at Solomon. She spoke first.

"Sergeant we were just having a bit of fun. We've just leased this building and were celebrating by having a quick kiss and a cuddle." Cass put her arm around Solomon.

"You can't blame us for that now can you, Officer?"

"Well it's just that she says she saw certain things –" The Sergeant was interrupted by Solomon.

"But as you can see, Sergeant, the windows are very dirty. Surely she couldn't see through those things," he said pointing to the windows. They hadn't seen a wet cloth since the day the shop closed twelve months ago.

"Well, they do seem to be very dirty."

"She probably thought she saw something, but honestly we've done nothing wrong," pleaded Cass.

"Well, this time I'm going to let you off with another caution." The policeman raised his finger in admonishment. "But if I have any more complaints, or hear that you've been out of order, I'll come down on you like a ton of bricks." The policeman looked at both of them and waited till they both nodded.

"Right, I'll bid you good day then." And with that the policeman turned round and went about his normal business.

Chapter 29

Margaret and her mother made their way through the town armed with enough information to set Broughton alight. Margaret was pregnant. If that were not bad enough, she was carrying the child of an incomer, a charge that meant social exclusion. Broughtonians slept with Broughtonians, and if they did stray, there was only one answer. They must leave town. Now Mrs Wainwright was upset that her daughter was with child, but she was more upset that her only daughter would now have to leave the town or face years of silence and abuse from an unforgiving bunch of townsfolk. It would be round the town that Margaret was a slag and had slept with the long-haired one. He who wore the multi-coloured jeans and smoked the fat roll-ups. The Permissive Society had impregnated itself amongst the female population and Broughton would never again be the same.

The two walked from the surgery in a silence only punctuated by the odd sniff and sob. Every time Margaret sobbed her mother just squeezed her a little tighter, trying to comfort her. Margaret wasn't crying because she was carrying the child of Solomon Tump. She was crying because of what her father and all the rest of Broughton Man would do to him once they found out that he'd been sleeping with her. They walked past the café.

Mrs Butterworth's radar was the first to react. "Ethel, isn't that your Margaret ?"

Mrs Hebblethwaite sprang up and peered out of the window.

"Yes!" she said, remembering Margaret was picking up the results of her pregnancy test. She was out the door quicker than you could say Full-Fat Fry-Up Please.

"You having a cup of tea?" she shouted down the street. The sunken shoulders of the two harbingers of bad news slowly turned round and immediately the grandmother knew the news was not good.

Margaret nodded at her mother in recognition that what she was thinking was correct. They would have a brew and relay the news. The sooner her family found out the better. Or so she thought. They followed Mrs Hebblethwaite into the café.

"What's up love?" said Mrs Butterworth, putting her size eleven hands around Margaret's shoulders. "Come on, it can't be that bad," she said. "Look, when I'm feeling like that, what I do is have a nice cup of tea and a chat. Problem shared is a problem halved," she said, not knowing that the problem was growing inside Margaret as she spoke. She went over to the tea urn and poured another four cups of tea. Mrs Platt moved closer. If what she saw in the face of Mrs Hebblethwaite was anything to go by, then her problems were minor. Ethel had a face that could stop a rhino at fifty paces. They all sat down. Margaret looked at her mother and smiled weakly. Mrs Wainwright coughed slightly and embarked on the bad news.

"We've just been to see Dr Brown." She cleared her throat. "And it's not good, mum." She looked across at her mother and could feel the pain and anguish coursing through her mother's veins. "Our Margaret's pregnant!" The gasps of amazement rippled around the table as the true horror of what had been said filtered through. Mrs Wainwright grabbed her daughter's hand. Everybody wanted to ask the obvious question, but etiquette dictated that the maternal head of the house had the dubious privilege.

"I take it, it's Solomon's?" Mrs Hebblethwaite said. Margaret didn't want to look at her Nan in case she turned into a pillar of salt or became another victim of instantaneous combustion.

"Yes," was the small and nearly inaudible reply.

Mrs Butterworth was aghast. Her mouth opened but nothing came out. She mouthed silence and shock. Eventually she said "Well, you won't be the first and you won't be the last!" It was in moments like these that platitudes rarely comfort those that need it. Margaret started to cry. Tears turned her face into a mascara'd trellis.

"Well, what's done's done. So, young lady we'll just have to make the best of a bad lot!" said her grandmother, shifting uneasily on her chair. What she would have liked to do was smite the Tump right there and now, but even as holy as she was, she couldn't achieve that.

Mrs Platt was also crying, not at the thought of another young woman from Broughton finding herself pregnant, but at the thought of being assaulted by what she saw through the Co-op window that morning.

Mrs Hebblethwaite had tried the long arm of the law, which in this case seemed exceedingly truncated. She had become frustrated by the police's efforts to stop The Permissive Society from gaining a foothold in Broughton. Mrs Hebblethwaite was at her wits end. She made a final call to the Bishop.

"They're at it again, Your Grace!" said Mrs Hebblethwaite opening her Pagan-Busting Diary at the correct page. She coughed to clear her throat, for what she was about to reveal to the Bishop would be, she thought, the final nail in the coffin of the vile impregnator. "They, and here I'm referring to the hippies, Your Grace, you know the ones."

The Bishop was irritated that his secretary had failed again to deal with what was becoming an increasingly time-consuming event. "Yes, Mrs Hebblethwaite, the flared-jeaned son of Lucifer and his progeny."

The sarcastic note in his voice was lost on Mrs Hebblethwaite who was nonetheless happy he was getting to grips with the problem.

"Them's the ones. Well, they're trying to open this shop, and it's not one of your ordinary kind of shops if you catch me drift, Your Grace, it's the kind we've not seen before In Broughton. You see, it'll be selling all kinds of things to aid in the practice ..." Mrs Hebblethwaite paused dramatically. " ... in the practice of Devil Worship!"

The Bishop had spent much of the last two and half weeks dealing with issues raised in the smallest parish in his constituency and was beginning to tire of Beelzebub and his new found home in Broughton. "And what kind of things would these be, Mrs Hebblethwaite?" he asked, humouring the caller.

"Well, they're selling these oils from abroad of all colours and smells that are supposed to entice evil spirits into the room while 'Goings-on' are going on, if you understand me Your Grace. And different oils to spread on your body to make the act of you-know-what more pleasurable whilst they light sticks of intent, I think that's what you call them, which are desired by the cloven-hoofed one if he is to make an appearance." Mrs Hebblethwaite took a deep breath and continued. "And, Your Grace, we've found out something that is worrying the good people of Broughton."

"And what would that be?" He wondered what on earth could be more worrying to Mrs Hebblethwaite than the Devil playing Bob Dylan late into the night.

"He has told one of me friends that him and his floozy of a partner are –" She braced herself. "That they are Vegetarians, Your Grace, and more than that, they don't eat meat!" Mrs Hebblethwaite was certain that this last piece of information would certainly force His Eminence to act.

"There is nothing wrong in not eating meat, Mrs Hebblethwaite," the Bishop said with some force. He hadn't eaten red meat since his ulcer became problematical in 1953, the day after the Coronation.

"Well, what about the vegetarianism then?" she asked, disappointed that a representative of the Catholic Church would openly admit that he didn't eat meat. She didn't eat meat on Fridays but that was different.

"They are one and the same, Mrs Hebblethwaite," the Bishop said rather pompously, happy that he had gained the intellectual high ground.

"What do you mean, one of the same?" said Mrs Hebblethwaite, worried that he was trying to tie her up in a theological argument.

"I mean," said the Bishop, "That a non-meat-eater is called a vegetarian." He indulged in a smile.

"Well, why didn't he say that? Trying to confuse us all with his long names." Mrs Hebblethwaite stopped for a second or two to gather her thoughts.

"Well tell me this, Your Grace, why is it these stick-burning, oil-rubbing, non-meat-eating people must run around naked?" If that didn't put him on the wrong foot, Canon Law or not, she'd be very surprised.

"I don't think they have a monopoly on these things, Mrs Hebblethwaite."

Mrs Hebblethwaite was thoroughly confused now that the Bishop had brought up playing Monopoly.

"Well, Your Grace, I think it's about time we got the troops in and exorcised number twenty three. We don't want the situation to escalate, do we?"

"Of course not," agreed the Bishop.

"Because if it did we'd have to call in a higher authority."

The Bishop, who was barely taking in what Mrs Hebblethwaite was talking about, suddenly became a little more interested. He wasn't interested in all the devil nonsense, he was concerned at what he thought was a veiled threat from a fellow follower of Christ.

"What do you mean, a 'higher authority?'"

"Well, Your Grace, the situation has certainly moved on apace ..." Mrs Hebblethwaite was playing her trump card. "... and I think that The Vatican should know."

There was a stifled cough on the other end of the line.

"Are you all right, Your Grace?" asked Mrs Hebblethwaite with genuine concern.

The Bishop was far from all right. In over thirty three years of administering the gospel to his flock, not once had anybody had recourse to the Vatican. He only had a few more years to do before he retired and he'd never needed to ask the Vatican for help. He wanted it to stay that way.

"The Vatican!" he said in a voice pitched rather higher than normal. "Why would you want to get the Vatican involved?"

"Well, Your Grace, without wanting to undermine what excellent work you are doing, I was thinking that the Vatican, what with all its knowledge and everything, they would know what to do."

"And I don't?" The Bishop was rather upset.

"It's not that, Your Grace. It's just they're in contact with priests all over the world ..." She paused, knowing that the Bishop had been caught off guard. " ... and they'll be knowing of similar situations with Satan riding into town and causing all the usual devilish problems." Mrs Hebblethwaite was no mean operator when it meant getting her way.

"I don't think that'll be necessary, Mrs Hebblethwaite," the Bishop barked down the phone. He was trying to remain calm. "I'm sure we can deal with the Tumps here in Broughton without worrying His Holiness," the Bishop said, trying to steer his parishioner away from phoning the Vatican. He knew several Vatican departments that would like nothing better to do than come to Broughton and do the whole Spanish Inquisition thing.

"So what will we do then, Your Grace?"

The Bishop didn't like the sound of the Royal We.

"What time does this shop open Mrs Hebblethwaite?"

"One o'clock, Your Grace."

"Right, if you meet me at the presbytery at twelve thirty we'll take it from there. OK?" the Bishop said.

"That'll be fine your Grace, I'll be looking forward to it."

The Bishop knew she would, but put the phone down anyway and returned to his office contemplating how thirty-odd years of unblemished service might blow up in his face. He didn't want the Press getting hold of what was going on down Broughton way

Mrs Hebblethwaite was extremely pleased with her morning's efforts, and even happier that she didn't have to divulge that her granddaughter had been impregnated by the Cloven-Hoofed one. She didn't even have to contact Mr Greenwood, the magistrate, and ask him for favours. Mrs Hebblethwaite made herself a pot of happy tea and celebrated with a Garibaldi. Soon, oh so very soon, Broughton would be Tumpless. She smiled and lifted her finest china cup to her lips, convinced that she had at last triumphed.

Chapter 30

Mrs Hebblethwaite went round to the café.

"Have you any boxes, Mary?"

Mrs Butterworth had just finished serving her tenth full-fat breakfast. She wiped her hands on a tea-towel. "What d'you want boxes for, Ethel?"

"Placards, Mary. We want hundreds of placards made before one o'clock," said Mrs Hebblethwaite.

"Placards?" queried Mary, frowning.

"That's right and as many as possible, because at twelve thirty I'm meeting the Bishop at the presbytery, and if I don't like what he has got to say then we're off to the Tumps' shop."

"Placards?" Mrs Butterworth took off her pinny and came round to join her on the other side of the counter. "And what will you be writing on these placards?"

"I thought we would have a mixture," Mrs Hebblethwaite said, trying to think on her feet. "Well, to be honest I haven't a clue but I saw it on TV that this fella in America was complaining about not having the vote and he was carrying round placards with slogans on them."

Mrs Butterworth was a little worried that they seemed to be straying from the spiritual nature of the problem and getting involved in politics. She didn't like politics and she hated politicians. To her all politicians should be put on the spit, preferably hers, and roasted until they came out with either the truth, which was unlikely, or promised never to hold office again. "Isn't this getting all too political?" she asked.

"I wouldn't say political, Mary, more of an act to get the Bishop fired up to do something, because I'm sure he wouldn't want a whole load of journalists hanging around taking notes and pictures," Mrs Hebblethwaite said like a true campaigner.

"No, I hadn't thought about that angle, Ethel." Mrs Butterworth nodded in agreement, acknowledging that her friend had moved on from just being a ball of fiery Catholicism and was becoming adept at rallying all to her cause.

"Well?" said Mrs Hebblethwaite.

"Well what?" asked Mary, temporarily distracted because Full Fat Fred was trying to leave the premises without paying. He should have known better.

"Oh no you don't!" she said, catching him by the top of his overalls. "That'll be three and six."

"Can I put it on ..." Fred murmured.

"Can you put it on the slate? " smiled the owner of the café.

Fred grimaced slightly. "Please," he replied.

"No you bloody well can't!" Mrs Butterworth went straight for his boiler suit pockets and found the requisite sum.

"And next time don't be so bloody cheeky." Mrs Butterworth walked round to the till and rang up three and six. Fred left disconsolate knowing he didn't have the right money for a beer after work. She returned to Ethel's table.

"Where were we?"

"Boxes," said Mrs Hebblethwaite.

"Right."

Mrs Butterworth went into the back to find as many boxes as she could. Ethel remained seated, keeping an eye on the two remaining customers lest they too try and make a dash for it.

She emerged out of the back room laden with boxes. She tottered gingerly to where she thought her friend was sitting. The thick dust that had accumulated over the years was playing havoc with Mrs Butterworth's asthma, and the coughing and wheezing let the rest of the café know that something rather strange was happening. The two customers kept their heads down for fear of attracting attention and the possibility that work may be involved.

"How long have you had all those?" said the Catholic activist as she stood up and took the top two or three boxes from Mary's grip.

"God only knows and he's not telling," spluttered Mary.

All the boxes were placed on the empty seats. There were twenty in all which would be more than enough, once they were cut up into sections.

"Right, Mary, what I was thinking . . ." said Mrs Hebblethwaite.

The two men got up to pay and suddenly the radical Ethel had an idea.

"Mrs Butterworth?" she asked. "Do you think these two lads would give a couple of old dears a hand in exchange for the price of their cups of tea?"

"I'm sure they would, Ethel," agreed Mary without having an idea what she was going on about. The two men looked at each other in that resigned fashion the married man of more than five years has. Capitulation or suffer the conjugal consequences.

"Right lads, would you cut these boxes up into largish squares, say two foot square?"

They both nodded.

"Good!" said Mrs Hebblethwaite. "I'm going out to muster some troops." She smiled, slapped both men on the back and walked towards the door.

"I'll be back in an hour," Ethel said, reaching the pavement outside. "And make sure you've got enough tea to drown an army." She laughed and scuttled up the street towards the market.

Mrs Butterworth nodded, slightly concerned at who would be footing the tea bill. The two men busied themselves in their new employ.

Chapter 31

Margaret sat in their battered armchair twiddling with the lace anti-macassar. She didn't give two hoots that her Mary Quant mascara was splattered across her reddened cheeks. What she was bothered about was telling Solomon. Or how to. Her father was out at work and her mother was clattering around the house, muttering under her breath about this and that and giving Jimmy Bloody Young a hard time. At least they both agreed on that one. Jimmy Young on the radio, what was the world coming to.

She stormed into the room. "People like that don't do responsibility, Margaret, they just . . ." She couldn't find the words; they were all tied up in a verbal traffic jam somewhere inside her head. "Look love, I know you say you love him –"

Margaret knew there was a 'but' that would follow.

"I *do* love him, mum." Margaret burst into tears again just as Ken Dodd burst into his one and only bloody awful hit. Her mother went into the kitchen and turned the radio off.

She came back and put her arm around her daughter.

Margaret tried to sob, but nothing came out, there was a hosepipe ban on tears.

"I know, love," her mother said.

"No you don't! How can you?" These were the reasoned arguments of a teenager in love. "You've been married for ever."

"I've not been a middle-aged trout all me life, you know," she replied, trying to bring some humour into the proceedings. "I was your age an' all once, you know," her mother continued, throwing the tea towel over her shoulder.

"You can't have loved Dad like I love Solomon!" Margaret said, delivering what she thought was the coup de grâce.

"Who said I was talking about your dad?"

Round one to mother.

Margaret turned round. "WHAT!" she said incredulously.

"Arthur Greenslade." She looked down at Margaret. "All the girls were after him. He had big green eyes, big as a camel's, with lashes to match, and jet black wavy hair. We all thought he'd walked off a Hollywood film set."

Margaret was sure she saw her mother blush.

"He tore my heart out, stood on it, jumped on it and then tossed it into the cut." She smiled weakly. "I'd been seeing him for three months and we'd not done anything, you know, like ..." She pointed to her daughter's ripening belly. Margaret nodded. "But he was my first proper, and I mean proper kiss. My chest was heaving that much I thought me bra was fit to burst."

Margaret laughed for the first time in over a day.

"What did Dad say?" Margaret asked, wiping some of the blackness from her damp cheeks.

"Oh, I didn't know him then."

"So was Dad your first ..." Margaret paused, knowing that the next question could prove difficult. "I mean, was Dad the first man you ever slept with ?"

Her mum twiddled with the end of the tea towel like children do their hair when asked a question they don't really want to answer. She looked at her daughter.

"No, he wasn't," she said truthfully. She moved around from the back of the armchair and sat down next to her daughter. Margaret wasn't as shocked as she thought she might be.

"Now, nobody knows this." Her mother shuffled her skirt down over her knees. "Your dad thinks I was a virgin when we got married, and I want to keep it that way," she said, pointing a finger at Margaret. "Because you know what men are like about all that." Margaret did but said nothing. She just listened. "For some reason, to them it's all very important to be the first. God knows why." Her mother looked out of the window then back at her daughter. "It's like men and their cars. When they first pass their test, they buy second hand and tootle around, very proud, but it's only when they get a brand new one that they really stick their chests out."

Margaret listened intently. "And that's why your dad's so annoyed." Margaret didn't like the thought of being likened to a second hand car. "You see, in his mind a pregnant girl out of wedlock is soiled goods." She took Margaret's hand. "I know it's stupid, love, but there you go, that's what he's like. Anyway, you won't be the first and you definitely won't be the last."

"Thanks, Mum." Margaret kissed her.

"But you're going to have to tell Solomon before your dad does."

"I know."

"Right, go upstairs get your new face on and then we'll go round and tell him. Together." She gave Margaret a hug and went into the kitchen to finish off the pots.

Margaret came down after about ten minutes. With a lot of heavy make up, she just about managed to conceal most of the damage of the last hour.

"Come on then," her mother said. "There's no time like the present."

They left their house and crossed the street. They looked at each other, took a deep breath and walked over to number twenty-three.

Margaret slowly walked down the path to the door. She knocked. No answer. She knocked again. Still no answer. She turned round and said to her mother "There's nobody home, Mum."

Her mother looked disconsolate. She wanted it all done and dusted, so they could move on and make plans. They needed to let Solomon know before her husband decided to tell him in one of his drunken 'I know what I'm doing, we all end up in a fight' ways.

"I forgot," Margaret said, putting her hand to her mouth. "They're opening the shop today!"

"Does your Nan know?" her mum asked, knowing that if she did, martial arts expert or not, Solomon would be on the receiving end of a severe handbagging.

"I don't think so," Margaret said, running down the path.

"Come on, let's get to that shop before she does."

Mother and daughter walked swiftly down Prospect Street towards the town centre, hoping beyond hope that neither Mrs Hebblethwaite nor Margaret's dad got there before they did. They walked passed the café and gingerly looked in to see who was in there. Mrs Butterworth was, of course, but there were also two men nailing bits of cardboard to brush handles.

"Bit odd," said Margaret's mum as they continued their walk towards Solomon's new shop. "What's that smell?" she asked her daughter.

"Perfume, oils?" she replied, not knowing exactly what it was.

"Smells like a Turkish Brothel!"

"And how would you know?" Margaret said. Her mother was about to answer but her daughter continued: "Don't tell me, I've had enough shocks already!"

"Well, you certainly don't get that smell at Boots."

"I hope the assistants don't have orange heads like they do at Boots," Margaret replied.

Turning into Water Street, they were lured like the Bisto Kids into Solomon' shop The East-West Emporium.

They walked inside and just stood in awe. Aladdin would have been impressed. Two of the four walls were racked full of bottles of all shapes and sizes. Colours and smells danced together in a spectacular floorshow that drew the customer into a world where their senses came alive. A small part of each continent had been delivered to this Broughton back street, where normally blacks, greys and browns were the colours of preference. Books, clothes, crystals, stones, rugs, carvings, pictures and posters complemented each other in surroundings that three days earlier housed only dust and distant memories of the Co-operative movement.

"Looks like a brothel," her mother said.

"Not again! Anyway, how would you know, or have you got something else to tell me?" Margaret laughed.

"And you know what they say about a woman who wears too much perfume?"

"You're going to tell me anyway." Margaret replied already knowing the answer.

"Tarts. They put it on to mask the smell of sweat and semen."

"Mum!" Margaret was very nearly appalled by this latest outburst from her once prim and proper mother. "You're a real eye-opener today aren't you?" Margaret pushed her mum gently in the back and they moved into the centre of the old shop. There were plenty of other sightseers from Broughton who'd come to see for themselves what hippies sold. Solomon was nowhere to be seen but Cass was standing behind the counter, eager to relieve Broughtonians of their hard-earned brass.

At the back of the shop was the produce. Vegetables, pulses and beans.

"Doesn't look very appetising does it?" her mother said, picking up a piece of celeriac.

"What the hell's this?" she asked Margaret, who was none the wiser. "No wonder they all look so funny, eating all this stuff." She put the celeriac down and picked up some capsicums. "Your dad'd moan blue bloody murder if I gave him this for his tea." She blew her cheeks out and stood with her arms dangling as though from a coat hanger and did an impression of her husband. *"Bloody 'ell, I do an eight hour shift an' I come home to this pot o' shite."*

Before her mother had finished Margaret was already laughing when Solomon approached.

"Good to see you both in such high spirits," he said.

Margaret's mum regained her composure and went and stood a little nearer her daughter. Margaret looked at him but didn't say anything.

"So," Solomon said, waving his arm around at all the wares in the shop. "What do you think?"

"Looks good, but where did you get all this stuff from, and so quickly?" Margaret asked, stalling for time before she had to tell him.

"Four van-loads came up yesterday morning and we worked through the day and night to get it ready for the grand opening, which is," Solomon said, looking at his watch, "In three hours time, at one o'clock."

"Good," Margaret said. Her mother gave her the eye.

"Will you be here then?" Solomon looked round at Margaret's mum who'd returned her face to that of the stern Broughtonian housewife.

She pursed her lips and said "No!"

"More wine for us then, Margaret!" laughed the flared businessman.

Margaret's mother was about to let fly some advice on things Margaret didn't want the rest of the shop to hear.

"Can I have a word, Solomon?" Margaret said.

"Of course," the harbinger of the Permissive Society said, rolling up another cigarette.

"If you'll excuse us," Solomon said to her mother and they went into the store room.

"Why is it always the polite ones who do all the damage?" said Mrs Wainwright to a distressed-looking mango.

Chapter 32

Father O'Dowd was tired. Not of life, not even of those in his parish that led him a merry dance, be it devil-worship or using the wrong prayer book. No, he was just tired and needed sleep. If only he could turn the Catholic clock off for a while and make himself invisible for two or three days, then he knew he could return with renewed vigour. He lay in bed. It was six-thirty in the morning and he knew that his mother would breeze in with a cup of tea and come out with some phrase or other. She mixed and matched phrases much like you do from the pick and mix at Woollies. The door opened.

"Morning!" she said, far too cheerily. "It's always the lark that can kill two worms with one stone!" She placed his cup of tea on the table next to his bed.

"Sleep well?" She didn't wait for the answer, parents never do, she merely carried on oblivious that he was there. "Right," she said and walked out. He could have been dead for all she would have known, but that wasn't the object of the exercise. The whole point was to tell those she knew that she woke her son up every day at six thirty in the morning.

UNFROCK YOUR PRIEST

Father O'Dowd often played this game whilst getting dressed. It was a bit of fun and passed the time whilst he was assembling.

"Father O'Dowd, if you weren't a priest what would you be?" asked Terry the host.

"Well, Terry, that's a difficult one." It wasn't really; he'd asked the same question over thirty times and he'd always given the same answer.

"I would have liked to be a pop star, you know, stood up there on the stage in front of thirty thousand screaming fans."

"Bit like the Pope on Good Friday, then."

"That'll be four Hail Marys, Terry, you wicked man."

Wry smiles from all and gentle chuckling from the crowd. Father O'Dowd walked past the full length mirror in his wardrobe. He winced because it reminded him of his expanding frame, which was beginning to look like the coastline of Nova Scotia on a foggy day.

"And celibacy Father. What do you think the church will be doing about it in the next fifty years?"

"Well, I think priests will be allowed to marry."

"Really? Would you get married Father?"

He pulled on his socks that needed a bit of darning, but since Miss Mahoney was still bedridden, suffering from delusions of a pathologically sexual nature, holed they would remain.

"I think so Terry. I think so."

He pulled on the uniformly dull black trousers.

"And to whom, Father? Name any woman in the world today who you'd like to marry?"

"Well ..."

On went the black shirt with optional dandruff liberally sprinkled around the collar.

"Go on Father, there's fifteen million viewers out there dying to know the answer." "There's also the Holy Father, a few Cardinals and loads of Bishops who wouldn't like me to answer."

He put on his hand-made dog collar; it was amazing what you could do with a washing up bottle. There was something to be said for watching Blue Peter.

"Whisper in me ear then Father, I won't tell."

"Well, viewers, Father O'Dowd would like to marry Marianne Faithfull. But the question is Father, would Marianne like to marry you, and would she be Faithful?"

CANNED LAUGHTER

"Are you getting up, or are you going to strut around all day talking to yourself?" his mother said as she began hoovering. There's no rest for the religious. He put his jacket on and went down stairs at too early an hour for breakfast that wasn't yet cooked. His mother had to clean and dust everywhere before they could eat.

"You don't know what kind of germs lurk around of an evening," his mother said, giving the kitchen table a good buffing. "And anyway, as the good Lord said, it's better to be safe than sorry."

Father O'Dowd had yet to find this piece of scripture in the Good Book.

Breakfast over, seven-thirty mass finished and time for himself before the telephone started to give him instructions for the day. He went upstairs to see Miss Mahoney. She had instructed him to cough loudly, say his name three times and announce his intentions before opening the door.

"Morning, Miss Mahoney, and how are we today?" he mouthed slowly as though she had lost all sense of reasoning.

"I'm not dumb, Father, and I can hear perfectly well," she said, her hand firmly attached to the mashie niblick her father had given her when she left Ireland for the shores of Perfidious Albion.

"I was just thinking –" The priest didn't have time to finish. His housekeeper's mind was several leaps ahead of his.

"I know what you're thinking, along with that Hebblethwaite woman." Her face contorted into a hell-racked gargoyle. "And His Grace. You're all in league with the Devil. Your minds should be bleached and Dettolled of all sin and . . ."

The parish priest didn't wait for her to finish her diatribe; it was the same every day. He closed the door behind him and went into his office with the intention of writing the Sunday Homily. He took the paper instead. Luxury. He lay on the battered cold leather Chesterfield that could freeze the trident from the hands of Beelzebub and dozed off with the paper over his face.

Mrs O'Dowd had given up on any kind of etiquette these days, and merely went where she wanted. She barged into her son's office and found him snoozing under a copy of the Manchester Guardian.

"Thomas!" she shouted, as though scolding a child.

Thomas was still in his game show. "What?" he tried to say, as if he were in control of the situation. He pulled the paper away from his face. "I was just –"

"I know what you where doing, m'lad," his mother said, trying to brush his hair with her hands. "Now think on, the Bishop's on the phone."

"What now?" he said gruffly.

"You can't use that tone of voice when the Bishop's on the phone, Thomas," his mother said, patting down his jacket and dusting the dandruff from his collar.

"It's a telephone, Mum, he can't see me!"

"That's not the point," his mother replied, continuing to dust him off as if he were some kind of leper. "What if a parishioner came in and saw you stood there all dishevelled? It doesn't give the right impression, does it?"

"Mum, they come for divine help, not fashion tips!" Thomas said, pulling his mother's hands away. He walked out of the office. She followed him to the phone like a theatrical dresser whose just realised there's a thread dangling from the star's costume.

"Hello," Father O'Dowd said. He was worried it would be another below the belt lecture from His Grace.

"O'Dowd," the Bishop said brusquely. "We have a situation occurring with Mrs Hebblethwaite." He sounded like a junior officer in the Home Guard.

"What kind of situation?"

"She wants me to exorcise the Tumps," the Bishop said matter-of-factly. "In fact, she wants me to run them out of town dressed in all me finery spouting forth great tracts from the Old Testament!"

"You mean Crosier, Mitre, retinue in purple and the life-size model of Christ on the crucifix carried by four unfortunate penitents from the local parish?" asked the parish priest, aware that such an operation wasn't only hugely expensive but it often led to the closure of several streets. The result: Catholic gridlock and Protestant protestations.

"I'm afraid so," said the Bishop. "As you know, I'm not averse to a bit of pomp, brightens up the day don't you know, but I'm afraid that I've already used up my quota of gold-laden processions."

Father O'Dowd was fully aware that the Bishop was only allowed three ceremonial processions a year, and he always had to keep one in reserve in case the Pope died. He would look a bit foolish using his reserve procession on the Tumps if His Holiness died the following week.

"I see," the priest said. "Can't you tell Mrs Hebblethwaite that you wouldn't want to draw attention to the Tumps and their lifestyle by having a huge procession marching through Broughton?"

"I'm not sure whether she'll accept that."

"But you don't have to do all the grand stuff, though." Thomas tried to give succour to his boss. "I mean, can't you just say a Mass, have a word and then be done with it?"

"She wants more," sighed the Bishop. "She wants Pomp, Thomas, all of it."

"And what if you won't or can't?" Father O'Dowd asked rather nervously.

"She says she'll contact the Vatican, and then where will we be?"

Where will we be indeed, thought the priest who had never heard the Bishop so down and lost for ideas.

"Do you want me to have a word?" As if Mrs Hebblethwaite would listen to him.

"No, she's asked me to do something and I will. If needs be I'll call in the Jesuits."

"That bad, Your Grace?" Father O'Dowd winced at the very thought.

"Needs must, Thomas."

Good Lord! thought Thomas, the Bishop just called him Thomas.

"I'll call you back in half an hour to let you know the plan," the Bishop said, putting the phone down.

Mrs O'Dowd ran up to her son, flung her arms around him and gave him a big kiss.

"What was that for?" he asked.

"Didn't you hear? The Bishop just called you Thomas." His mother finally let go and walked towards the kitchen muttering about bishoprics and cardinal's hats. As she closed the door he was sure he heard his mother mention the Papacy.

Father O'Dowd had just sat down to read his crumpled paper when the phone went again. His mother didn't have time to get to it, which satisfied him in strange kind of way. It was, after all, his home. He picked the receiver up. "Father O'Dowd."

"I've been thinking, O'Dowd," said the Bishop.

Must have been a very short thought, said Thomas to the nicotine-stained picture of The *Hay Wain* that hung just above the telephone. A bequest from a parishioner before his time.

"You know you proposed to tell Mrs Hebblethwaite about not having a huge process because it could draw attention to the Tump's alternative lifestyle?"

Well, well, Thomas thought. This was a first, the Bishop listening to one of his ideas.

"Do you think she'll go for it?"

"I would have thought so," Thomas replied confidently. "She just wants rid of the family and if the church can help, then all well and good."

"Right, I'll leave that up to you then," the Bishop said, glad to delegate for the first time one of his problems. "I will be arriving at around twelve thirty. A pot of tea and something light would go down very well."

"The Bishop's messenger," Thomas said loudly as he walked into the kitchen. He grinned as though he'd just taken the cream from the top of the milk bottle. "Mum," he said in the grand style of the operatic performer. He gestured to his mother. "We shall be having a guest for dinner."

"I've only got two chops," said Mrs O'Dowd. "I've not been out shopping yet."

"He doesn't want a cooked meal, Mum, he wants something light."

"Who does?"

"The Bishop," her son said, beaming from ear to ecclesiastical ear.

His mother dropped the cup she was drying. "The Bishop! But we haven't got anything in, and look at me hair it looks like birds nest soup, and I haven't even hoovered the hall. Polish. I'll polish it and then he won't look at the floor because he'll like the smell. Flowers. We need some flowers." She was running round the kitchen. "Why didn't you tell me before and I could have had all this spick and span?"

"Don't worry, all he wants is a cup of tea and a slice of cake or whatever," her son said, trying to calm her down.

"You can't give a Bishop Whatever. He's only two down from you-know-who and you certainly wouldn't give him Whatever, would you?" His mother was talking in tongues. She was all of a quiver and very excited, that excited she wasn't actually doing anything bar get worried. She'd never met a Bishop before; she'd seen them from afar but never spoken to one. "Will you do me confession before he comes, Thomas?" she said with a pained expression. "I can't make the Bishop a Victoria sponge while still in a state of sin, now can I?"

"If it'll make you feel better."

"It will, it will," she said. They both disappeared into the church.

*****

Armed with the mashie niblick and a set of rosary beads, Miss Mahoney took her first tentative steps out of her bedroom. She made sure that nobody was around. Nobody had seen Miss Mahoney in her nightgown and she wanted to keep it that way. She knotted her dressing gown a good few times, lest anybody thought this spinster was fair game. Easing up and down the landing, she began to feel the confidence slowly seep back into her body.

"Feeling better?" said Mrs O'Dowd, fresh from confessing all to the Lord. Sin-free fingers make the finest Victoria sponges, she would later tell her friends after the Bishop had commented on the lightness of her cake.

If it hadn't have been for her resolute constitution and mashie niblick, Miss Mahoney would have fallen straight to the balding carpet. She clutched her chest and rosary beads. "You could've killed me, woman," she said. There was no love lost between the two women. They both vied for supremacy of Father O'Dowd's kitchen.

"Sorry, I didn't mean to give you a fright," Mrs O'Dowd said, swishing past her with a feather duster. "It's just that the Bishop will be arriving soon and I want the place shining like a new pin." Mrs O 'Dowd carried on her way, whistling a tune and gaily dusting at the same time. She didn't mind moving her son's private parts around. Well, she'd seen enough of them when he was a little boy.

"*The Bishop's coming!*" Miss Mcafferty shrieked. She froze.

The Bishop, Mrs O'Dowd and her son locked together in an unholy trinity of troilism.

She pictured the scene and shuddered.

"I'll have to get out," she whispered. "I won't be any part of their shenanigans." Miss Mahoney unfroze and tiptoed back into her bedroom. With tears in her eyes she began to pack her meagre belongings into her holdall. A lifetime's service to the priesthood and it all fitted into this one bag. From the window sill she picked up her crucifix, held it to her chest, kissed it and placed it gently on top of her clothes. Although she was sad to be leaving, she knew that if she stayed any longer she would become the victim of something that would ultimately end up on the front page of The News Of The World. She finally got dressed and picking up her bag left the room, still clutching her mashie niblick.

Chapter 33

Now all Father O'Dowd had to do was find Mrs Hebblethwaite. He donned his black Dannimac and headed into Broughton. Walking swiftly down Millgate he noticed there seemed to be quite a crowd gathering outside the old Co-op. Obviously Solomon's new enterprise was causing something of a stir. He would pop in there later once he'd found the ball of Catholic fervour called Mrs Hebblethwaite.

Several men doffed their caps and ladies smiled gently in acknowledgment of the collar. He returned their smiles. The town was busy with women and baskets looking for the best bargains and cuts of meat. A few men who'd lost their jobs but as yet hadn't told their wives sat on benches reading newspapers. Those that dared not show their faces headed for the security of the library, where they spent their time trying to force the hands of the clock round to five o'clock.

"Good day, Father," said Miss Mahoney, enjoying her new found freedom and celebrity.

"Good day." Father O'Dowd returned the compliment. "We won't be having any more trouble, will we?"

"I wouldn't have thought so, Father," came the reply as she went into the greengrocers to get her supply of carrots.

The priest laughed, although at the time it wasn't a laughing matter being called down to the police station to give your word that the prisoner wouldn't repeat the offence.

He couldn't help but walk into 'Everything but the Squeak,' and was surprised to find that two men were busily constructing what he could only make out to be placards.

"Morning, Mrs Butterworth," he said.

She turned round. "Tea is it, Father?" she asked the cleric.

"No thanks, Mrs Butterworth. I was wondering if you'd seen Mrs

Hebblethwaite this morning."

"I'm sorry, Father, I haven't," she said, giving one of the placard makers the eye as he was about to tell the priest that she had been in the café not half an hour since.

"It all looks very industrious," laughed the priest, making his way out of the café. "When does the revolution start?"

"Sooner than you think!" said the fryer of full-fat breakfasts.

He headed straight for Prospect Street and for the Hebblethwaite residence. He knocked on the door several times but there was no reply. He stood back and cupped his hands over his eyes to see if there was any sign of movement upstairs. There was. It was Mr Hebblethwaite and he'd been on nights. A bedroom window opened.

"What the bloody hell do you think you're playing at?" Before he had time to realise who was disturbing his sleep, he'd let out a fusillade of four letter words. "Sorry, Father, I didn't know."

"It's OK. It's my fault I should have known you might have been on nights," said the priest apologetically. "I'm looking for Mrs Hebblethwaite."

"Not seen sight nor hair of her since I got in."

"Not to worry, I'm sure I'll find her," Father O'Dowd said as he turned away from the house. "Sorry about waking you."

His apology wasn't heard because Mr Hebblethwaite had already closed the window and had returned to his pillow.

"Hiya, Father! Looking for me Nan?" said Gary.

"Yes," said Father O'Dowd, shocked to see Mrs Hebblethwaite's grandson dressed in flares and a CND tee shirt.

Gary hadn't had time to grow his hair as long as Solomon's, so he just went for the unkempt 'I couldn't give a toss' look. He was gainfully employed trying to roll a cigarette. His effort looked more like a badly chewed carrot.

"I saw her this morning flying up the street like some distressed cat, man," said Gary in true flared jeans parlance.

"Oh," said the priest, somewhat taken aback by her grandson's language.

"Yes, I know she's been kinda hot under the collar ever since the Dude arrived." Gary was nothing if not a trier but his attempt to immerse himself in the lore of the hippy was grating and unconvincing. You can lead a man to flares but you can't make him think.

"But she's totally lost it, man, you know. I think it's this thing with the Dude and Margaret." Gary put the badly manufactured cigarette into his mouth. "I think it's because my sister's carrying the Dude's baby," the apprentice hippy said.

"You mean Margaret's pregnant?"

"Let it not be said that the men of the cloth do not possess the razor mind." Gary was getting into the language. Slowly.

"Holy mother of eternal joss-sticks!" Father O'Dowd said. "Where's Margaret now?"

"I saw the Mummy Bear and Baby Bear head for the man's new shop in town."

That rolled-up carrot contained far more than just Virginia shag, thought Thomas as he walked down Prospect Street towards Solomon's new emporium.

Gary Carrot, as he was later to be called, tried to cross his legs in recognition of the new religion he had wholeheartedly embraced, and fell off the wall.

Work at the café was now reaching a feverish pitch, with all customers who purchased a hot drink receiving it free on condition they joined the placard production line. There were only five of them but they had knocked out twenty-seven placards already and were awaiting further instructions from their leader when Scoop Norman appeared. They asked him to tone down his jumper but he refused.

"What's all this in aid of?" said the scribe, unfamiliar with the hardware of the revolutionary.

"Don't know," came the reply from Mrs Butterworth, whose activities with the hammer had rendered her brow awash with perspiration.

"Looks like you're getting ready for a march," Scoop said after a blinding light had kick-started his brain.

"Could be."

"Anything to do with long hair and flares?" The scribe was going for the kill.

"Don't know what you're talking about!" she lied badly.

Father O'Dowd came into the café and walked up to Mrs Butterworth.

"If you see Mrs Hebblethwaite," he said, slightly out of breath. "She mustn't go to Solomon's new shop." He looked at Mrs Butterworth and then realised that Broughton's paparazzi stood next to him. "OK?" Father O'Dowd rushed out of the café.

Norman was getting excited; he could feel a story ebbing up his arm like a column of mercury slowly rising to the top of a thermometer. He got quite red and sweaty. His jumper twitched and he was off.

"Bloody hell!" Mrs Butterworth said under her breath. "Right, I think we've done enough of these placards," she said to the five artisans. "Free teas for all." The revolutionary cry went up for Mrs Butterworth. "Tomorrow." The revolutionary cry dimmed. "Right, I'm shutting up now."

The five hardened activists left, full of tea and revolutionary fervour.

Mrs Butterworth was hard on their heels, waddling along all ruddy face and anticipation. She didn't have time to stop and acknowledge all those customers who waved. She didn't even stop in recognition of their 'Good Mornings' or 'How are you's'. When the Devil's to be run out of town there's no time for glad-handing or tittle tattle. She did explain later on, but because their greetings were summarily dismissed there were a few residents who were of a mind not to frequent 'Everything but the squeak.'

Chapter 34

S olomon looked stunning in his flares and multi-coloured waistcoat. Margaret felt fat and blotchy.

"So what do you have to tell me?" he asked, already knowing that it would probably have to do with their night of passion. He hoped for the best. He already had one child and two would be, well, inconvenient, especially with the shop just opening. The idea of staying in Broughton with two children and being double wived was becoming less appealing by the minute.

"You know I went for that test the other day?" Margaret said quietly, fearing somebody might hear. Solomon nodded.

"Well." She coughed and looked down at the ground and said "It was positive." She looked up at Solomon. He didn't say anything. His face remained impassive.

Eventually, he said "You're pregnant?"

Margaret didn't reply immediately to this obvious statement. She thought that Solomon, possessor of mystical gifts and talents could work this one out for himself.

"Yes, Solomon. Pregnant. With child. Carrying your baby."

"Oh," he muttered under his breath.

"Is that it, Oh?" Margaret said scornfully.

"It's just that it's a bit of a shock."

"Solomon, you must know that when you sleep with somebody the chances of getting pregnant are much higher than if you don't." Suddenly it was her turn to be the wise one.

"So you're pregnant," he said sarcastically, moving uncomfortably from side to side. He scratched his nose and looked away from Margaret. He thought he loved her but this news, although expected, changed things.

"YES, I AM," she said through gritted teeth. "AND IF YOU ASK ME WHO THE FATHER IS, I WILL KILL YOU."

Solomon emitted one of those strangulated laughs people do when they've been caught out. It was a fearful titter.

"So, Solomon The Wise, what are you going to do?" Margaret took the initiative, becoming stronger by the minute. She thought she better had, because if she didn't her dad would, and the result wouldn't be pretty.

"Que sera, sera." Solomon said.

"You know I don't know what that means!"

"It's Latin for what will be, will be," Solomon explained.

"You mean you learned Latin to say the bleedin' obvious?"

"What do you want me to do, Margaret? You're pregnant, I'm the father. I'm not going to get married just because you're pregnant."

Margaret didn't hate him because he wouldn't marry her but it was at that moment she decided she didn't like, or love him. In fact he appalled her because he couldn't make a decision. The man who prided himself on his in-depth knowledge of eastern religions didn't have an original thought in his head.

"It's all a game, isn't it Solomon?" Margaret said, shaking her head.

What is?"

"This," she said pointing to her stomach. "You. You're a long-haired joke." Margaret was angry, not crying angry but hitting I-hate-you angry. "I thought you were different but you're not. You're just the same but packaged differently." Margaret moved towards Solomon. "You had the bottle to take my virginity but you haven't got the bottle for this." Margaret hugged her stomach, knowing that all she cared about now was the baby that was growing inside her. She stood and stared at those eyes that had left her jellified.

"But you're the joke, Solomon, because we've all sussed you out." Margaret was beginning to get into her stride. "I bet even Cass is laughing at you now."

Solomon didn't say anything.

She now knew why he wore flares, because whichever way the wind blew, so did his jeans along with his opinions and values too. She stood in front of him and with a ramrod back of defiance laughed at him.

"It doesn't matter, Solomon, whether you're there or not. I will have this baby and when the time comes for your child to ask where his father is I shall tell him. He's wherever the wind takes him because he is shallow, feckless and without a spine." She grinned. "And you know what? You're so transparent with your one-liners and mystical speech." Margaret pointed the famous family digit at him. "I bet in two or three years' time when you've used up all your Mysterious Solomon Tump material here, you'll be on your way to the next town to play the maverick, strange, long-haired roll-up god."

She laughed at her own clarity, annoyed that she hadn't seen through him before.

"But Solomon, there'll come a time when you'll have to stop in one place. You'll have run out of mystery and then there'll be you. Just you." It was Margaret's time to become the sage. "You, a mirror and your soul. D'you know what a soul is, Solomon? It's that empty place you try and stay clear of by getting stoned."

Margaret started to walk slowly towards the door. "And I know why you do all the drugs and drink. It's not to get to a higher plane is it? No, it's to get as far away as possible from yourself. You, Solomon The Transparent." Margaret stopped, turned round and pointed at her child's father. "Because you don't like yourself really, do you? You don't like what you see and from where I'm standing, neither do I!"

Solomon stood there like a chastised child. The colour had left his face, even the famous Tump eyes had visibly drained. They were one-dimensional, just like their owner.

"And yes, I will answer your next question. No, I will not tell Cass. You will have to, if you've got the balls, that is." She stood there for a few seconds and before she left she said "Oh, and thanks for the sex." Margaret had become a woman.

Even the colour had gone from his rainbow waistcoat. He was annoyed, not that he had got a young girl pregnant, but that he had underestimated her. She had got under his skin and found out how he ticked and that meant he was vulnerable. He'd not been vulnerable since his father died. That was the last time he cried, too. He vowed after his father's funeral that he wouldn't he let people in. He'd keep them at arms length. People let you down or die. People can't be trusted and so he treated them accordingly. Yet here in this northern outpost somebody had managed to clear his defences, get in and attack from the inside. A nineteen year old factory girl had sussed him out. He felt shit.

Solomon took a deep breath and entered the fray. He walked into the shop all smiles and bon viveur. Glad-handing all those who were nosing around looking, gawping or laughing. After what Margaret had just said he would have to become, again, Solomon the Chameleon.

Margaret walked up to her mother with tears in her eyes. Though she knew Solomon was a bastard she still fancied the pants off him, but at least she'd had the courage to walk away before she got truly messed up with his rolled-up ideology.

"What did he say?" her mum asked, taking her arm.

"Que sera, sera."

"And what does that mean when it's at home?"

"Whatever will be, will be."

"Is he trying to be funny, because if he is I'll knock his bloody block off."

"Mum, it's OK. I've sorted it and I don't want him around. He's a shallow charlatan," Margaret said, squeezing her mum's hand.

"I thought he was a hippy."

Margaret laughed and then burst into tears just as she was leaving the shop.

Father O'Dowd was coming towards them and saw Margaret crying.

"Are you all right?" he asked.

"Why is it," Margaret's mum said, "That men always ask such stupid bloody questions when they can see that NO, she isn't all right, otherwise she wouldn't be bloody crying now would she, Father?"

"I suppose not," Father O'Dowd said.

"She's not all right Father, because that long-haired excuse for a clothes horse has got her pregnant, and all he can do is spout Latin or some other stupid language." She put her arm round her daughter and they made their way back home.

"I don't suppose you've seen Mrs Hebblethwaite?" There was no reply.

He was about to enter the shop when he was joined by Mrs Butterworth and the five elves. "What are you doing here?" he asked the café owner.

"Free country!" she said and stood outside the shop.

"Are you not going in?" the priest asked.

"No!" came the reply from all six.

"Why not?" the cleric asked.

"Don't want to," Mrs Butterworth said. "And anyhow, we're waiting for Mrs Hebblethwaite."

Suddenly it dawned on Father O'Dowd. "The placards. You're going to picket the shop!"

"The saints needn't worry about being deposed just yet with you around, Father!" Mrs Butterworth said sarcastically.

"But the Bishop's coming at half twelve ..." A thought lodged itself just above his right eye, and it twitched. PICKET. CAMERAS. CROWDS. NEWSPAPERS. PUBLICITY. BISHOP. EXORCISM. HIPPIES. TROUBLE.

"I'd better find Mrs Hebblethwaite."

He walked up to Mrs Butterworth. "You've got to tell me where she is," pleaded Father O'Dowd.

"I do not!" replied Mrs Butterworth robustly. "I have to answer to nobody but the Lord."

And the priest knew that she was right.

"Shit," Father O' Dowd said quietly and ran down the street in search of Broughton's number one Catholic. As he navigated the corner, he nearly knocked Scoop Norman over. They both said 'Sorry' at the same time.

"Have you seen Mrs Hebblethwaite, Norman?" asked the priest.

"You can't miss her, Father" Norman said, pointing down the road. "She's heading this way with about forty others."

Father Thomas looked over the journalist's shoulder and saw a group marching down the centre of Broughton High Street. They were carrying placards and singing.

"Just what the Bishop wanted." The cleric sighed. His new-found favouritism would be short-lived if his Grace walked into this lot, thought Father O'Dowd.

"The Bishop's coming?" The Scoop was onto it in a flash and dashed off to phone a reporter from one of the nationals in Manchester.

It was all going terribly wrong. They were supposed to have a quiet exorcism finished off with a Mass and then a wave goodbye to the Tumps. At this rate they were bound to be on local news, if not the BBC at six o'clock.

The marchers were getting nearer and their singing louder. Mrs

Hebblethwaite was leading the Revolutionary chorus. A Plump Emily Pankhurst.

"DOWN WITH DRUGS
DOWN WITH HAIR
BROUGHTON PARENTS
DON'T WANT YOU HERE !"

Their banners had all manner of slogans written on them:

HIPPIES OUT!
SPAWN OF THE DEVIL!
BE WISE SOLOMON AND LEAVE BROUGHTON!
FLARED JEANS OUT!
ROLL UP AND ROLL AWAY!
TURN ON, TUNE IN, TUMP OUT!

The group finally reached the priest who stood dumbfounded, unable to take in what he was witnessing.

"I told you Father, if you didn't do anything, we would!" Mrs Hebblethwaite said. She halted her troops just as they were about to launch into their civil rights song.

"But you know the Bishop's coming at one," Father O'Dowd said.

"It's back-up, Father, just in case we don't get what we want."

"You mean you don't trust a man of the cloth ?"

"It's not about trust, Father, it's about evil and drugs and long hair and the Permissive Society opening shops in our high street so they can have sex in the window. Him walking down the high street all hair and crotch as though he owns the damned place," Mrs Hebblethwaite said. She wasn't in a compromising mood.

"You know, Father, he's even got our Gary wearing them damned silly clothes and talking as though he's off his head. And I'm not having it, Father! There comes a time when the meek shall inherit the streets. And today, Father, the streets of Broughton are ours." This was greeted with a tremendous roar initiated by Mrs Hebblethwaite's cheerleader, Miss Mahoney.

"You won't solve things by marching round Broughton carrying banners and placards!" Father O'Dowd was stalling for time. He looked at his watch; it was a quarter to eleven. He had an hour to quell the streets of Broughton before the Bishop and his small entourage hit town.

Father O'Dowd was all for going into Solomon's shop and telling him what was afoot. He needn't have bothered, because Broughton's newest recruit to the alternative society, Gary, had done it for him. Brotherly Solidarity he called it.

Gary came out first to speak to his Nan. "Cool it, Nan. What blows?" he said.

His grandmother ignored him. First, she couldn't understand a word he said and second, she thought he may have been on mind-altering substances.

Gary persevered. "Nan, the man's OK. He ain't no trouble!"

"No kind of trouble is it, Gary? Have you looked at yourself in the mirror lately?" His Nan pointed at his clothes. "You look like some bloody clown who hasn't worked for years with coloured this and coloured that. Even your bloody brain's coloured," she said, to general applause from the throng.

"The man's trouble Gary, can't you see through him with his Eastern thoughts and mystical goings-on? He hasn't an original thought in that head of his. He comes here all flared and rolled-up with his fancy ideas, and what does he do?"

Gary stood there hands on his flared hips wondering what other gems his grandmother would come out with.

"He charms the bloody knickers off our Margaret with tales of the world and travel and rock concerts and ley lines. You could stick a pig's bladder on stage that whistled and they'd still dance around as though they'd found the meaning of life."

"YEAH!" shouted Mr Shawcross from the back of the marchers. He hadn't heard what had been said but wanted to keep the momentum going.

Solomon spoke and a wind of OOOOOHS went round the crowd in expectation. *The Tump versus Hebblethwaite!*

"Mrs Hebblethwaite, I can understand –" He didn't finish.

"You can't understand anything, me lad, with your tousled hair and your flared genitals. Your brain's that addled with drugs you don't know what's right from wrong. You come here make our Margaret pregnant, put my other grandchild in tie-dyed T-shirts and expect us not to do anything." Her face was seared with anger like a hot cross bun. "You play the Devil's music until Mr Hebblethwaite can't sleep and gets ideas, and you have Percy Filth in the shop window." Utter disbelief from the crowd, who hadn't heard of that particular incident.

Solomon didn't have time to answer because Father O'Dowd stepped in.

"Mrs Hebblethwaite, I appreciate your concerns –"

"How dare you appreciate it, Father! This pain is mine and mine alone. Let me suffer it for the good of my soul . . ."

"Is that what it's all about? Pain and suffering?" questioned Solomon. The crowd sat down awaiting a theological debate on pain and suffering.

"No!" Mrs Hebblethwaite said emphatically. "It's about sin, The Devil and the corruption of our youth."

"I think the established churches do a good enough job of corrupting our youth without my help," Solomon said with a wry smirk on his face.

"Why, you cheeky –!" Mrs Hebblethwaite was about to launch herself at him with her placard but was stopped by Father O'Dowd's quick thinking. However, he couldn't stop Miss Mahoney who, hearing that the church was being attacked by a long-haired devil-worshipper, took over and belted The Tump with a placard that denounced Satan and all his works. Solomon was cut, but not badly. It was the first blood drawn in The Battle for the Souls Of Broughton's Youth.

"Heavy, Man!" said Gary, who was feeling the effects of the cannabis he'd just smoked.

"Will somebody take him home before he gets hit by something other than drugs?" his grandmother said. Gary was led away, flares dragging in the midday sun.

HIGH NOON

"Mrs Hebblethwaite, I ask you to disband this group. We don't want any more trouble or fighting. I'm sure the Bishop wouldn't be impressed if one of his more devout parishioners was arrested for a violation of the peace," Father O'Dowd pleaded.

Mrs Hebblethwaite harrumphed and got into a huddle with the other leaders of the march. They agreed to disperse for now, return to the café for a cup of tea and a bun and reconvene as and when Mrs Hebblethwaite gave them the sign.

This they did.

"I'LL BE BACK!" she said as she led her troops down the high street and back to the café. Revolutions were good for business, thought Mrs Butterworth, and hoped this wasn't an end to evil in Broughton.

Father O'Dowd turned his attention to Solomon. Fortunately he wasn't aroused.

"Solomon, for your own safety I'd advise you to keep your head down for a couple of days."

"Thomas, I've already had one warning from Margaret about what I should do and I'm not going to be pressured by her grandmother to leave." He turned round and pointed to his shop. He was less than convincing.

"Look! This is what we came here to do, and I'm damned if I'm going to let some religious crank stop me doing it," Solomon said without any passion. It was a matter of principle. Or so he thought.

"The shop isn't too much of a problem, Solomon," the priest said. "Margaret's pregnancy is another issue." The cleric stood next to Solomon. "I take it you're not going to marry her?"

"You guess right, Father."

"Her father's going to be very angry."

"So, he hates my guts."

"He'll have your guts for garters when he finds out that the tests were positive."

"Father, I can handle Margaret's' dad."

"Maybe, but you won't be able to handle the entire male population of Broughton," Father O'Dowd said with concern. "And, Solomon, that's what this amounts to." The priest took him inside the shop. "This has very little to do with getting a local girl pregnant and everything to do with you being different. You're challenging the status quo here in this town that for hundreds of years has followed its own tradition. It may have changed over the years, but only very slowly. It took decades for things to change and then you come with your long hair, flared jeans, drugs, different music. You more than anybody must realise that people are tribal and if anyone comes in and tries to change it, there's bound to be trouble."

"I'm not trying to change anything!" Solomon pleaded.

"Your very existence in this town is like saying 'Hey you lot, you've got it all wrong and I'm right. ' You know what I mean."

"I've done nothing wrong. OK, I got a local girl pregnant. Big deal!"

"Not any old local girl, Solomon," the priest said. "She's the grand-daughter of the Mrs Hebblethwaite who just happens to have direct contact with God and the Bishop."

Solomon shrugged his shoulders, thanked Thomas and returned to his shop.

The priest sighed. Frogs, pestilence and drought he could handle. Long hair and flares he couldn't, especially when Mrs Hebblethwaite was on his case.

He was already late for dinner, so his mother would be in a foul mood. If the cakes hadn't come out like she expected all hell would break loose. If there had been a saint that overlooked the rising of cakes, he would have prayed to them.

This meeting with the Bishop meant so much to his mum that it almost hurt. To her this was the culmination of over sixty years of devotion. She'd done the pilgrimages to Fatima and Lourdes and every European town that laid claim to some piece of bone from an apostle, but to shake hands with an alive, here-and-now, mitre-clad son of the church, well, you could open those pearly gates now as far as Mrs O'Dowd was concerned.

He looked at his watch, ten past twelve. He'd just go down to the café and have a word with Mrs Hebblethwaite, tell her what the Bishop was proposing to do. He was just about to enter the café when he was joined by Scoop Norman, all excited with his front page banner headline already etched in his pie-filled head.

"Mrs Hebblethwaite?" the cleric said. "Can I have a quick word?"

The leader of the revolution was nursing a mug of tea and talking tactics to her Broughton Gauleiters.

"We're not backing down, Father, until that flared, drug-fuelled excuse for a human leaves this town today."

Father Thomas was about to say something, but he was silenced by the leaderenes voice proclaiming.

"And that's final. We will not compromise," she said emphatically, to 'hear hears' from her followers.

"Not even if Mother Church asks you?" said the priest, going for her Achilles heel.

Mrs Hebblethwaite didn't reply immediately, which gave some sort of comfort to Father O'Dowd because it showed there was a chink in her armour.

"You're playing a dirty game, Father," she said, upping the ante. "I suppose next you'll be saying that if I continue I'll burn in HELL FIRE for defying the Bishop."

"Something like that," Thomas said half smiling, half hoping it might work.

"Well, Father, my conscience is clear about all this. Now I can't say the same for him with the roll-ups and pipes. Can you?" Mrs Hebblethwaite was getting rhetorical and surly.

It was nearing twenty past twelve and his mother would be panicking by now and so he chickened out from a direct theological debate. He didn't even tell her about the Bishop and his small exorcism team that was to land in Broughton in ten minutes. He didn't thank her or say goodbye, which was rather churlish; he just left the journalist to interview Mrs Hebblethwaite and her followers.

Chapter 35

He marched purposefully up Millgate, his cassock blowing in the wind. He looked like a one-winged bat. He opened the door of the presbytery and was assaulted with a volley of questions and answers all rolled into one.

"Have you seen the time, you know the Bishop's coming and I don't know if the sponge will have risen and you promised you'd be here, and look we've got five minutes and my hair, you know how much this means to me and what do you do, you stay out all morning and, God, look at my face!" She was all raw nerves.

"It'll be OK," her son said stupidly because he didn't have the eye of Cassandra, although he sometimes professed he did.

"Since when have you been a pastry chef?" his mother asked, applying only the slightest hint of blusher. She didn't want to appear too tarty when His Grace came. There was nothing worse when you were given a sliver of sponge cake than to be overpowered by cheap perfume and anxiety.

"How do I look?" she asked her son, who told her she looked all right without actually looking at her.

"Mrs Hebblethwaite's leading a march to try and get Tump out of the town! Our journalist friend is on to it and has contacted the Nationals in Manchester. The Bishop thinks I've sorted it and is expecting a low key exorcism, and he'll go to Purgatory and back when he finds out what's happening," Father O' Dowd said nervously. "So everything's going swimmingly!" he said.

His mother hadn't heard a word. "I'll get the cake out," she said in solidarity.

Father O'Dowd heard a car draw up on the drive. He looked at his watch; it was dead on half past twelve.

THE BISHOP HAD ARRIVED

The Cape. The Walk. The Pomp. The Ceremony. It was all there and it had arrived at the presbytery, all in one man. Bishop Bone. He was doing it for Hollywood and Mrs Hebblethwaite. He was out-golding gold. He was the Vatican's peacock and he loved it. His fellow exorciser did not, as he wasn't used to Glam Church do's like his boss. He walked meekly behind, concerned, worried and embarrassed. Father O'Dowd too looked a trifle non-plussed as he opened the door. His mother loved it. She'd not seen a frock like it since the Queen got married.

"Hello," said Father O'Dowd, stumped for words.

The Bishop merely waved a bejewelled hand. Thomas did not kiss it, much to the consternation of his clerical superior.

"Your Grace, I must tell you there have been some problems with Mrs Hebblethwaite since I last talked to you," the priest said.

"I thought you had it all sorted!" His Grace said, perturbed that his plans were beginning to fall apart.

"I had, but Mrs Hebblethwaite decided that a march through town is what it will take to throw Solomon out of Broughton."

"We'll see about that!" the Bishop said. "There have been many who have tried Thomas, and they've all failed." There was a brief silence. "The Tumps are no match for The Mother Church."

"It's not the Tumps I'm worried about," Father O'Dowd said, walking beside the servant of Christ. "It's Mrs Hebblethwaite."

They both entered the kitchen where Thomas's mother was busy being busy, aided by a pinny and a nervous smile.

"I'm sure that once we've managed to have a chat about Evil, she'll come round to the ways of the Mother Church," the Bishop said confidently.

Father O'Dowd wasn't too sure. Over the last few weeks this stalwart of the Catholic faith had made somewhat of an about-turn. Theologically she was as devout as ever, but when it came to observing the Church and those that administered pastoral care, she had deviated.

"A sliver of sponge, Your Grace?" his mother said, bowing slightly as she backed towards the oven. She was hoping and praying to any saint that would listen that her Victoria sponge would rise and be adequate for this special occasion.

"That would be most generous, Mrs O'Dowd." The Bishop managed to sweep up his vestments and perch himself on a chair at the table. The parish priest followed suit and sat opposite his boss. Mrs O'Dowd tentatively opened the oven door and beamed when she saw that her creation had risen beautifully. She put it on top of a doily, which was protecting the silver cake stand and brought it over to the table.

"I would love a cup of tea," the Bishop asked Thomas's mother. "If that's not too much trouble?"

Mrs O'Dowd giggled like a pubescent girl who'd just found out what the birds and bees are all about. "Of course, Your Grace," she replied, noting that since the Bishop had arrived his ring had remained unkissed. Catholic etiquette had been ignored.

"Remind me again what time we're to meet this woman and her fellow conspirators," His Grace said, placing the warm cake on his plate.

"One o'clock," Thomas replied. "Although I think it may be better if we got there slightly earlier. You know, to outmanouvre the enemy."

*****

Mrs Hebblethwaite was still in the café surrounded by followers and a journalist.

The Scoop was in full flow. For once in his journalistic career he was around when something big was happening, and this was big. Very Big.

"So you're fighting for the souls of our children?" he asked.

"The souls of a nation. We can't sit idly by and watch these people wander into our towns and villages and corrupt our youth with their Bob Dylan records and mystical ways. It starts with a rolled-up, cross-legged discussion on this and that, but mainly that. Before you know it they start growing their hair and taking drugs that make them sound as though they're talking through blotting paper." Scoop was finding it hard to keep up, his shorthand being very rusty.

"And once they stop eating meat, well, all hell lets loose, they start dancing around naked, sleeping with anything that moves and embracing any culture that's East of the Urals." Mrs Hebblethwaite was the only one who knew where the Urals were, but it was nearing one o'clock and she didn't have time to explain.

"As you might know, my grandson started asking questions, which is fatal because they get answers and what do answers lead to, more questions. It's a vicious circle that leads to sin, long hair, drugs and unwanted pregnancies. He wanders around these days calling everyone 'cat,' or 'man' and says he doesn't do time anymore. He says time is for the oppressed masses who pander to the will of the evil capitalist system. I said if it wasn't for time, Gary, you wouldn't get fed, get money from the dole or get served in the pub at opening time."

Mrs Butterworth interrupted her friend.

"It's nearly one, Ethel. I think we should be getting round there, don't you?"

Mrs Hebblethwaite looked at her watch and said. "Let the battle commence."

They left the café and walked to the Tumps' emporium . . .

Scoop Norman would later describe the stand-off between the two main protagonists as a latter-day version of 'High Noon'. There were over a hundred people present that day and even given the atmosphere and expectant nature of the crowd, nobody would describe Bishop Bone as Gary Cooper, or Mrs Hebblethwaite as a young Grace Kelly. Even with the best soft-focused lens.

As the Anti-Hippy element rounded Market Street and into Water Lane they met the Exorcists who, although much better dressed, were outnumbered ten to one. It was like the joining of the waters at Avoca, two turbulent rivers vying for supremacy. Nothing was said, but if looks could kill then the Bishop would have been up for mass murder.

Walking behind was a large golden crucifix that tested the strength of the Monsignor who had been chosen for the thickness of his biceps rather than his expertise in exorcism. Two altar boys followed, waving their baubles full of incense. It wasn't intended to provoke or irritate, it being a traditional Catholic order of service. However there were many in the Anti-Hippy marchers who thought it was a religious ruse to smoke-bomb the opposition into submission.

The Bishop said something in Latin and his retinue stopped. Mrs Hebblethwaite also stopped by raising her hand and asking her followers to cease their singing.

"We can be civil about this, Mrs Hebblethwaite, or we can call on the Almighty to administer justice." The Bishop came straight in and played his trump card. Although he didn't smile, he knew that for a religious like his opponent, this was now major league stuff.

"Justice?" she cried. "Where is the justice in my granddaughter being impregnated by the seed of Beelzebub?" A huge gasp went up from her followers as this news hit them for the first time. "Fornication and drugs, Your Grace," she shouted, turning round to her followers. "I don't remember the Ten Commandments promoting such things." This was greeted by a cheer, which soon turned into derision and abuse as The Impregnator came out of his shop.

Solomon Tump was a bit of a film buff but not even he had witnessed such a scene. Zeffirelli, Renoir and Bergman would have been hard pressed to come up with the script for what was unfolding outside his shop. He looked at Father O'Dowd: either he was walking behind someone very high up in the church or Broughton was witnessing its first gay Mardi Gras.

He looked across at Mrs Hebblethwaite, slightly alarmed that the baying mob had a revolutionary air about them. Fortunately there was no Madame Guillotine. The Catholic Crew were impressive in all their regalia and quite rightly gained all the marks for artistic merit.

"At last, the man who's been at the heart of all the problems," Mrs Hebblethwaite said.

She started to walk forward but was stopped in her tracks by a film crew from Look North who'd just arrived. She didn't want to be captured on celluloid striking Tump, even if he was a cloven-hoofed harbinger of evil.

The Bishop nearly spat. He turned round and gave Father O'Dowd such a look that the parish priest thought he would turn into a pillar of salt. The Bishop was worried about what the Archbishop would have to say about all the commotion when he saw it on the evening news. If it did all blow up in his face he could expect a visit from the theological clean-up squad who would smooth everything out and then send him to some Mediterranean isle where life would consist of saying Mass to toothless locals and ignorant tourists.

A man in his mid thirties, all fake sun-tan, flossed teeth and ego rushed into the centre of the street holding a microphone in one hand and a sheaf of papers in the other. He was followed by an overweight cameraman who was sweating nearly as much as the Bishop.

Solomon stood there with a huge grin on his face, wondering how the two factions would handle this new addition to the proceedings.

"Thomas," the Bishop whispered.

The parish priest strolled over, trying not to alert anyone that something was afoot.

"Yes?"

"We need to get out of here as quickly and quietly as possible."

Father O'Dowd was not a man of science but even he knew that trying to retreat discreetly with a six foot cross of gold, two altar boys, a Bishop in ceremonial garb, a parish priest and his mother would not be easy. He thought for a couple of moments and came to the same conclusion. It would not be easy. Although the Bishop was in full regalia it wasn't apparent whether he was celebrating a Holy Day, parting the waters or just trying to drum up support for the church.

Word had leaked out on the journalistic wires, however, that there was to be some devil-bashing down old Broughton Way. The television front man walked up to Mrs Hebblethwaite and was about to thrust the microphone into her face when he noticed a slight shuffling of the Catholic Praetorian guard.

"Your Grace," the journalist said. "I'm led to believe that you are here to exorcise an inhabitant of Broughton?"

The Bishop concentrated on shuffling backwards. He remained tight-lipped.

"Is it normal Catholic practice to process through Broughton when it isn't a Holy Day?" The journalist was nothing if not persistent. The Scoop was taking notes. The camera crew finally reached the exorcists.

"I've also got it on good authority that one of your priests is a practising homosexual."

The Bishop, slightly disorientated by the incense and stressed from the occasion, fainted. Father Thomas was the first to react and caught His Grace before he hit the floor.

"You should wash your mouth out with carbolic young man, going round talking all that smut just so's you can get on the news." Mrs O'Dowd strode purposefully, knowing that what she was about to do would be absolved by a greater authority. She slapped the news reporter round the face.

"Did you get that?" he asked

"Sorry," said his cameraman.

"Shit!"

"But I've got the Bishop fainting."

"I suppose that'll have to do."

The Bishop was carried into the nearest shop, which happened to be the Tump Emporium. Solomon helped Thomas settle him down. The film crew followed. So did the Anti-Hippies.

"What the –?" said Cass. She'd stayed in the shop whilst the demonstration was going on and was shocked to see a dead pope enter the premises. The Pontiff was followed by a film crew and Mrs Hebblethwaite waving a banner denouncing Satan and all his works.

"He needs a hot drink and some air," Solomon said.

Father O'Dowd wasn't too worried about the tea bit of the order but bringing him into a shop doused in enough perfume to stop a bull elephant at fifty paces was worrying to say the least.

Mrs Hebblethwaite was now frantic. Not only had she been initially thwarted in her attempt to rid Broughton of the long-haired opium seller, she now had to bear witness to the devil himself manhandling one of the Vicar of Christ's flock.

"AAAAAAAAAAAAAAAARRRRRRRRRRRRGGGGGGGGGGGGGHHHHH-HHHH!" she screamed as she tore through the crowd.

"And now Mrs Hebblethwaite, the leader of the anti-hippies is launching a one-woman attack on Solomon Tump, alleged spawn of the Devil and Impregnator General," the journalist said in his earnest, dulcet, 'there's a tragedy afoot' voice. The Great-Grandmother managed to get her ample frame through a section of the crowd before her parish priest stopped her in her tracks. Thomas O'Dowd fell at her feet and launched into the Lord's Prayer.

"Please, Mrs Hebblethwaite, we don't need this," Father O'Dowd pleaded as he got to his feet. "The Bishop's suffering, you're suffering, we're all suffering." He gestured to the crowd that stood around in a semi-circle, a human amphitheatre of drama, concern and bewilderment. Thomas carried on.

"The only people who are benefiting are the media. Do you really want

Broughton on the TV for this?" He was never that great at oratory. His sermons were less than inspiring but he was infused now with a passion born of fear that his trip to the gay bar in Manchester would be broadcast live on air tonight.

Two days ago Mrs Hebblethwaite would have gladly accepted every camera and journalist in Western Europe to witness the event, but she had never realised that others too might suffer.

"I still want him out," Mrs Hebblethwaite said defiantly. "But she can stay," she said, pointing to Cass. Cass nearly dropped the mug of tea she was carrying for the Bishop. Sisters of the world indeed unite. Mrs Hebblethwaite had begun to realise that Cass wasn't all that bad. Yes, her breasts were in your face and she did make a lot of noise come the witching hour but the grandmother was convinced it was Solomon who was the main instigator of evil. Even if Cass had taunted her with midnight nakedness and music, no women should suffer the indignity of betrayal.

"But *he's* got to go," she added firmly.

Father O'Dowd had become a resourceful diplomat in the last three weeks or so but he knew that this was probably the best he was going to get from Ethel Hebblethwaite.

"And if he's not gone by five o'clock then Margaret's father and his mates will force him to go."

Broughton's motto had always been 'when all else fails, hit 'em'.

Solomon lifted his head away from the Bishop, whose condition was still causing concern.

"I'm sorry about Margaret," the hippy said.

He could have said anything else in the world and got away with it.

"Sorry? You're not sorry. You're not sorry about anything you do," Mrs Hebblethwaite said, putting her banner down much to the relief of everyone. "That girls gonna have to bring up that kiddy all by herself and you can bet your last roll-up that you won't be around to hand over so much as a penny piece."

"I have this place," retorted Solomon.

"Oh, so you're going to give your child a quarter equal are you?"

"Well . . ."

"Wells that are empty are no use to anyone." Which confused everyone bar Solomon, who looked on thoughtfully.

"Look, even your bloody girlfriend of how long is getting sick of yer. Can yer not see with your own eyes? You're living in your own head, in your own time and that time is running out, especially in this town." Mrs Hebblethwaite received an ovation.

A smile of contentment flickered across the mouth of the Bishop when he heard the roar of angels coming to welcome him into the Kingdom of Heaven. He sat up, awaiting St Peter.

Solomon Tump was no St Peter.

"AAAAAAAAAARRRRRRRRRRGGGGGGGGGGGGHHHHHHHH-HHHH!" the Bishop said.

"He's gone into shock." Father Thomas said.

He wasn't wrong. When the Bishop awoke expecting a host of angels to carry him forth to his rightful position, all he saw was BEELZEBUB, BANNERS, Mrs H, AND A BAYING MOB OF IGNORANT NORTH-ERNERS. This was his worst nightmare.

"Would you take a financial settlement to leave Broughton?" said a lone voice from the middle of the throng.

"Sorry?" said Solomon, trying to see whether the Bishop had relapsed or merely fainted again.

"I said, would you take a financial settlement?" the benefactor repeated. It was the landlord of the Flying Horse. Mrs Hebblethwaite had never liked him, although she would grow to.

"You can't buy me off just because you don't like my hair or my music," replied Solomon earnestly.

"Everyone has their price, and it'll be a lot more than ten pieces of silver," Mine Host said.

Solomon didn't immediately reply, which annoyed but didn't surprise Cass.

Everybody turned to Solomon. Even the Bishop woke up.

Solomon thought. And thought. He looked round at the baying mob and knew that it was him and him alone that had aroused such hatred and fear. The demonstration wouldn't be taking place if he hadn't come to Broughton. He looked at Cass. She was still beautiful but he had known for some time that their relationship was floundering. If he stayed, and it was a big IF, the best he could hope for was Cass leaving, Margaret leaving and her dad and his mates beating him senseless. Solomon didn't do bruises. He'd managed for thirty-three years to avoid confrontations like this and his instincts told him to keep it like that. He quickly weighed up the situation. One: There was an unconscious Bishop on his lap. Two: Father O'Dowd lay prostrate on the floor in an attempt to stop any violence. Three: A TV crew was present, just waiting for an almighty bust-up to start so they could fill two minutes on the evening news. And the plusses were?

"How much were you thinking of?"

"Fifty quid," the landlord said.

"Hundred," Solomon countered.

"Seventy-five."

"Eighty?"

"Done!" The landlord of the Flying Horse had been willing to go up to a hundred but knew his bargaining skills were much better than anybody who listened to Bob Dylan.

"Power to the people, hey Solomon?" Cass walked over to her ex-boyfriend.

"LONG LIVE THE REVOLUTION!" She stood in front of him with a clenched fist and brought her knee up quickly into his testicles. Martial arts expert or not, he went down in a bundle grabbing his crotch with both hands. He hit the floor to tumultuous cheers from everyone except Father Thomas and the altar boys.

"I think that's were you belong, down amongst the dirt and filth."

Solomon tried to get up but she gave him a slap around the face. Buddhist or not, she knew how to dish out a good old beating. "Well, you know what they say, Solomon, where there's muck there's brass." She started to laugh. She didn't know it yet but she had more in common with the women in Broughton than she thought. Solomon the Mystic was just a mystified boy in man's clothing.

"And if you think you can see your son," she said as Solomon gingerly got to his feet. " . . . you'll have to go through my solicitor." She didn't have a lawyer but it sounded good. Solomon finally sat up and put his fingers through his hair. Cass continued in the hushed silence. "And as you know, all the money that went into setting up this place was mine so if you think you're entitled to any of it, you can just whistle."

Solomon stood up, looked at Cass and shook his head. He'd been found out, caught red-handed after all this time. He was a Fraudulent Mystic. A Sage who'd run out of things to say. He brushed his trousers down and walked over to Father O'Dowd.

"Thanks for all your help, Thomas." He kissed him on the cheek. The film crew responded with a close up shot and the Bishop turned away. He walked straight past Mrs Hebblethwaite. "Tell Margaret I'll be in touch."

"Dead bloody right you will," said Mrs Hebblethwaite, puffing out her chest in admiration for her granddaughter.

The crowd parted and let Solomon through. There was no hissing or bad language. It was far worse. There was silence. The silence of defeat and complete humiliation. Solomon would later tell anybody who would listen that it was a tactical withdrawal. He'd managed to get away without receiving a good beating and eighty quid in his pocket. He thought it was a result.

Cass was nearly in tears, but she managed to hold them back.

"That must have been hard, love," Mrs Hebblethwaite said, putting her arm around her former Number Two Enemy. Cass just smiled.

"I know what it's like to have to throw somebody out that you still love, but as they always say, better out than in."

Cass wasn't really up to platitudes and clichés but as a peace offering it worked.

"If you don't mind, everybody, I'm going to shut up shop now. But –" She put her arms in the air. "We'll be open first thing tomorrow morning, at ten o'clock sharp." Cass thought that was early enough, but Broughtonians knew that most of the workforce had already put in half a day's work by then.

Mrs Hebblethwaite led her followers and crew out into the afternoon sun. Mrs Butterworth was in close attendance, there was the matter of sixty-four teas to pay for.

"If it's any consolation, I think he's done the right thing, Cass." Father Thomas realised the full extent of what he had just said. "No, I don't mean leaving you and Leo, I mean leaving Broughton. Not because of what he looked like or stood for, but there are times when such full-on confrontation is not good for anybody." Cass nodded. The priest put his arm round her. "Change can be for the good, but it can also be catastrophic if pushed too hard and in the wrong place."

Cass chuckled and a lone tear wended its way down her left cheek. "You mean that old battleaxe next door."

"How did you guess? "I know she seems like some firebrand but I think underneath all that Mrs Hebblethwaite does have a heart."

"Margaret's going to need a lot of help, Thomas. I've known ever since we moved up here that he wasn't for me. In fact, if it hadn't been for Leo eighteen months ago I think we would have split up then." Cass wiped the solitary tear away. "Don't get me wrong, he wasn't a bad dad. In fact, compared to some of our mates he was bloody good."

The parish priest smiled and squeezed her hand.

"But he was never good at settling down in any one place for any length of time, so when he said he wanted to open up a shop I thought, well, not my cup of tea really, what with money and profits and mortgages and things, but we had Leo and I thought come on, give it one last shot. Let's see if there's any of that spark left. And of course there wasn't."

"Come on love, come to the presbytery for a cup of tea and a sliver of sponge cake," Mrs O'Dowd said, understanding the recuperative capacities of cup of tea served with a sliver.

"I'll have to go and get Leo." And then she suddenly thought that Solomon may have gone to try and get him. "Shit! What if Solomon kidnaps him?"

"Is he at home?" the priest asked.

"Yes."

"Right, let's go." Thomas grabbed hold of her hand. "Mum, can you take the Bishop, the monsignor and the two altar boys up to the house? We'll see you later." His mother nodded. Thomas and Cass ran down the street.

Chapter 36

M rs O'Dowd went over to the Bishop and helped him to his feet. "And you lot can clear off! The show's over." His Grace got to his feet with a little help. "And if I see or hear anything on tonight's news then I'll be having a word with your producer." As he passed the crew he admonished them with a delicate finger. "Because he comes to my confessional every week," the Bishop said, exhausted.

"I bet he does," the newscaster said under his breath. They left, their cans empty. Scoop was physically sick. He had been there and reported it in full and what happened? It became a non-story. With the rest of the crew he went to the Flying Horse to try and get the real story of the 'Eighty Pound Tump,' as it was to become known.

The walk back up Millgate was less Pomp than their descent into Broughton. The Bishop, still decked out in his official exorcism outfit, was feeling under the weather.

"As soon as we get back I'll make us some dinner. I'm sure once you've got something hot inside you, you'll be fine." Mrs O'Dowd was revelling in her Florence Nightingale role, especially when the victim was too tired to respond. The monsignor's arms were burning with fatigue and as they reached the middle of the brow he collared the two wee altar boys and told them it was their honour to ferry the golden crucifix the last few hundred yards up to the presbytery.

Mrs O'Dowd, new custodian of the presbytery, unlocked the front door.

"Where's Miss Mcafferty?" asked the Bishop, summoning up enough energy to walk into the kitchen.

"I think she may have gone," replied Thomas's mother, knowing full well that the Irish spinster had left that morning, mouthing obscenities and full frontal allegations against anybody who entered the presbytery. She didn't want to get the old dear into any trouble and didn't mention any of the carryings-on.

"How strange," His Grace said, slumping into a chair. The Monsignor sat opposite, his brow running with rivulets of sweat. The two altar boys hadn't yet made it into the kitchen. They sat down in the hallway. It was a long and arduous road to Calvary, mused the older boy, impressed that Our Lord had made it all the way.

"Will soup be all right, Your Grace?" The Bishop nodded.

"With lots of hot crusty bread." She scurried over to the bread bin to make sure there was enough to go round. "Well, you can't be having soup without bread, can you?"

Chapter 37

Father Thomas and Cass walked hurriedly back to Prospect Street. The café was full of revellers crowing over the victory, each story becoming more and more embellished. History is always written by the victors.

"You did have a thing for Solomon, didn't you Thomas?" Cass said as they turned into her street.

"I suppose I did." he replied, slightly embarrassed that she was so up-front about the whole thing.

"Well, it wouldn't be the first time. Solomon had this way with both sexes, kind of androgynous, I suppose," Cass mused.

"Did he ever have affairs with men?" Thomas asked forthrightly, strong enough now with his own sexuality to pursue this line of questioning.

"I don't think so. It always seemed to me he had this kind of Svengali effect on young men, what with his good looks and all that mystical stuff. They hung on to every word as though it would change their worlds. And some it did," she said, passing the hedge that had captured Mrs Hebblethwaite two weeks ago. "Was it like that for you, Thomas, or was it a pure sex thing?" she laughed. So did he.

"I know that when I saw him in the first few days you arrived things happened under this cassock that would have made the Bishop blush."

"Is it still like that?" Cass asked.

"No," he said emphatically.

"Not about Thomas, about me!" Cass punched him on the shoulder and they fell about laughing.

"What would you do if I said yes?"

"Pour cold water over you and hit it with a spoon."

"I know some priests who'd enjoy that," he laughed.

"Steady, Father, you don't want to be giving away too many church secrets."

"You're taking all this pretty well, you know, Solomon leaving," the priest said, impressed with her

"To be honest, Thomas, Solomon left us years ago. He only stayed out of some sense of obligation, which was a first. He felt he owed it to his son. He still carried on much the same though, screwing as many women as possible. You see, Thomas, like most men Solomon tried to create a false environment for his relationship with me. He thought he could do what he wanted without fear of contradiction. He was trying to go through life without the threat of responsibility."

"And you put up with it?"

"Those were the rules we laid down at the beginning, so those were the ones we played by. It was only in the last three years or so that I started thinking all this free love shit, was just that, SHIT."

"How did you put up with it?"

"When you've been with somebody as long as I have, it's easier to stay than go. Going is transition and that's hard when you've relied emotionally on somebody else."

"At least I've got Him Upstairs to speak to," Thomas said gratefully.

"Have you?" Cass said.

"So who are *you* going to rely on now?"

"Thing is, Thomas, I really don't think I need anybody. Not at the moment anyway. Isn't it weird –"

"What is?"

"Well, I came here all hippied out and yet now I think I have more in common with the women of Broughton than all those screwed-up professional women who try to juggle work, parenthood and orgasms. There's more to life than a clean hostess trolley and the constant threat of wrinkles. Wrinkles are there to tell you to stop worrying and slow down. Nirvana may not be Broughton but it certainly isn't in North London." Thomas smiled. "And to be honest, Thomas, they're not that bad really."

"Even Mrs H?"

"Especially Mrs H."

"Why?"

"Because they just get on."

"Is that enough?"

"It has to be!"

They approached number twenty-three and could see that Solomon was loading the van. It didn't seem so bright and vibrant these days. The Rainbow seemed to lack sparkle. They walked past him and into the house where the baby-sitter was bouncing Leo up and down on her knee. Cass smiled and then cried. She picked him up and gave him a big hug. He giggled. Thomas went outside to see if he could help Solomon.

"Need any help?"

"Please," Solomon replied. "Seems you're the only round here who doesn't detest me."

"Yes, well, part of the job."

"Cheers," Solomon said.

"Joke. Humour, remember it?"

"Bit hard to now." Solomon was all truncated sentences, gone were the free-flowing elegant phrases that took you to places you didn't know existed.

"What you doing, Man?" Gary asked. The effects of his giant roll-up were wearing off.

"Heading off west. Exiting left, Gary." Solomon put another load of albums into the van.

"Can I come with you?" Gary said. "I've had it with this joint!"

"Gary, I've already had a run in with your Nan, your sister's pregnant and your dad would like to castrate me without the use of surgical instruments." Solomon came out of the van. "I don't think taking you would be a good idea."

"Neither do I," Father O'Dowd said.

"I'm seventeen," the youth replied with all the conviction his tender years could muster.

"I tell you what." Solomon said. "You ask your mum and if she says yes then I'll think about it."

Solomon and Thomas went back into the house where Solomon gathered his bag of clothes and took down four posters that were still on the wall.

"Thomas, do you mind?"

The priest took the holdall and posters and went out to the van.

"This is it, then." He grabbed hold of Leo and hugged him. His son played with his long curly hair as he always did. He kissed him and gave him back to his mother.

"Daddy's going away now Leo, but he'll be back soon." Solomon's eyes, those huge translucent orbs of mystery, were filled with tears and they fell onto his cheeks like bricks falling from a demolished house. He sobbed and kissed Leo again. He hugged both Cass and Leo and walked out of the house and up to his van. He couldn't bear to turn round.

"Take care Solomon," the priest said. "And next time try not to find somewhere like here!"

Solomon nodded and got into the van.

Gary rushed over with a bag. "She says it's all right, I can come."

Solomon was too tired to argue and Gary jumped in all smiles.

"Me mum says that at least if I'm with you they'll know where you are." Gary said reverting back to Broughtonian.

The van that brought the Permissive Society to Broughton left Prospect Street to its future. Father Thomas hugged Cass and with Leo they walked slowly over to see how Margaret was getting on.

Mrs Hebblethwaite turned into the street just in time to see the multi-coloured Hippymobile depart.

"That's a wonderful sight! " she said, still clinging onto the placard. Her mouth was just about to break out into a smile as wide as the Nile delta, when she saw her Gary in the passenger seat waving at her.

"JESUS, MARY AND JOSEPH!" she shrieked.